Jackson stumbled out of the wreckage. He made it five steps before collapsing to his knees. "That was . . . immensely difficult."

Uncle Steve's shadow loomed over them. "That was also more than enough to draw unwanted attention, I'm afraid."

Gabe stood and followed his uncle's line of sight, scanning the skyline. "Where're the bats? How many?"

"It's not bats, Gabe," Uncle Steve said. His voice sounded strange. Flat.

Defeated.

A dozen gigantic, golden, six-winged creatures like nightmare versions of dragons plummeted out of the sky.

THE CRIMSON SERPENT

DAN JOLLEY

HARPER

An Imprint of HarperCollinsPublishers

For Tracy

Always.

www.harpercollinschildrens.com

Library of Congress Control Number: 2017954083

ISBN 978-0-06-241171-6

Typography by Torborg Davern

18 19 20 21 22 BRR 10 9 8 7 6 5 4 3 2 1

❖

First paperback edition, 2018

PROLOGUE

Around Jonathan Thorne, San Francisco trembled. Buildings shuddered, asphalt cracked, and people screamed in an earthquake of his own making. The horror of the disaster was a delight to him, but these magickal tremors were far more than a bit of fun. They were the final piece in a plan he had been engineering for over a century.

For all the chaos in this quaking city of concrete and glass, it would soon pale against the audacity of Thorne's dream—a vision of the future that was now so close he could almost taste it. Though he had spent lifetimes planning for this moment, not even he knew precisely what would happen next.

What will be wrought when Earth and Arcadia finally merge?

He imagined commonplace creatures transformed by Arcadia's magick into eyeless, skinless beasts. He envisioned grand citadels of twisted stone rising high above the clouds of every city. He dreamed of every nation of the world bowing in submission to him.

Most of all, he relished the shock of the ordinary people of the earth, waking to a world that was no longer their own. Confused. Afraid. *Powerless.*

He had done all this—with the unwitting aid of a circle of young elementalists. By manipulating them in his guise as their friend Brett Hernandez, he had twisted a ritual meant to destroy the shadow realm of Arcadia to do the very opposite. Instead of obliterating Arcadia, he had orchestrated a series of events that had fooled the children into realizing his deepest and darkest desire.

He watched with satisfaction as the glass of a nearby skyscraper buckled and showered the street below with deadly shards, and then—he *felt it.*

A change in the vibrations of the earth. The tremors of soil and concrete amplified, but it was more than that. The air around him seemed to *swell.* The colors around him appeared to both dim and deepen.

At last!

Then a pulse of energy jolted through him. Its charge of heat and power was alien to the earth, but very familiar to Thorne.

Arcadia on Earth. Two worlds made one!

Thorne smiled. His teeth grew and multiplied as he thrilled at the fresh Arcadian magick that flowed through him. New strength and power filled his body as he sensed the realms merge into a single reality. He had plotted an aeon to reach this moment! His dream had finally been realized, but there was work to do. There was a new world to build—one in which he was both god and emperor.

He had to find the others. But first, he wanted to look upon his new domain.

He wished for his legs to lengthen, and so they did, stretching into long stilts of black shadow. Thorne could make himself look like a man, but he hadn't been human for many decades. He was darkness and power and hunger itself. On his towering strands of shadow, he rose ten feet, then thirty, then fifty, and soon loomed over the surrounding buildings. He gazed upon San Francisco—only it wasn't San Francisco anymore. The changes had already begun, some of them most intriguing. Neither Earth nor Arcadia, this was something different. Something new.

Something *his*.

Thorne rose higher through the air, his shadow stilt legs broadening and lengthening as he soared above the city. He wanted to see it all. What *fun* he would have here! His gaze swept over Oakland in the east, and the Diablo Range to the south, and . . .

What is that?

A red circle enclosed the Bay Area. It was only from this height that Thorne could see it. This was not part of his design. Whatever it was, it had no place in his plan.

He bounded over a block of buildings in a single massive stride and then stopped and grew his bright green eyes until they were the size of wagon wheels in order to get a better look at the unexpected sight. The red circle was not simply a circle, he realized. It seemed to be *moving*. But that wasn't the worst part . . . the worst part was that the world beyond the red boundary seemed frozen. The hills there still green, the waters and sky still pure blue. Arcadia hadn't spread to all the earth— it had not gone beyond the strange red circle. Its magick was contained. Leashed. *Trapped*.

Impossible.

A spark of anger lit within Thorne and quickly flared into a furnace of rage.

IMPOSSIBLE!

Out of pure fury, he stomped two buildings a hundred feet beneath him. He shrieked his wrath into the amber clouds swirling above.

Stop. Stop. He forced himself to calm down. His dark mind whirred and calculated and schemed. This infuriating red circle was only a minor setback. He had crossed dimensions and remade reality itself. He would not be thwarted by anything. Not now that he was *so close.*

He adjusted the length of his legs so that he could stalk across two blocks at a time, and then three in a single step. He must find the others. The child elementalists as well. Perhaps their usefulness to him had not expired quite yet.

No matter what, Thorne knew he must break the cursed red circle that stood in the way of his dream. Once this final obstacle was dispatched, the convergence of Arcadia and Earth would be complete, and this world would truly be his kingdom.

1

The city across the bay darkened and changed, and Gabe Conway stood rooted to the ground in pure horror.

He tried to focus on the voices of his friends in hopes that it might distract him from the hideous amber streaks burrowing through the sky overhead, the distant calls of the inhuman monstrosities wheeling and diving over San Francisco, and the awful tinge of gold growing slowly but steadily clearer in the waters of the bay.

We failed. The words pulled at the edges of his mind, demanding to be given their full, proper weight. *We failed, and now the world is ending.*

"You guys, look at it," Kaz Smith said. Gabe didn't need

to look at his friend to know he was crying. "Look at the city."

Already barely recognizable, the skyline was slowly changing. Gabe watched an office tower blacken and torque into a grotesque parody of itself. Then his stomach knotted as the armored, bloated bulk of a leviathan rose from the building's roof, its dozens of repulsive tentacles reaching for the streets below. The leviathan drifted inland, leaving a slow rain of golden ooze in its wake.

"We screwed up," Brett Hernandez said. Only minutes ago, they'd finished performing a complicated ritual to destroy Arcadia. Using their complete circle of five elements—fire, water, air, earth, and magick—they'd hoped to wipe away the corrupt shadow realm forever, but Thorne had duped them. He'd changed the ritual to accomplish the opposite of what it was supposed to do, and now Arcadia had been combined with San Francisco. "Thorne played us. Guys . . . I think we just destroyed the world."

Brett's twin, Lily, silently put her arm around her brother's shoulders.

Jackson Wright, the fifth member of their circle and the wielder of magick itself, had wandered off from the group soon after the ritual backfired on them. Gabe guessed the pale boy was coming to grips with what had happened on his own. They'd all been through the wringer, but none more than Jackson. He knew better than any of them the kind of evil Jonathan Thorne and his cult, the Eternal Dawn, were capable of.

Gabe glanced over his shoulder at Aria, standing next to Uncle Steve.

My mother.

When Gabe had first met her, in the nightmare dimension called Arcadia, she wasn't quite . . . well, quite *human* anymore. Her skin had turned an odd kind of translucent, and she'd gotten taller, and *way* too many pointy teeth showed when she grinned. But now that Arcadia and Earth had converged, at least she *looked* like his mother again. Pretty and slender and dark haired, with big blue eyes and perfect white teeth.

Next to her, Uncle Steve stood quiet and shell-shocked. But Aria—*Mom*—her eyes darted around like a frightened rabbit, at the sky, at the ground, even at her own hands. Yes, Aria looked just like Gabe's mom, but the way she trembled and looked so afraid and confused, she wasn't at all like the mother he remembered.

Although the truth was that Gabe had never known his mother. Not really. He knew she and his dad and Uncle Steve and a woman named Greta Jaeger had tried to destroy Arcadia ten years ago, when Gabe was three. That attempt went horribly, disastrously wrong, costing Uncle Steve his leg, Greta Jaeger her sanity, and his parents their lives.

No. It cost Dad *his life. Mom just got trapped in Arcadia and . . . turned into something else.*

Gabe closed his eyes and wished that when he opened them this would all end up being a dream. That he and his friends had never been bound to the elements or found the Emerald Tablet or walked the streets of any world but the one they'd been born to. But no such luck. Across the waters, a building stretched for the amber sky, and its upper stories seemed to unfurl like the petals of an impossible and sinister black flower. As unrecognizable as it was, this was reality.

To Gabe's surprise, it was Aria who broke the silence. She stepped forward, putting a hand on his shoulder.

"Gabe, is your . . ." Aria faltered. She squeezed her eyes shut and made an impatient gesture with one hand. "Your . . ." She touched the side of his head, then the center of his chest. "I'm sorry. It's difficult to find the words. It's been so long. Your brain, and your heart . . . are they good?"

Uncle Steve gave Aria a little smile. "I think she wants to know if you're feeling okay, Gabe."

"Am I feeling okay?" *Does she even understand what's going on right now?* "Well, let's see if I'm missing anything. One, Jonathan Thorne possessed my friend to trick us into merging Earth with Arcadia, and now evil magick is, like, *everywhere*. And *two*—" He thought for a second. "Uh . . . I guess it's really just the one thing."

Uncle Steve grimaced. "In this case, one thing is more than enough."

Aria nodded and might have said something else, but a horrible howl sounded from across the waters, and she grabbed Uncle Steve's arm and hid her face in his chest. Uncle Steve stroked her hair. "It's all right, Aria. You're all right."

Gabe put a comforting hand on her shoulder, but he had no idea how to help his mother. He didn't even know if she *could* be helped. Seeing her so distressed made him feel utterly powerless.

As the others moved to join him, Uncle Steve, and Aria, Gabe looked to them for support. But they were all clearly every bit as stunned and lost as he was.

Kaz muttered, "All those people in the city. I mean, what's happening to them? Do you think they're even still—"

"Our grandmother's over there!" Lily said, turning to Brett in horror. "That's if—" Her voice caught for a moment. "That's if she survived the—"

"Oh my God," Brett said, looking stricken. "What do we do?"

"What do we do? We stop gawking and start *moving*." Lily gestured toward the far shore, across the choppy waters from Alcatraz Island where they stood. "We can't just stay here while the city turns into—into *that* with Abuela in the middle of it! She's all by herself, and who knows what's happening over there!"

"Lil's right," Gabe said. They could stand here on Alcatraz's rocky shore and watch their city darken. They could feel bad about how royally they'd screwed up, and how many thousands of people were in terrible danger because of them. But Lily and Brett's grandma needed their help.

Gabe had no clue how to undo the damage Thorne

had tricked them into causing, but helping find his friends' grandma? That was something he *could* do.

"We have to find her," he said. "We've got to help her and everyone else who needs it." He turned to his friends, and each of them nodded in agreement. "Let's find Jackson and get over there."

"Looks like another ride across the bay," Kaz said, trying for a smile. "Hey, maybe now that the dimensions have been mashed together, I won't get seasick. That'd be a silver lining, I guess?" Kaz's grin couldn't quite mask his desperation and fear, but Gabe appreciated the effort.

Uncle Steve offered his arm to lead Aria toward the water, and Gabe hurried to help him with her. She wasn't weak, exactly, but very disoriented. She constantly cocked her head and then swiveled it as if she heard voices that no one else could hear and saw things that no one else could see.

"Whatever's going on in the city can't be any worse than Arcadia," Gabe said to his uncle. He tried to smile. "Right?" he added hopefully.

"I don't know," Uncle Steve said as they neared the waterline. "This is a whole new reality. All new rules. We have to be ready for anything."

"And we shall be," said a higher-pitched voice.

Gabe turned to see Jackson Wright leap off a rock outcropping and land beside them—the pale, frail boy who wasn't really a boy at all.

However worried and afraid Jackson might be himself, he didn't hesitate for a second as he conjured a large golden disk of pure magick with a few gestures of his hands. The disk blazed into being within a moment. It was as impressive a display of his powers as Gabe had seen, but the smaller boy looked confused.

Jackson wasn't like Gabe and Lily and Kaz and Brett. They'd bonded with fire and air and earth and water. Real things, solid things, things anyone could understand. But Jackson controlled the magick itself, the fifth of the five elements, and Gabe knew they would need him if they were going to stop Jonathan Thorne from—

No. We did *need him. But Thorne beat us. He got what he wanted. He merged the magick of Arcadia with this world.*

"Everything okay?" Gabe asked. He wondered if he'd ever completely trust Ghost Boy. They hadn't gotten off on the right foot, and in Gabe's book, Jackson still wasn't normal, not by a long shot. But at least he wasn't actively insulting and unpleasant anymore.

"Yes," Jackson answered after a moment. "But I thought creating our conveyance would be more strenuous."

Gabe shrugged. Jackson's powers had always been a mystery to him. He positioned himself so he stood at the leading edge of the disk. Icy salt water sprayed his face as Jackson began to speed them toward the mainland, but he was too mesmerized by the twisted horrorscape of what had once been San Francisco to feel it.

"What if we're too late?" Brett asked Lily.

"We're not," Lily answered. "Abuela's tougher than both of us put together. If anyone survived over there, it's her. We're going to get to her as quickly as we can. Just try not to worry too much."

Brett harrumphed and folded his arms. "Easier said than done."

"It would probably be wisest to stand as close to the center of the platform as possible," Jackson said.

Brett gave him a quizzical look. "I'm bound to water, remember? If one of us falls, I can just pull them out."

Jackson's eyes shimmered gold, unblinking, as he answered. "It's not the water or your mastery of it that I question, Brett. But considering the strange beasts we've seen in the air, I fear what might lurk beneath these waves."

No one said anything, but they all huddled closer to the center of the disk.

"Gabe," Uncle Steve said as he stepped forward, and that's when Gabe noticed with some surprise that his uncle still had both of his legs. When Uncle Steve had been thrown into Arcadia—and Gabe still hadn't forgiven Jackson for *that*— the shadow dimension's magick had grown his missing leg back. The fact that Steve still had it proved just how messed up this merged reality had become.

"Do you know what Thorne changed to make the ritual go so wrong?" Uncle Steve asked.

Gabe's shoulders slumped. "When Thorne had control of Brett, he made us think we had to use Jackson's family's ring to finish the ritual. Except it wasn't really a ring at all. It turned into some kind of . . . red snake. The snake grew and grew and . . ." He waved his hands helplessly at their surroundings. "And this happened."

Aria moved closer, and this time she put her arms around Gabe and hugged him. She didn't say anything, just held him. And for a second or two, Gabe wanted nothing else in the whole world.

This is the first time. The first time since I was three years old that my mom has really held me.

Gabe hugged her back.

After a minute, Aria let him go and turned to Uncle Steve. "Do you think . . ." She sighed raggedly. "My *mind* won't work. Do you think, all of this . . . Can we stop it? Undo it?"

Gabe kept his eyes closed as Uncle Steve answered, "I wish I knew."

Gabe didn't think he'd ever heard Uncle Steve sound so uncertain. About *anything*.

He didn't have time to give it any further thought, because Lily shrieked, "*Watch out!* Over there!"

Gabe whipped around to look, and suddenly wished they were much closer to the shore.

Six dark shapes were hurtling across the waves toward them. In the same way that Arcadian monsters began as normal earthly animals—normal dogs became hunters, ordinary bats became abyssal bats—Gabe felt sure these things had once been otters. *No, wait . . .* they were too big.

Seals!

He could only see their heads. Gone were the seals' big, dark, soulful eyes. These atrocities just had muzzles filled with hooked, razor-sharp fangs. Gabe trembled. Had every seal in the bay turned into one of these monsters?

"Jackson!" Uncle Steve barked. "We need to move faster!"

Jackson didn't reply, but gold radiance spilled from his eyes, and the disk picked up speed, smashing through the cresting waves on its path to the far shore.

Still, Gabe could tell that it wasn't fast enough. The seal creatures were gaining on them.

"Brett!" Lily shouted, dragging her brother closer to the disk's edge. "Do something! Make a waterspout, freeze them, *something*!"

Brett nodded, and swallowed hard, wiping his hands on his pants. "You got it." He adjusted his footing, threw out one hand in the creatures' direction, and then frowned.

Nothing happened.

Brett's frown deepened into a scowl. He hooked his fingers into claws, straining, and still nothing happened. The water between the disk and the rapidly approaching creatures didn't even bubble.

"What's wrong?" Kaz came to Brett's side. "Do your water stuff!"

"I'm trying!" Brett said through gritted teeth. "It's not—I don't know, it's not working!"

The seal creatures made a chilling sound, half bark, half roar. Gabe tried to think of a way to help. He could target their heads with fireballs, or try to make the water hot enough to scare them off. But before he could, Aria stepped over to the disk's edge, and her eyes went a solid slate gray, just like Kaz's did when he was about to channel the power of earth.

"No one is going to hurt my son!" Her words seemed to reverberate through the sky, and green light flashed from her eyes and out along her limbs. Now the water *did* bubble. It began to churn, and then a massive spike of stone erupted from the surface right where the seal creatures had been.

Kaz's mouth dropped open. "That's right! Gabe, your mom's an earth elementalist!"

Uncle Steve nodded. "She was, before she was trapped in Arcadia. And Gabe's dad's element was fire. Just like Gabe's."

Gabe had never thought of it that way before—that by becoming a fire elementalist, he had followed in his father's footsteps. It reminded Gabe of the dreams he'd been having of his family. How the three of them would be on a nice outing one moment, and then in the next, everything was burning. His father himself like an inferno made flesh, his eyes as hungry as burning embers.

The thought gave Gabe chills. He wondered if the flames had hissed in his father's ears the same way they did in his own. Had his dad ever had to face the hungry furnace inside him the way Gabe had in the Library of Mirrors, where he'd found the Mirror Book?

More bark-roars from the bay shook Gabe from these thoughts. He saw the seal creatures round the pointed rocky obstruction and come after them again. He thought Aria had speared them with the rock, but all she'd done was slow them down.

"Uh, ma'am?" Kaz said. "Could you maybe do a few more of those?"

Aria gave no sign that she'd heard him. But the green light flashed brighter from her eyes, the water churned again—and huge stone spikes erupted all around them, one after the other, punching up from the floor of the bay. Jackson yelped as a spike appeared almost directly in their path, and the golden disk lurched to one side as he veered around it.

"Gabriel!" Jackson said through clenched teeth. "Could you please ask your mother not to kill us all?"

Gabe said, "Mom—"

But Uncle Steve had already gone to her side. He had one hand on her shoulder, trying to pull her back from the water, and he spoke softly and quickly into her ear. Gabe couldn't hear what Uncle Steve said, but he heard his mother's words plainly:

"I—I can't— Something's wrong, Steve. I can't get it to stop!"

Aria trembled with the effort of controlling her element. Then, with a sobbing cry, she collapsed, her eyes blue again. The water stopped churning.

And the closest of the seal creatures burst out of the water, jaws gaping, fangs aimed straight at Uncle Steve's neck.

2

Gabe saw the seal lunge in what felt like slow motion. Its body was skinless, covered in gold slime, and *grooved* with channels that spiraled back from the tip of its snout. *It's like a screw . . . or a drill.* Now that he was up close, he realized it was also a whole lot bigger than any seal he'd ever seen.

Before the creature could sink its fangs into Uncle Steve, Jackson grunted, and the edge of his magickal golden disk expanded and curved upward. The seal slammed into the rim and disappeared beneath the waves with a howl of pain.

But the impact knocked the disk off balance, and as more seals smashed into its now-exposed underside, it began to tip over. "I could use some assistance here!" Jackson yelled.

Gabe wasn't sure what to do. He'd seen his mother's powers back in Arcadia—they were incredible. If she couldn't control her element, then how would Gabe be able to handle fire? *What if I try to hit one of those things with a fireball and accidentally burn us all to a crisp?*

THUD. THUD. *THUD!* The creatures kept bombarding the disk, knocking it further off keel. There was nothing to grab on to, so Gabe slid sideways, trying not to knock anyone else over. He wiped a spray of salty water out of his eyes and squinted at the shore. "Jackson! We're almost there! Can you go any faster?"

Golden light flashed and shimmered all around the smaller boy. "Do you not think that if I could increase our speed, I *would have by now?*"

"Everyone get down!" Uncle Steve shouted "I'm going to give us a push!"

Gabe watched Uncle Steve move to the center of the disk and saw his eyes turn a shimmering silver-white. As he raised his hands, a sudden wind rushed around them—and the disk lifted out of the water. Gabe let out the breath he'd been holding. The disk rose fast, riding on a column of air, and the twisted city spread out below them. It was just like staring out the window of a plane at takeoff, the bay and the shore and the gnarled buildings rapidly growing smaller as they lifted into the sky.

That'll get us out of reach of those monsters!

But no sooner had that thought formed in Gabe's mind than the disk began to spin. Not just spin—it started *whirling*. Gabe and everyone else slid to the edge of the disk, hanging on for dear life.

"Steve!" That was Aria, panic in her voice. "Steve, it's happening to you, too! You have to stop!"

Lightning flashed around the disk as Uncle Steve shouted, "I'm trying! I'm *trying*! It won't let me go!"

Kaz slid over near Gabe, his arms flailing. "So much for hoping I don't get sick! This is why I don't get on whirly rides at theme parks. Oh God, stop. I'm gonna hurl!"

Somehow still on his feet, Jackson shouted, "Someone do something or we shall spin ourselves to the moon!"

Gabe's stomach was doing flip-flops, and he felt nausea rising in his chest. But he knew Jackson was right. Groaning with effort, Gabe pushed himself away from the edge of the disk, braced his feet on Kaz's back—"Sorry!"—and clamped a hand around one of Uncle Steve's ankles. Letting the centrifugal force work in his favor, Gabe heaved, pulling his uncle's legs out from under him. Steve crashed to the floor of the disk, his eyes flickering back to their normal blue-gray.

The spinning finally stopped.

Jackson bared his teeth and screamed, "It would be wise for everyone to brace for impact!"

It still felt like a theme park ride. But instead of the spinning teacups, the disk was now the front car on a superhigh roller coaster, and Gabe's stomach lurched again as they plummeted toward the ground.

Everyone slammed together as they dropped from the sky. Gabe didn't even have time to try to figure out whose elbow was digging into his shoulder blade before they crashed into the rocky shoreline in an explosion of gravel and dirt.

Gabe spat out a mouthful of grit and slowly, painfully sat up. As the ringing in his ears faded, Gabe patted himself, noting with relief that he didn't think he'd broken or ruptured anything.

He untangled himself from the knot of limbs and glanced around. Cautiously, he asked, "Is everyone okay?"

All seven of them lay in the huge rut the disk had carved, but the disk itself had vanished. "Define 'okay,'" Brett grumbled.

Gabe got to shaky feet and started helping other people up from where they'd fallen. Lily bounced to her feet like a spring, and Jackson followed her half a second later. Kaz sat in place, though, holding his head with both hands. When Gabe got close enough, he heard Kaz saying, "I will not throw up. I will not throw up. I will not throw up."

Jackson knelt next to Kaz and put a hand on his shoulder. "Kazuo. If you need to vomit, go ahead. But we must be on our guard."

"Jackson's right," Gabe said. It looked like they had crashed near Pier 39—about a hundred yards from the shore—though it took a few beats for him to recognize the area. The closest building to them was a parking garage, but it had buckled and crumbled in on itself, leaving little more than a huge pile of concrete chunks and pulverized cars. At least there weren't any seal creatures around. "We have to be ready for anything."

"Our grandma lives in Sunset," Brett said. "Which is—"

"That way, I think," Lily said, pointing inland and to the west. "And, yeah, let's be careful and really quiet."

"No!"

Gabe spun around at the sound of his mother's voice. She was a dozen yards away, down on her knees, beating her fists against the ground. Uncle Steve knelt beside her. Aria threw her head back, tears running down her cheeks. "Why won't you listen to me? *Why?*" Her eyes turned solid slate gray as she pounded her fists into the dirt again.

Gabe realized who she was screaming at. The earth. Brett and Lily came to stand on either side of Gabe. Softly, Brett said, "Dude, what's going *on* with your mom?"

Gabe wished he knew how to respond.

"You guys!" Lily grabbed Gabe's arm and pointed.

In the distance, dirt and concrete buckled as something burrowed underground—and started heading straight for where Gabe and his friends stood. Then Gabe noticed another rumbling, moving mound of earth and pavement nearby. And another. And *another*. They looked like moles skimming just under the surface. Except these things were *way* bigger than moles.

He counted six. All headed straight for them. Gabe drew in a breath to call over Uncle Steve, but before he could, one of the earth mounds burst open. Gabe's heart kicked into hammering overdrive as one of the seal creatures from the bay leaped up out of the ground, torqued through the air, and burrowed underneath again, like a great white shark breaching as it tore after its prey. Gabe could see now that along the length of its grooved, bear-size body, the seal had sprouted row after row of long, sharp, rocklike spines. *Those spines must help them dig through the earth!* As they rotated themselves, the beasts would cut through the ground like a drill through wood. *"Hey!"* Gabe shouted over his shoulder. "We've got company!"

That snapped Aria out of whatever kind of argument she was having with earth. She angrily wiped her tears away and scrambled over to join the group, Uncle Steve right behind her.

Steve said, "Where?"

The creatures had halved the distance between them. They were slower tunneling through earth than skimming over the water, but not by much.

Brett said, "There! The—the seal things! The *spike seals*! The things that attacked us on the raft! They're coming after us!"

Gabe could tell when Uncle Steve spotted the creatures; his expression went tight. "We need to run!" Steve said. "We can't take them on with our powers behaving so unpredictably!"

Another spike seal breached, smashed its way through a hot dog stand as if it was made of Kleenex, and ripped into the ground again.

Gabe shook his head. "Uncle Steve, they're too fast! We can't outrun them."

Brett stepped forward, his eyes shifting to blue-green. "You're right, Gabe. They'll be here in a few seconds. But I can feel a water main right underneath us. Kaz? Jackson? You with me?"

Uncle Steve shook his head. "Don't, Brett. You saw what happened when Aria and I tried to use the elements. You couldn't even channel water when we were on the bay."

Jackson's eyes turned gold again, and magickal energy danced and crackled around his hands. "Dr. Conway is correct, Brett. My element seems to be the only stable one. You should let me handle this."

Brett shook his head. "No way. I'm connected now! I can feel it! C'mon, guys! Let's do this!"

Two spike seals exploded from the earth not twenty feet in front of the group, and two things happened at exactly the same time: Brett summoned a broad column of water up from beneath the crumbled concrete, and Kaz, his eyes slate gray— *Just like Mom's,* Gabe thought—made the ground erupt in a broad, high wall, blocking their view of the vile Arcadian monsters.

But the water that Brett wielded looked different than any

Gabe had seen before. Not just sparkling with reflected light from the amber sky, it seemed to hold a luminescence of its own. Arcs of blue energy jittered along the column. Kaz's barrier of rock looked as if it was charged, too, with faint veins of green incandescence laced through the stone.

Gabe noticed all this in the space of a moment, and that was all the chance he got. Because when Brett's column of water brushed against the top of Kaz's rock wall, there was a surge of power that sent his ears ringing and his eyes dancing with the afterimage of green and blue fireworks.

There were some things that only elementalists could see, and when Gabe blinked and saw the surreal way that column of water and wall of earth *twisted together*, he wondered if this was one of them. Then steam burst from the surface of the pillar, which whirled and swayed for one second, maybe two, before it exploded, sending Gabe head over heels and flat into the ground. He screamed in shock and pain as tiny particles of scalding mud plastered themselves to his face and neck, burning like lit matches. He frantically scraped them off his skin, but blisters were already rising where the mud had stuck to him.

The spike seals fell back, but only for a heartbeat. He could tell from the moving mounds of dirt that the creatures were about to charge for them again, then Gabe almost choked as a hand grabbed the back of his collar and pulled. "Don't just stand there!" Lily screamed in his ear. *"Run!"*

Gabe did run, and as Lily veered toward where Brett was laid out on the ground, Gabe almost collided with Kaz, who was just picking himself up. They helped each other through the chaos. His friends and uncle and mother scrambling after them as seal after seal burst up in the air, fangs gnashing as they tried to sink into flesh. Gabe couldn't see Jackson, but off to his left golden light flared over and over, and spike seals squealed every time it did. He spotted Uncle Steve and Aria taking shelter behind a caved-in dump truck, and Brett and Lily running as two spike seals tunneled after them. Gabe was so disoriented that he nearly ran into one of the pillars of the ruined parking garage.

Bracing themselves against the column and catching their breath, Gabe and Kaz stood on a pile of cracked asphalt and shattered concrete. For a second, Gabe thought maybe, *maybe*, they'd lost the spike seals, but no sooner had the thought crossed his mind than the pavement and debris beneath them began to shudder and buckle. A spike seal was drilling right for them.

"What do we do?" Kaz shouted as they scuttled to the side. With mounds of rubble around them, there wasn't anywhere else to go. "Earth is a no-go, and, no offense, I'd rather you didn't try fire and torch us all to ashes!"

The spike seal broke through the pavement. It was bigger than any they'd seen before, easily the size of a car, and it hissed as its yawning mouth searched for them. Gabe had no answers. He knew Kaz was right. He didn't dare try to use fire. But he wasn't about to just stand there and let some Arcadian freak have him for lunch.

Desperate, Gabe grabbed a fist-size chunk of broken concrete and threw it as hard as he could at the spike seal's head. His aim was better than he'd expected. The chunk hit the monstrosity's gnashing fangs and snapped one of them cleanly off. The seal recoiled, shrieking in pain. Gabe shouted, "Throw stuff at it! *Throw stuff at it!*" He snatched up more loose rocks and heaved them, bouncing them off the creature's head and body. Out of the corner of his eye, he saw Kaz throw something as well—and Gabe couldn't help but frown in puzzlement as Kaz's tea thermos disappeared completely down the spike seal's throat.

"Kaz, what are you *doing*?"

Kaz had his backpack open. As Gabe threw another chunk of concrete, his arm already getting tired, Kaz flung a notebook at the spike seal, and then an assortment of pens, and then an apple. His voice spiraling up toward hysteria, Kaz said, "You've got all the good concrete bits over there!"

The spike seal didn't seem to mind being fed Kaz's school supplies, but then it convulsed and coughed the thermos back out. Gabe landed another chunk of concrete on its muzzle, and that made the creature *really* angry.

Kaz wrenched the Mirror Book out of his backpack. "This is all I've got left! Should I throw it? I shouldn't, should I?"

"No, you should *not*!"

The spike seal seized its opportunity, screamed, and lunged for them.

Gabe threw his arms up, bracing for impact, hoping

it wouldn't hurt for very long when the creature's fangs tore through his flesh . . .

. . . but nothing happened.

Gabe lowered his arms.

The spike seal was *gone*.

He looked over and saw Kaz, eyes squinched shut and the Mirror Book held open in front of him like a makeshift shield.

Numbly, Gabe realized none of them had actually opened the Mirror Book before. In fact, all he knew about the artifact was that it was some kind of twin to the Emerald Tablet, which meant it was soaked in magick, and really powerful, and probably insanely dangerous. He and Uncle Steve had retrieved it from the Library of Mirrors in Arcadia in their effort to stop Jonathan Thorne from combining Earth with the other dimension. *For all the good that did.*

Gabe said, "Kaz. What did you do?"

Kaz opened his eyes and lowered the Book. "Great crispy Tater Tots . . . did that *work*? We're not dead?"

Gabe repositioned the Book in Kaz's hands so that they could both see the pages. Unlike the Emerald Tablet, whose pages were covered in glyphs of elemental magick, the interior of the Mirror Book seemed to be composed of . . . a broken mirror? No, Gabe realized, it *looked* broken but it was actually carefully pieced together like a collage.

Kaz stared at the Book with wide eyes. "What are we even looking at?"

Gabe's breath caught in his throat, and he pointed mutely. There, visible in a single shard of mirror, was the spike seal. After a moment it scurried away and appeared on the opposite end of the page.

That's when Gabe realized that the mirrors weren't a collage . . . they were a *maze*.

The spike seal was caught in whatever kind of labyrinth lay within the Book's pages, dashing from one part of the maze to another. Disappearing from one part of the page and then reappearing somewhere else. Panicked. Searching for a way out.

"I'm not sure, exactly, but the library where Uncle Steve and I found this book, in Arcadia? This reminds me of it." Gabe couldn't help but sympathize with the creature, if only a little. "You should close it."

Kaz glanced up at him. "Why?"

"The library in Arcadia was an illusion. A trap. It was made of mirrors, just like these pages, but the books there . . . they reflected bad things back at us. It was a place where your inner demons sort of . . . come and find you. If that book opens up to a place anything like that library . . ."

Kaz took that in. "What, like that island in *The Voyage of the* Dawn Treader? Where dreams turn real?"

Gabe nodded. Without another word, Kaz carefully closed the Book.

Jackson hovered up to them on a floating disk of magick.

At least someone's element is working.

"Are you two all right?" Jackson asked.

Gabe and Kaz exchanged brief looks, then nodded.

"Good. Come on. I've dispatched the last one of these creatures, but there are more coming out of the bay. More than we can handle. We need to leave the area."

Gabe needed no further prodding. He and Kaz wordlessly followed Jackson to an avenue embedded with streetcar tracks. Uncle Steve, Aria, and the Hernandez twins were already waiting for them. *God, they all look like they've been through a war.* Blisters dotted their exposed skin from the disastrous mud explosion Kaz's and Brett's powers had caused, and they all had the same golden ichor splotched all over them. A dozen dead spike seals lay around them.

"Hi, guys," Kaz said hollowly. "What's up?"

"That's a good question," Lily said. "Dr. Conway? Um . . . Aria? You guys have any idea why our powers've gone all wonky?"

Uncle Steve rubbed the back of his neck. "As I told Gabe before, this is a new reality. A new balance among the elements. Thorne's original plan had been to increase the amount of magick on Earth, so maybe that's why Jackson's power is so effective while our terrestrial elements are so . . . unpredictable."

Gabe looked around at the dead spike seals. *Did Jackson do all this on his own?*

Brett turned in a slow circle. "This isn't even San Francisco anymore. Not really."

"Nope." Kaz shook his head. "We're in *San Arcadia* now."

Gabe let those words sink in. *San Arcadia.* He hated the sound of the name, but he could feel how appropriate it was all the way to his bones.

"Come on," Uncle Steve said. "We need to get inland. As far away from these things as possible."

"Our grandma's apartment is this way," Lily said, and started off.

"Wait." Brett squinted at the waterline. "I don't see the spike seals anymore."

"Oh God," Kaz said. "Then where are they!?"

As if in response to the question, the ground trembled beneath their feet. Gabe looked back toward the parking garage, and his stomach dropped into his shoes. At least two dozen seal trails buckled and shattered their way toward the group. As they charged through a sea of parked cars, they knocked everything from sedans to SUVs up in the air as if they didn't weigh a thing.

Brett's voice trembled. "Too late to run, and I'm afraid to try anything with water again. Jackson, you're the only one worth anything in this fight. Can you handle all of those?"

Like Brett, Gabe was still too afraid to try to use his

element. Even on a good day he had trouble controlling the furnace inside him, and now, in San Arcadia, fire was sure to be even more dangerous.

But without our powers we're completely helpless!

Jackson was still breathing hard. The gold in his eyes flickered. "I can certainly try."

"No." Aria stepped out between the group and the onrushing spike seals. "Let me."

Uncle Steve caught her elbow in his hand. "Aria, no! What if you lose control again?"

She shook his hand free. Her luminous blue eyes turned solid gray; green light flashed around them as they lingered on Gabe. "I will let no harm come to my family."

The earth rumbled beneath them again, but it felt different this time, and Gabe knew his mother was the cause of it. As the spike seals drew nearer, Aria knelt and placed both hands flat on the ground. Her skin took on a grayish tone.

Gabe had seen his friends' eyes change color when they channeled their powers, but he'd never seen their entire bodies change like this. What did it mean? Was this another unpredictable side effect of San Arcadia? Or was this something else?

Aria arched her back, and the streetcar tracks in front of them tore completely out of the ground.

Greater and greater lengths of the metal rails uprooted, and as Gabe watched, they flattened and sharpened, until fifty yards' worth of metal was whipping through the air like ribbons.

Gabe had seen something a little like this before, when Kaz had summoned columns of rock up out of the ground and transmuted them into metal. That had been impressive, but didn't come close to matching Aria's power. He'd never seen anything like it.

But what if she does lose control again? What if something crazy happens like when Brett and Kaz tried to use their powers? We'll be sliced to pieces! Gabe glanced at Uncle Steve and saw that he wasn't retreating—he was watching, just as curious as Gabe—and that made him feel a little better.

As soon as the spike seals came close enough, the animated rails attacked. They speared into the earth, living, whiplike swords that plunged and sliced and gouged. One after another, moving faster and faster, the tracks found seal after seal, and it didn't matter whether the creatures were aboveground or below. Within seconds, every spike seal had been sliced apart, and the razor-sharp streetcar tracks sprayed golden ooze as they cut through the air, seeking another target.

Gabe held his breath, waiting for more of the creatures to come. All he could hear was the bladelike rails creaking and groaning as they swayed in the air above them.

Barely above a whisper, Aria asked, "Is that it? Did I get all of them?"

Eyes wide, Uncle Steve said, "I believe you did."

The tracks froze in place as Aria fell over sideways.

Gabe and Uncle Steve rushed to crouch beside her. Now

that he was closer, Gabe was horrified to see that his mother's skin had not only turned gray, but also had taken on a stone-like texture, with a fine webwork of cracks running all across it. Aria blinked, tears in her eyes, and Gabe finally exhaled as her skin faded back to normal, the cracks and the stony texture disappearing.

Gabe helped Uncle Steve pull Aria back to her feet. His uncle said, "That was too much. You're asking too much of yourself. You know the risk you're taking."

Aria grimaced in pain.

"Mom? Can you walk? I don't see any more spike seals, but we need to get out of here."

She nodded. "I'm . . . I'm all right. Come on. I know we need to move."

It didn't seem to take long for her equilibrium to return, and Gabe and Uncle Steve and Aria joined Gabe's friends as they made their way inland, away from the shore.

The city changed, slowly but steadily, as they moved deeper into it. After the first block, Gabe noticed a golden tinge in the air. It was disturbingly similar to the air in Arcadia. It grew more noticeable as they walked, and the colors of the buildings and sidewalks and streets began to warp and darken. It wasn't quite the rich, intense, oil-painted look of Arcadia. More as if San Francisco—*San Arcadia*—was slowly being tainted. Spoiled.

The city is rotting. The city is dying.

Normally, at a time like this, Brett would have been the

first one to strike up a conversation, or at least crack a joke to try to break the tension. But silence descended on them as they walked, and Gabe's head swiveled side to side, looking for threats. The spike seals could come at them from the ground beneath their feet. Gabe wondered, against his will, what other horrors were creeping around—what other city creatures had been grotesquely changed. Cats? Rats? *Pigeons?*

Nowhere is safe now. They can come at us from any direction.

"Look! Up ahead!"

Gabe had gotten so used to the silence that his feet almost left the ground at the sound of Uncle Steve's voice.

Two streets ahead, a knot of fifteen or twenty people had gathered in the middle of an intersection, between a couple of blessedly undamaged apartment buildings.

We're not the only survivors!

They broke into a jog   even Aria, who seemed to be more or less in control of herself again—and as they drew closer, Gabe heard several of the people crying.

From teenagers to senior citizens to businessmen, none of the survivors seemed to know what to do. They just huddled together, frightened eyes darting like rabbits.

"I never thought I'd be this glad to see a bunch of regular, ordinary humans," Gabe said, mostly to himself.

A middle-aged Asian man, wearing a work shirt with the name "Carlos" stitched over the left chest pocket, spotted them approaching and warily broke away from the group. "Who are you? What do you want?"

"We're just trying to get someplace safe," Uncle Steve said. "What are you doing out here in the street?"

Carlos raised a shaky hand and pointed at one of the apartment buildings. "We all live in there. Or, we *used* to live in there. But it tried to . . . to . . ."

Another of the survivors, a thin blond woman, came and clutched at Carlos's arm. "It tried to *eat* us!"

Kaz's brow furrowed. "It tried to *what* you?"

Carlos put his arm around the thin blond woman, gesturing toward the building with his chin. "Look at the entrance to the parking garage."

Gabe did—and wished he hadn't.

What had once been a broad, empty opening leading from the street down to the building's underground parking structure was now filled with *teeth*. At first Gabe had mistaken the long, distinctive Arcadian fangs—the same kind of fangs that filled the mouths of hunters and spike seals and abyssal bats— for some kind of gate. But once he had made out that detail, others sprang out at him: the golden ooze seeping out from the cracks in the walls. The malevolent light glowing from the windows. The sense that the building, in a vast, lethargic way, was *breathing*.

Close to his ear, Lily murmured, "Oh God . . . the whole block . . ."

Gabe saw what Lily meant. Every building around them

had come alive. Massive giants made of brick and steel and mortar, waking from a deep sleep. Waking *hungry*.

Gabe squeezed his eyes shut and pressed the heels of his palms into them. *Hunters and bats, sure. Spike seals, fine. But this?*

How do you fight a city?

"Over there."

Gabe opened his eyes again to see Aria pointing down the street to their left. "I don't think the buildings along that street have been affected. At least, not yet."

To Carlos and the blond woman, Uncle Steve said, "Can the two of you get everyone moving? We can't stay here. It's not any safer out in the open than it is inside one of those . . . things. We've got to find shelter."

Carlos turned to his neighbor. "What do you say, Holly?"

Holly nodded, her expression resolving into something more determined. "I say, let's get out of here. I'll get the others into gear."

Together, she and Carlos gathered the other survivors, and they all fell in behind Uncle Steve and Aria as they headed down the street, staying as far away as possible from—Gabe shuddered at the thought—any of the *living buildings*.

Kaz and Lily walked closest to him. Softly, Gabe said, "Do you guys think the whole world is like this?"

Lily just shook her head. But it didn't look like a "No." More like a "Who knows?"

Kaz frowned darkly. "Thorne kept saying he wanted to

merge Arcadia with Earth, right? Like, the whole earth. I don't think we can do anything but guess . . . but if that was his plan, then yeah, it might be like this everywhere."

Gabe clenched his jaw. He'd moved all over the country with Uncle Steve. *New York. Washington, DC. Seattle. Are all of them gone? Or worse than gone?* "All because of what we did. Because of our screw-up."

"It's *not* our screw-up," Brett said. "Thorne used me, and he tricked all of us. We were trying to do what was right."

"I know. I know." Gabe searched for the right words. "But how do we *fix* it?"

He didn't have time to think about it any further. Jackson had hardly said a thing since leaving the ruined parking garage, but now he hissed, "Overhead! Abyssal bats!"

Gabe craned his neck toward the sky. The winged monstrosities were shaped more or less like bats, but the similarities ended there. They were as big as large dogs, had no eyes or noses, and instead of skin were covered in the same golden slime as so many other creatures befouled with Arcadian magick. The flying marauders weren't directly above them, but they were getting closer, and fast.

"Everyone!" Uncle Steve shouted. "Inside that store!"

A ripple of frightened whispers made its way through the survivors of the living apartment building. Holly shook her head vehemently. "What if it tries to eat us?"

Lily snapped back, "I don't know if the store will eat us, but

I *guarantee* those things in the air *will*!"

Gabe spied an overturned streetcar down the street. "Everybody! Hey! This way!" He pointed to the vehicle. "That should be big enough! We can all get inside it!"

The survivors seemed unsure, but Uncle Steve and Carlos and Holly all started waving them toward the streetcar. Within a few seconds, moving in a tight cluster, everyone reached it and crowded inside.

Next to Lily and Brett, Gabe peered up through the windows that faced the sky. The abyssal bats wheeled overhead but seemed to take no notice of them. Soon they turned as a group and glided off to the east, vanishing from sight.

Kaz whispered, "Do we keep going now?"

"Let's give it a few minutes," Uncle Steve said. "Make sure they're gone."

Gabe didn't mind taking a breather. If he pretended the streetcar was right side up, he could further pretend that he and this terrified knot of survivors were just normal people on a normal day going about their normal lives.

If only.

Jackson spoke quietly. "I understand these people's reluctance to enter another building, but something about our current location . . . troubles me."

Lily conjured up a tiny smile. "You mean like how we're in the middle of a city that literally wants to eat us?"

Jackson shook his head. "No. Well, yes, yes, of course,

but something about this streetcar is peculiar. We know that magick is everywhere in this new reality, but I sense more in some places than in others. And its strength is changing—growing—around us, as if the metal is becoming permeated with it."

Their conversation caught Uncle Steve's attention. "Jackson, what are you saying?"

Jackson opened his mouth to answer, but whatever words he might have spoken got drowned out by the sudden ear-splitting screech of rending metal and a brittle explosion of shattering glass. As golden ichor abruptly oozed from every joint and rivet in the streetcar, the far end of it crimped inward, and the shredded metal curved down and became teeth.

Jackson's voice boomed as brilliant golden light flared from his body. "Everyone out! *Everyone get out!*" Amid shrieks of terror from the passengers, Jackson thrust both hands forward, and a disk of golden energy materialized in the middle of what had rapidly become the streetcar's mouth. Jackson grunted, and the disk expanded, forcing the teeth back.

"I can only hold it like this for a few seconds!" Jackson snarled. "Evacuate everyone! *Now!*"

The survivors, and for that matter Gabe and Lily and Kaz and Brett, needed no further prodding. Everyone dashed out of the streetcar, and Gabe turned to see Jackson's golden light blasting from every one of its windows. The metal writhed and rippled, and the streetcar reshaped itself into something like a huge, twisted caterpillar.

"Jackson's still in there!" Lily screamed. "We've got to save him!"

Gabe thrust out a hand, ready to summon the power of his element, but caught himself. He'd grown so used to relying on his element in moments of danger against the Eternal Dawn and its creatures. But now, in San Arcadia, fire itself might be the worst danger of all. He hated how helpless he felt without it. *Should I risk it?*

But before he could decide, the immense metal monstrosity whipsawed back and forth, bent double, and ripped in half as a massive, spinning, golden saw blade cut it from the inside out. The separate halves slammed into the street and lay still.

Jackson stumbled out of the wreckage. He made it five steps before collapsing to his knees. Immediately Gabe and Lily rushed to help him, but Jackson sank down to the ground and waved a weak hand at them. "I cannot stand," he gasped. "Not yet. Please give me a moment." He looked around at the ruined—deceased—streetcar. "That was . . . immensely difficult."

Uncle Steve's shadow loomed over them. "That was also more than enough to draw unwanted attention, I'm afraid."

Gabe stood and followed his uncle's line of sight, scanning the skyline. "Where're the bats? How many?"

"It's not bats, Gabe," Uncle Steve said. His voice sounded strange. Flat.

Defeated.

A dozen gigantic, golden, six-winged creatures like nightmare versions of dragons plummeted out of the sky. Gabe recognized them—*null draaks!*—a second before realizing each of them had a *rider.* A rider dressed in a long, flowing robe.

No. No no no! The Eternal Dawn!

The magick-worshipping cult led by Jonathan Thorne had dedicated itself to uniting Earth and Arcadia, and in the process had tried to kill Gabe and his friends so many times he'd lost count.

Gabe threw up his arms to shield his face against the violent downdraft as the lead null draak beat its massive wings. The creature's momentum slowed, but not by much; and when it slammed into the street, the shock wave sent Gabe and everyone else flying like bowling pins in a strike.

3

Kaz clutched his backpack. It occurred to him to hop into Uncle Steve's arms and pray for safety, but he clamped down on this impulse. Terrified beyond all reckoning or not, Kaz did his best to avoid embarrassing himself more than was strictly necessary. His backpack would have to give him the comfort he needed, *and, holy cow, did he need comfort right now.*

He thought the massive null draak looked even bigger than the one they'd encountered before. It unleashed a full-throated roar so loud he thought it might liquefy his bones. The beast whirled, its long, armor-plated tail sweeping right above them—*Good thing it already knocked us to the ground*—and the impact of its footfalls felt like earthquake aftershocks.

A burst of intense heat washed over him, and Kaz turned just in time to see Gabe get to his feet, pure elemental fire dancing around his hands and his head. Gabe's eyes blazed, and flames shot from his mouth as he screamed:

"Get away from us!"

In that moment, Kaz wasn't sure who to be more afraid of: the null draak or the wild nature of Gabe's fire.

Should I break out some graham crackers and chocolate for when Gabe toasts us all like marshmallows? Kaz thought hysterically.

The null draak's rider yanked hard on its reins, pulling the creature's enormous head up and away, but Gabe had already followed through. Thrusting both hands forward, he summoned a five-foot ball of fire and sent it rocketing toward the great beast. Kaz immediately noticed there was something different about Gabe's fire. It burned just as you'd expect, but it also seemed to dance with scarlet energy that almost looked electric. He never saw if it hit the null draak, because with an eye-searing flash, the recoil of launching the fireball knocked Gabe backward, tumbling head over tail as if he'd been flung out of a giant slingshot.

Kaz shouted, "Gabe!" and scrambled after him, but two more null draaks slammed into the street between them. Kaz staggered, lost his balance, and fell backward—but stayed on his feet, thanks to the disk of golden light that materialized and caught him. Kaz struggled to regain his balance. When he did, he saw what he'd almost fallen on—what he *would* have fallen on, if the disk hadn't stopped him: a sharp piece of rebar poking up out of the ground like a rusty dagger. As he realized how close he'd come to being skewered, Kaz's knees got a little weak, and he bent over to steady himself. He wanted to kiss the ground. *Is that what people do when they almost get turned into a human shish kebab?*

Jackson crouched beside him. "Are you hurt, Kazuo?"

Kaz blinked a couple times and tried to steady his breathing. "You just saved my life."

A smile touched Jackson's eyes. "That is what we do, is it not? Save each other's lives?"

Kaz tried to think of something to say, but he couldn't stop staring at the length of rebar. Instead, silently, he held up a fist. Just as silently, Jackson reached over and bumped it with a fist of his own.

Kaz looked back to check on Gabe, but all he saw were five more null draaks. The ground trembled as they landed on the street.

But it wasn't just the null draaks causing the street to shake.

Kaz couldn't keep his jaw from dropping as the entire length of Stockton Street seemed to disintegrate. An army of spike seals headed toward them, buckling the asphalt as they charged.

Right. Of course. Because just a dozen null draaks would have been way *too easy.*

Kaz spun in place, looking around. The Dawn's null draaks on one side and a herd of spike seals on the other. *Maybe we can get inside a building that won't eat us? Maybe they can't get to us if we're up high!*—but he could see the golden ooze of Arcadian magick rolling down the sides of every structure in sight.

"That's it," Brett said, his words also ringing hollow. "That's game over. We're done."

"No way!" Lily's eyes flared silver-white as she shouted into her brother's face. "After all we've been through, no *way* am I just going to roll over for those things! My powers might be out of control, but I bet I can still take a bunch of them with me!" She whirled to face Kaz. "Come on, Kaz. Let's at least send these creeps out with a bang."

Kaz didn't like the way earth had felt when he connected with it earlier . . . and that was *before* it somehow combined with Brett's water and exploded like some weird volcano-geyser.

But he knew they only had seconds.

He reached his senses down into the earth and felt his eyes turn gray.

We're not going down without a fight!

But then something happened that brought a seriously bizarre day to a whole new level of weirdness.

He had horrible memories of the first time he'd witnessed a null draak in full attack, when he and Gabe and Lily and Brett had accidentally summoned one in the middle of an abandoned theater. That one had sprayed a ghastly, supercorrosive acid instead of dragon-fire, and the eight in front of them now were doing the same thing.

Except instead of coming after Kaz and his friends, the null draaks were attacking the spike seals.

Every time a spike seal breached the earth, it caught a full blast of null draak acid, and soon the air filled with squeals that Kaz knew would haunt his nightmares for years. The spike seals' shrieks sounded like tiny rocks being ground into powder, and they echoed up and down the streets for long, agonizing minutes. Kaz caught a glimpse of one of the seals dissolving into a bubbling glob of gold-and-green goo, and *really* wished he hadn't.

A spike seal with bristling fangs burst from the asphalt right in front of Kaz and Jackson, but no sooner did it reveal its nasty dental situation than a null draak stomped on it, pounding it right back into the ground.

Its rider, clad in the flowing robe of the Eternal Dawn, gave Kaz a little salute and then charged down the street toward where more spike seals were closing in.

Are they . . . they can't be . . . is the Dawn on our side?

Jackson must have had the same thought, because Kaz heard him say "What the devil?"

In the midst of the chaos, Kaz had momentarily forgotten about Gabe. He caught a glimpse of his friend's shoe sticking out from a heap of rubble and hurried over to him. "Gabe! Can you hear me? Are you all right?"

Gabe's voice floated up weakly from the other side of the pile of bricks. "I'm still breathing."

"Hey! You! You two!" another voice called down to them.

The voice belonged to the rider of the first null draak, a tall, thin woman with close-cropped, honey-colored hair. She stood on a leather-and-wood platform buckled to the broad back of one of the null draaks between the three sets of folded wings.

Kaz blinked at her. "You mean me? Us?"

The rider scowled, but she didn't seem angry. More like impatient. "You're Kazuo Smith, yeah? And that pasty little dweeb beside you is Jackson Wright. Correct?"

Kaz and Jackson exchanged a brief look. For once, Jackson seemed as clueless as Kaz felt. "Dweeb?" he echoed, mystified.

Kaz didn't have a comeback, but he did the best he could. "Who wants to know?"

The rider rolled her eyes. "My name is Myra Willis! Look, I'm supposed to get you and your little friends, okay? Now climb up and let's get you out of here!"

"Wait," Kaz said. His brain felt like a scrambled egg. "What?"

"We're here to rescue the five of you, so climb aboard," Willis said.

"Are you *serious*, lady?" Scraped and bleeding, Gabe picked himself out of the rubble. "You've kidnapped me, tried to sacrifice me, sent me to another dimension, and tricked us into destroying the world, and that was *just this morning*! Now you want us to, what, go on a *scenic dragon ride* with you?"

The screams of the spike seals had finally died away, and the null draak Willis stood on swung its head around. Kaz flinched, and Jackson's eyes flashed gold, but the null draak made no move to attack them. It just seemed to be looking at them. Sort of curiously.

Wait. Looking?

Kaz had spent enough time staring at the first null draak they'd encountered, and enough time running from hunters and abyssal bats and now spike seals, to know that creatures borne of Arcadian magick didn't *have* eyes. Their heads were always missing eyes and noses and ears entirely, and were only left with those huge, god-awful, fang-filled mouths.

But this one *did* have eyes, and as it pushed its head closer, Kaz saw with a deeply unsettling feeling in his guts that the eyes were blue.

Blue and *human*.

A dim memory surfaced. Greta Jaeger telling him and his friends that the first null draaks had originated as members of the Eternal Dawn, and were trapped in Arcadia back in 1906 and overwhelmed by magick.

And the differences didn't stop there. Now that he was studying the creature, truly seeing it, Kaz saw that it wasn't skinless. It was still golden, but it seemed to have traded in the sickening ooze for a kind of segmented skin. *More like armored plate.* Kaz realized he had noticed the armor right off, when the creature's tail had almost smashed them flat. He'd just been too busy almost dying to understand what it meant.

It's not just the city that's changing now. It's not just our powers. Everything *is changing.*

But did that mean the Eternal Dawn could change, too?

"It's a long story," Willis told Gabe. "And the streets are dangerous. There are worse things out there than these creatures. I've already lost three of my people looking for you."

"Three? I believe we can do better than that, can't we, Gabriel?" Jackson said.

Kaz glanced at Jackson. Judging by his steady, measured breathing and the tiny flickers of gold flashing from his eyes, the "pasty little dweeb" was trying to build enough strength for a major assault. Kaz put a hand on Jackson's arm. "Hey. Calm down for a minute, okay? Maybe we should listen to her."

Jackson never took his eyes off Willis, even as the other null draaks approached, their riders pulling carefully on their reins. Every one of the beasts peered at them with disturbingly humanlike eyes.

Kaz looked around, trying to find his friends. *Okay—there's Brett and Lily.* They were hunkered down behind a huge section of upturned pavement. He spotted Dr. Conway and Aria, too, several dozen yards away, facing down three null draaks of their own. Even at this distance, Kaz could see Dr. Conway's eyes flickering silver-white—ready to attack, but holding back for now. Kaz met his anxious gaze and raised a calming hand.

We're okay is what he wanted to communicate, or *I think we're okay, or at least I really hope so, because getting dissolved by null draak spit is not at the top of my to-do list.* Past Dr. Conway and Aria, Carlos and Holly stood with the rest of the survivors, frozen and staring in shock at the otherworldly null draaks.

Another of the giant beasts stepped forward at a nudge from its rider, a burly man with iron-gray hair and two ragged scars across his face. The rider snapped, "This area won't be clear for long! Grab 'em and let's go!"

A burst of heat flared over Kaz's shoulder, but Kaz raised his hands to his friends. "Guys, guys, hold on, okay? Just for a second." Kaz cleared his throat and looked back up at Willis. "Why should we trust you? Why should we believe anything you say? From the second we found out about you, the Dawn's done nothing but try to kill us."

Willis narrowed her eyes. "How about the fact that we just saved your malnourished butts? Or would you rather we left you stranded out here?"

"You will have to do a good deal better than that," Jackson said. The boy summoned a trio of gold disks. They looked like smaller versions of the craft that had brought them across the bay from Alcatraz, except Kaz could see these had edges as sharp as blades.

Kaz tried to square his shoulders. He wasn't sure he pulled it off, but it wasn't for lack of determination. "Jackson's right. Why help us now?"

"Because, believe it or not, you're the only ones who can undo this disaster," the burly man said.

"Undo it?" Gabe asked incredulously. "*You're* the ones who've been trying to merge Arcadia with Earth for over a century!"

Willis and the man exchanged glances. Kaz tried to read the look that passed between them. Embarrassment? No . . . it was something stronger than that.

They're ashamed.

"We were tricked by our Great Founder—by *Jonathan Thorne.*" Willis spat out the name as if it were rancid. "Thorne killed our Primus. Just to prove a point. To prove he *could.* We wanted to make the world a better place. Not be part of a senseless slaughter."

Kaz almost snorted. "But the Dawn *was* part of a senseless slaughter! I watched you—watched your Primus sacrifice people!"

"Yeah, like *me*," Gabe said. "And him." He tapped Jackson on the shoulder. "*And* him!" He pointed to where Dr. Conway stood.

Willis snarled, "That was for a *purpose*! We wanted to create a new Earth! A *better* Earth! Why do you think we called ourselves the 'Eternal Dawn' in the first place? We were meant to harness Arcadia's power, to bring forth a utopia! And instead . . . instead we unleashed a monster. And all the horror that came with him. This is an apocalypse. We don't know if it can be undone, but if it can be, then you're the ones to undo it.

Now you five—and *only* you five"—she glanced to where Dr. Conway, Aria, and the cluster of neighbors were huddled—"get aboard."

Gabe and Jackson started talking over each other with some pretty unfriendly words to Willis about just what they thought about *that*, but Kaz connected to earth, hoping like crazy that his element wouldn't go haywire on him. He used just enough of it to give his own voice a deep, gravelly tone.

"You want us to trust you?" He could feel words resonate through the ground at his feet and crush the sounds of all other voices. "You want us to come with you willingly? Then you've got to take all of us." He swept a hand toward Aria and Dr. Conway as well as Carlos and Holly's group. "Nobody gets left out here to die."

The scar-faced rider growled, made a truly disgusting noise in his throat, and spat a sizable wad of sputum on the ground at Kaz's feet. Kaz wanted to make a face or at least stick out his tongue at the man, but he was pretty sure that would ruin the tough-guy thing he was going for.

"Not a chance," the man said. "We pick up the five of you. Those are our orders."

Kaz glanced back at Gabe and Jackson. Gabe's eyes blazed, and Jackson's golden disks glinted menacingly. Kaz was used to Gabe taking the lead on stuff like that, but his friend gave him an encouraging nod.

Brett and Lily came over as Kaz spoke, squaring up behind

him and Gabe and Jackson. All five of them were now facing down the bunch of dragon riders. This was Kaz's show, and he was both excited and nervous.

This would be the worst possible time for a case of the giggles.

"If you take everyone to safety, we'll come with you," he rumbled. "If you don't agree to that, then we're staying right here. And I'd hate to be the ones who tried to move us."

I can't believe I just said those words out loud!

The scar-faced man snorted and turned his head away. Willis rolled her eyes with impatience but also, Kaz thought, a bit of amusement. Maybe even a touch of respect. She dropped back into her saddle. "Fine. *Fine*, you can all come." She spoke to the scar-faced man. "Norton, collect the others." To Kaz she said, "But *you* five are coming with me."

Kaz insisted on watching the survivors from the apartment building be collected first, which earned him a fair amount of grumbling from Norton and the other null draak riders. The survivors were on the fence, too, what with the whole riding-on-the-backs-of-giant-dragons thing, but once Dr. Conway explained the plan to Carlos and Holly, it didn't take long for them to decide that "someplace else" was better than "here."

As the survivors carefully climbed up onto the other null draaks under the supervision of Myra Willis and Dr. Conway, Gabe nudged Kaz with an elbow. "Hey, who died and made you leader?"

Kaz felt himself blush. "Oh, sorry, Gabe, I just thought that, you know, since I was right there and—"

Gabe grinned. "Relax. That was *awesome*. I wish I could do that earth thing with my voice. I think if I tried to sound that badass, I'd just end up setting my face on fire."

Kaz rubbed at the back of his own neck. "I just— I mean, we barely survived our first *ten minutes* in San Arcadia, and for people who don't have any powers—I figured we had to get them to the safest place possible."

"People like Abuela," Brett said, looking at Lily anxiously.

Kaz saw that the last of the survivors from the apartment building had boarded the null draaks, and Myra Willis was walking back toward them.

"We'll find her, *hermano*," Lily said, determined. "But she'd want us to get these people to safety first. And if the Dawn's headquarters is as safe as we hope it is, then we'll have somewhere to bring Abuela once we find her."

Willis stepped up to them and cleared her throat, her impatience back. "All right. Conditions met. Now will you please, pretty please, with a freaking cherry on top, *get up there?*"

Gabe grinned at Kaz again and made a grand gesture. "Lead the way."

At Willis's direction, Kaz very, very carefully climbed up the null draak's tail and settled onto the passenger platform. Thick leather loops were evenly spaced around its perimeter. Kaz gripped one as tightly as he could.

"Wait for us," Dr. Conway said as he and Aria hurried toward them

"We're all loaded up," Willis barked. "Take that one." She pointed to a nearby null draak whose passenger platform was completely empty.

"Ms. Willis, was it?" Dr. Conway said. He smiled, but Kaz couldn't find a single friendly thing in the expression. "I believe that going with you right now is the best of a series of terrible options, but I don't want you to be under the impression for even one moment that I trust you. I will not demean you with threats. I simply ask you to remember who I am and what I can do, and to pray that you don't give me a reason for a close-up demonstration of my abilities. Am I understood? Excellent."

Kaz bit down on a smile, then stole a look at Gabe, who didn't even bother to hide his grin. *I'd hate to forget my homework in Dr. Conway's class!*

"Kinda sounded like a threat," Willis muttered.

Dr. Conway finished climbing onto the creature's back and helped Aria up behind him.

Once they'd boarded, Willis turned back to them. "All right, now everybody grab a strap and hold on tight." She tapped both sides of the null draak's neck with her heels, and the gigantic creature spread its six vast wings.

Kaz's stomach dropped as they left the ground. But as the city fell away beneath them, he surprised himself by relaxing, if only a tiny bit. The null draak's flight was—he searched for the word—effortless? smooth? . . . *silky.* For such a huge, terrifying monster, it sped through the air with perfect, flawless grace. If not for the wind rushing past him, Kaz might have felt as if he were sitting still.

In between the velvety downstrokes of the null draak's sail-like wings, Kaz peered cautiously over its side at the city spread out below. Except it wasn't the city Kaz knew. Not anymore. It was San Arcadia, and even as he watched, Kaz saw more buildings succumbing to the evil, twisted magick threading its way through the streets. Concrete and brightly painted wood darkened to the black of soot, the black of wrought iron. Structure after structure shuddered and twitched and started to *breathe*, the buildings' shapes rising and altering as they transformed to reflect Jonathan Thorne's vision for the world.

We did this. He couldn't shake the thought. *We got used. Tricked. This is our fault.*

Thank God my family got out before it happened.

He and his friends had to fix this situation. This *crisis.* But before they could even start putting it right, he knew they had to understand it. Leaning far forward, he said, "Excuse me!" The rushing wind seemed to carry his words away. He raised his voice as much as he could without calling on the earth. *Would my powers even work this far off the ground?* "Hey! Hi, hello! Where are we going?"

Willis turned her head and fixed him with a baleful glare. She didn't have to shout as much since she was upwind. "The

Presidio. Fort Scott—or at least what used to be Fort Scott. It's a safe zone."

"How is it safe? Is the whole rest of the Eternal Dawn there? Did all of you turn on Jonathan Thorne? Who's in charge? Who told you to come and get us?"

Willis twisted around in the saddle and regarded Kaz with a level of condescension that made him grind his teeth. "You're an inquisitive little guy, aren't you?" She rolled her eyes again. "Fort Scott is safe because the Eternal Dawn have *made* it safe." She glanced down, past the null draak's head. "We're almost there. Hold tight."

Kaz peered forward, and his hands tightened involuntarily around the leather strap.

The Golden Gate Bridge wasn't golden anymore. It wasn't even a bridge. Instead, it had become some kind of . . . plant? The twin support towers had thickened, their surfaces growing dark and rough, and become what looked like two impossibly tall, warped trees. The bridge was broken in the middle, what was left of the roadway curling back toward the trunks like diseased branches. The huge support cables dangled lifelessly into the waters of the bay like enormous vines.

But that wasn't their destination. Kaz had seen plenty of aerial shots of Fort Scott on postcards and commercials. He knew what it was supposed to look like: a series of low white buildings with terra-cotta roofs, surrounding a huge green field. It was barely recognizable now, and if it hadn't been so close to the bridge, he wouldn't have had a clue where they were. The buildings had shifted, clumped together where the field used to be, and all of them were now five stories tall and a dull iron gray with black roofs. The trees surrounding the campus had either wilted or burned.

Something flickered in the air. Kaz squinted and could just make out a dome of wispy energy, like faint, golden filigree, surrounding the entirety of the Presidio, ringed by a dark band close to the ground. The dome revolved, very slowly, and as Kaz stared even harder, he saw radiant purple glyphs woven into its fabric.

As the null draak dipped and drew closer to the dome, Kaz saw other things in the sky: abyssal bats. More and more of them.

One of the dome's glyphs flared with brutal violet light.

Holy crap. It's like a giant bug zapper!

He shouted, "Uh, Ms. Willis? Watch out for the bats!"

Myra Willis turned to him again just as one of the bats swooped past. On its chest Kaz saw a glowing violet glyph just like the ones woven into the energy dome below. "The bats are on our side," Willis barked. "It's the sawjaws you have to worry about. They just *love* the dome."

The null draak dropped sharply—along with Kaz's stomach—and banked to the left. Off to their right, Kaz saw what Myra Willis meant: the abyssal bat that had come so close to them flew straight into a swarm of creatures the size of large house cats. Except they were reptilian, with wide heads, and membranous wings stretched from their forelegs to their hind legs. *It's like a hang glider and a hammerhead shark had a baby.* The abyssal bat ripped and tore its way through five of the sawjaws, and for a moment Kaz thought it might take out the whole swarm.

Instead the swarm curved in on itself, the sawjaws revealing ghastly, ravenous mouths, and the abyssal bat disappeared in a flare of purple light and a spray of golden slime.

A wave of nausea washed over Kaz, unrelated to their flight. But he forgot about that when they got near enough for him to get a closer look at what was clustered at the base of the energy dome.

People.

As the null draak cruised closer, Kaz saw hundreds of people—civilians, not Dawn members—huddled against the edge of the dome. Every now and then, one of the sawjaws broke away from tangling with the abyssal bats, swooped down into the crowd, and—

Kaz looked away, sick again, as a horrible scream sounded out and cut off abruptly. He grabbed a handful of Willis's robe. "Why are all those people outside? They're helpless! They're getting picked apart!"

He could barely hear her words. "We have our orders. Can't save everybody or we'd get overrun. And we've got enough problems as it is."

Willis's callousness struck Kaz dumb. He could only shake his head as the null draak dropped and flew through a circular gap in the dome that slid open just as they arrived.

Their landing was nothing like the null draaks' dramatic arrival in the street. The creature's six great wings slowed their descent so gracefully and gradually that, when they touched down, it was like dropping onto a big, soft pillow. The other seven null draaks landed out of sight, around the corner of the nearest iron-gray building. Banners of the Eternal Dawn were draped from several of Fort Scott's windows: a golden sunrise against a sea of black, just like the symbol many of the cults' members wore on their robes. Dozens of the cultists milled around—some moving back and forth between buildings, some on patrol, others coming forward to tend to the null draaks.

Kaz peered between robed individuals, trying to take in their surroundings. Instead of green grass, or any vegetation at all, they'd landed on dark-brown, hard-packed dirt. This bare earth appeared to surround the clustered structures of Fort Scott in a fifty-yard-wide band between the buildings and the slowly revolving barrier dome. Kaz couldn't help wondering if any plant life would ever grow there again.

He saw Gabe shiver as he jumped down from the null draak. "If I never, *ever* have to take a ride like that again, it'll be just fine with me. Those lizards were crazy! It's a miracle none of us got our head taken off!"

Brett grabbed Lily as soon as his feet had touched the

ground. "Lil, what if Abuela is out in that crowd? Stuck on the wrong side of the shield?"

Lily's face paled. "Oh God. With those sawjaw things!"

"I doubt very much that the Dawn will lower their shield to let these people in," Jackson said. "We should approach their leader and—"

His words cut off at the sound of a shrill scream. Not just a scream, more of a howl that made Kaz's bones vibrate. He couldn't tell where it came from because it sounded like it was coming from everywhere.

"What the heck is that?" Kaz asked. "I thought this place was supposed to be safe!"

"Maybe some sawjaws flew in when we did! We better check it out," Gabe said. "Uncle Steve, can you stay here with— Wait. Where's Mom?"

Dr. Conway had just hopped down from the null draak himself, and he looked back in confusion. "She was—she was right here a second ago."

The terrible sound doubled in volume. Even with his hands clutched tight over his ears, Kaz thought he might pass out.

"Mom? Mom!" Gabe took off in a panic.

Kaz ran after Gabe, with the others close behind. They rounded a corner of one of the compound's buildings to see the survivors from the apartment building fleeing toward them with looks of pure terror on their faces. Holly and Carlos were shepherding them away from something. But it definitely wasn't null draaks or Dawn members—they all seemed as confused and alarmed as Kaz and his friends.

What could be scaring everyone here, inside the safety of the dome?

Kaz's stomach dropped when he saw the answer.

"Mom!" Gabe shouted.

Kaz caught up to Gabe and saw that Aria was standing in front of the huge banner of the Eternal Dawn. She was swaying back and forth, wailing that inhuman cry. Kaz realized that her scream—roar? shriek?—sounded like it was coming from everywhere but was actually coming from the ground.

She's connecting to earth again!

"THE DAWN." The earth resonated with Aria's voice. Shards of razor-sharp rocks lanced the ground around her. With a wave of her hand, she shredded the cult's golden-sun banner. But she didn't stop there.

She reached down to the earth, and the ground cracked, breaking the building itself in half.

Gabe ran to Aria, trying to calm her down, but the crevasse she'd made continued to shudder and widen.

Ten cultists armed with some kind of crossbows approached from across the courtyard. Aria wheeled on them, and with a twitch of her stone-gray eyes, huge rock hands emerged from the ground to grab the first four Dawn members around their midsections and shake them as if they were no more than dolls.

"THEY DID THIS. THEY DID IT ALL. THEY TOOK MY FAMILY."

Gabe threw himself in front of his mother. "I'm here, Mom. They didn't take me. I'm still here!"

Aria's gray-eyed gaze wavered for a moment, and the armed cultists seized their chance to loose a volley of arrows pulsing with strange purple light. Gabe and Aria were both right in the line of fire, and Kaz started to scream, but then a gust of wind so powerful that it felt more like a wall knocked him onto his behind.

He squinted against the gale as it weakened, and he saw Dr. Conway kneeling alongside Gabe, his arms around Aria. His blast of air had knocked away the arrows as well as the cultists. His eyes flashed silver-white as he glared at the tumbling Dawn members. "Stay back! Stay *back*! Give us some room!"

Kaz saw Dr. Conway's fists clench with the extraordinary effort of controlling his element in the new weirdness of San Arcadia. As tough as it appeared to be, Gabe's uncle seemed to be holding strong. But Gabe's mom . . .

Aria's skin had again turned rough and gray. Stone-like. Green light flashed from between her closed eyelids for a heart-beat. Kaz could feel from the earth under his feet that she was still tapped in.

She's losing control. Aria had already destroyed a building with barely a thought.

What will she do if the earth takes her over completely?

Kaz clearly wasn't the only one wondering this. His fears were echoed in the murmurings coming from the Dawn members closing in from all sides—murmurings that coalesced into a single voice near where Uncle Steve still held Aria: "Surround her! Don't let her get her bearings!"

"Whoa!" Brett shouted. "Stop! Give her a second!"

But the Dawn paid no attention to him. The scar-faced null draak rider, Norton, led a group of seven Eternal Dawn members. Just as he'd ordered, they spread out around Uncle Steve, Aria, and Gabe, all of them focused on Aria, as if . . .

As if she were another San Arcadia monster. A dangerous menace to be contained.

One of the robed men brought out a pair of shackles. Kaz recognized the design: the same kind of elemental power-sapping bonds the Dawn had used on Gabe when they'd kidnapped him. That was bad enough, but on the far side of the circle, a woman pulled a *brand* out of her robes—a brand in the shape of a control glyph, just like the glyphs Kaz had seen burned into the abyssal bats protecting the Presidio.

They want to brand *her like an animal!*

The Dawn member with the brand had produced a small acetylene bottle. She ignited the torch and ran the narrow blue jet of flame over the control glyph, heating the metal to red-hot within seconds.

Kaz knew he had to stop this, but he was nervous about calling on Earth, and before a plan could fully form—

BOOM! The brand and the torch both flew from the woman's grasp, and she stumbled backward, frantically slapping out small fires that had sprung up along the sleeve of her robe.

"Nobody touches my mother." Gabe's voice hissed and crackled, his eyes blazing red-orange with a terrifying intensity Kaz had never seen.

Jackson, Lily, and Brett hurried to meet Gabe in standing against the Dawn. Kaz joined them, even though a pit grew in his stomach.

This is getting way *out of control.*

"Everyone just take a breath, okay?" Kaz said. He turned to face the Dawn members. "You need us, remember? That's why you, like, gave us free rides on Null Draak Airlines?"

"Yeah, we invited you. Not this—*creature*," Norton said. "She'll take this whole place down. She's gotta go."

A flare of firelight and a wave of heat told everyone Gabe's thoughts on that.

The truth was, Kaz understood the Dawn's position. In fact, with their powers being as unpredictable as they were right now, Kaz was pretty sure every single elementalist here was a serious danger to themselves and others.

"If you try to take her on, you'll have to go through all of us," Lily said.

"A course of action I do not recommend," Jackson added, his eyes glinting gold.

"Elementalists," Norton spat. "We're not exactly on our

own here, either, you know." He let out a high-pitched whistle.

Oh, this cannot *be good.*

Kaz remembered a time when he'd have been surprised at the sight of a pack of skinless, faceless wolflike creatures running along the sides of buildings as if gravity were only a suggestion. *Those were such good times.*

A dozen hunters responding to Norton's call scurried into position, facing off against Kaz and his friends.

Here we go again. But not quite. There was something else coming, something bigger. Kaz could feel its steps before the creature lurched into sight. *What on earth . . . ?*

In spite of himself, Kaz felt a gasp escape his mouth. This new creature looked like a cross between a hunter and a triceratops, and its body was larger than even that of the null draaks. Like the abyssal bats above and the hunters that escorted it, the monster was branded with a Dawn glyph of control.

"It's a behemoth," Norton said.

Yes. Yes it is.

"Uh, guys?" Brett said uncertainly. "What do we do?"

Dr. Conway, Gabe, and Jackson had connected with their elements; but Kaz hadn't missed the fact that Brett and Lily hadn't.

They must be just as freaked out about it as I am. But without our powers, how can we fight this thing?

"What do we do?" Gabe's voice flared and crackled. "We *fight!*"

The cultists aimed their bows, the hunters prepared to pounce, and the behemoth bellowed at an impossible decibel level that made Kaz wince and turn away. And when he did, he saw Aria's eyes settle on the creature.

"LEAVE MY FAMILY ALONE!" Aria screamed with the roar of the earth.

But the behemoth charged, heading directly for Gabe.

With a deafening sound like a mountain collapsing, a wave of force boomed out from Aria, through the ground, and surrounded the behemoth. A circular wall erupted from the earth and, pulsing outward like a ripple in a pond, swept every Dawn member away from the creature.

The behemoth growled as it turned in a circle, and the growl deepened into a threatening rumble as its eyeless face pointed toward Aria. It crouched, digging one foot into the earth, golden ooze slopping from its gaping mouth as it prepared to charge.

And then Aria *changed*. Kaz had seen her skin had become gray and stone-like, but this was completely different. Her body lengthened, elongating until she looked like a skin-and-bones scarecrow of herself, and her skin turned translucent, revealing the fine, pulsing tracery of veins beneath it. Veins that pumped *golden fluid*. Aria's mouth opened, and opened, wider and wider, all her teeth needle-sharp spines, and her eyes flickered between green and slate gray as she *howled*.

The force of Aria's shriek struck the behemoth like a shell

from a cannon, and it *detonated*. Not with the kind of splattering, horrible mess that Kaz had come to expect when an Arcadian monster died. It simply vaporized, leaving only a cloud of black and gold particles in the air.

There was a moment of perfect silence following Aria's attack.

Neither elementalist nor cultist made a sound as Aria stood there, panting, staring at the place where the behemoth had been.

And between one heartbeat and the next, her body changed again, and Aria became human once more. Her eyelids fluttered, and she fell, senseless, straight into Dr. Conway's arms. He held her and stroked her hair, whispering soothing words in her ear, but the pain and sadness and desperation on his face made Kaz's heart ache.

She's . . . she's not really human anymore. Not at all. And now everyone knows it.

He knew that ache was nothing compared with what Gabe had to be feeling. Gabe had turned his back on everyone, but Kaz could see his face reflected in a nearby window. Gabe stood like a statue, his fists clenched white, his eyes sealed shut against the rest of the world.

4

The calm after Aria's storm didn't last long. Once the cultists picked themselves up they moved on the tight cluster of elementalists, with Norton again leading the group, though moving a whole lot more cautiously than before. If Kaz hadn't been in their line of attack, he might have even been impressed by their bravery. But a glance back at Aria told him that she was totally spent.

The Dawn's lost their behemoth, but so have we!

Kaz was about to reach for earth—he knew he didn't have any choice but to risk it. But then Gabe strode past him to meet Norton head-on. Kaz watched his friend's hands move through the air, creating small, spherical patterns, and a protective ring of fiery orbs the size of baseballs leaped into being around them.

Kaz was thrilled to see the fire defenses, but this only lasted until he saw the sweat pouring from Gabe's face. Gabe was struggling to maintain control.

How long can he hold on to fire?

Maybe Norton wondered the same thing, because the man raised his hands. Not surrendering, but just kind of like he was asking for a time-out.

"Listen, we don't want any trouble, son. All we're doing is taking precautions. We have to guarantee the safety of the Presidio."

Fire licked up and down Gabe's arms. "By treating my mother like an animal? I don't think so."

"You saw what she did! She needs to be put in check!"

Gabe stared Norton down. "No one. Is going. To *touch her*. Do you understand?"

Kaz felt the blast of pure heat riding on Gabe's breath, forcing Norton to back away.

Norton scowled but motioned for the other robed men and women to move away. "You think you're doing the right thing, son. But what happens when she goes berserk like that and blows up a *person*?"

Gabe gritted out, "Don't call me *son*" as the slowly spinning, circling orbs flickered from red-orange to blue. "We'll calm her down. Now leave us alone!"

"Yes, Norton," a new voice rang out across the courtyard. "Leave them be." It was a woman. Kaz turned to trace her voice to a high window in the compound's main building. He couldn't get a good look at her, but she sounded young. "These elementalists have trusted us, and now we must put our trust in them. Lower your weapons. I'd like to meet our new friends."

Norton didn't look happy about it, but he obeyed the woman's orders. He waved off his squad of crossbow wielders, and Kaz was relieved to see the pack of hunters withdraw as well. Almost as relieved as he was to see Gabe pull away from fire, though he saw how hard it was for his friend. Kaz could see that Gabe had to detach from fire incredibly carefully, like moving a full-to-the-brim pot of boiling water off the burner of a stove. Any wrong move, the slightest twitch, and it would spill and scald them all.

He wasn't the only one to exhale in relief when the ring of blazing spheres faded until it was no more than wisps of smoke.

Gabe swayed, weakened from the exertion, but Jackson shored him up.

"Gabriel, of all of us, I believe I have the clearest understanding of magick," Jackson said. "Perhaps I can help you keep your mother calm?"

Myra Willis startled all of them by reappearing behind them. "Primus wants to talk to you. Follow me."

"No!" Brett shouted. "Our grandmother might be right there

outside the dome! Open it up so we can go try to find her!"

Willis scowled. "Out of the question. The dome only opens for null draak riders."

Lily got right in Myra Willis's face. "I don't think you understand. Our *grandmother.* Could be in *danger.* Now open the dome and *let us look for her!*"

Willis stared her down. "No, *you* don't understand. The only one who can give the order is the Primus. You want to get outside the perimeter? You ask the Primus. *Respectfully.* Now. Do you want to go talk to her or not?"

Is this new Primus as big a jerk as the last one? Kaz wondered. *Maybe not, if she's the one who ordered Norton to stand down.*

A long, tension-filled moment passed as Brett and Lily faced off against Willis. Finally, her words clipped, Lily said, "Fine. Take us to her."

Gabe cleared his throat. "Listen, guys. Jackson, Uncle Steve, and I need to stay outside and keep an eye on Mom."

"*And* on the Dawn," Uncle Steve added, looking at Willis meaningfully.

Willis gave Aria, who still crouched, sobbing, an analytical stare. "Yeah, that's probably a good idea. Kazuo Smith, Lily Hernandez, Brett Hernandez. Correct? Come with me." She turned on her heel and headed for one of the iron-gray buildings.

Kaz spoke softly to Gabe. "Join us when you can?"

Gabe nodded. "Thanks."

Kaz didn't know what the main building of Fort Scott was supposed to look like, but he was pretty sure it wasn't meant to resemble a dungeon. That was the only way he could describe the place Willis led them into: stone floors, black-metal walls, charred wooden beams across the black-metal ceiling. Other Eternal Dawn members moved around inside the place, pausing only to give him and Brett and Lily the occasional nasty look. Willis led them up three flights of stairs. Kaz was breathing hard by the time they reached the top and walked out into a broad, loftlike room, the center of which was taken up by a circle of heavy wooden tables.

Tables, and *maps*. Maps everywhere. He had to take care not to step on any, as they lay all over the floor and covered every bit of the tables' surface. In the middle of the circle, another robed, hooded Dawn member stood, facing away from them.

Willis said, "Primus. I have brought the elementalists as you requested."

The robed figure turned. Long, slender fingers pulled the cowl down, and for a moment Kaz forgot to breathe.

The new Primus looked to be in her early twenties. Wide hazel eyes raked over them from beneath a dazzling mane of wavy auburn hair.

Kaz had faced hunters, abyssal bats, and leviathans, but nothing stole his breath quite like the beauty of this young woman. At the periphery of his vision, he finally noticed other robed figures standing at the room's dozen windows, peering outside with glowing violet-rune-inscribed binoculars.

"I'm sorry about the rough introduction," the new Primus said. "I was hoping we could get off to a smoother start." And Kaz *loved* the sound of her voice. He instantly wanted to kick himself as hard as he could.

What is WRONG with me? Oh shoot . . . did that squeaking sound come from me or from somewhere else? Oh please let it have come from somewhere else!

But Kaz didn't worry about this for too long because Myra Willis started talking to Primus.

"Gabriel Conway and Jackson Wright are outside. This one"—she pointed at Kaz—"insisted that we bring along a cluster of survivors, which apparently included Gabriel's uncle and mother."

Primus nodded, looking thoughtful. "Yes, his mother was away for too long. The convergence must have put her in terrible distress."

Willis quirked her eyebrow. "That's an understatement. Dr. Conway and the others are trying to keep her from destroying any more buildings." She scowled at Kaz. "I knew you were going to be trouble."

As Primus walked slowly over to them, it struck Kaz how petite she was. She only had a few inches on him, and she was right at eye level with Brett. "You can leave us, Myra."

Willis made a sound of protest, but Primus waved one hand in a tiny dismissive gesture, and Willis bit off whatever she was going to say and stalked out of the room. A couple of the look-outs turned to give them curious once-overs, but none of them said a word.

"First off," Primus said, a gentle smile revealing perfect white teeth, "I want you all to relax. I am not your enemy. Second, please, don't call me 'Primus.' My name is Eva. Eva Terrington."

Eva. What a pretty name. Don't say that out loud! Don't say that out loud!

Kaz felt sure that if he *did* try to say something it would come out as gibberish, so he was happy when Lily spoke up.

"I remember you. I saw you, in the Transamerica Pyramid, when Thorne killed the old Primus. How'd you get to be the new one?"

Eva Terrington's smile vanished. "The old Primus was my mother. And yes, I was there. I watched that monster slaughter her." She turned, her face filled with what Kaz had to believe was genuine pain, and beckoned them toward the circle of tables. They followed, stepping around more of the maps. Kaz noticed an especially large one in the middle of one of the tables that appeared to show the entirety of the Bay Area—with a huge red circle drawn around it.

Something about the circle seemed familiar to Kaz, but he couldn't quite put his finger on what.

"The Eternal Dawn followed Jonathan Thorne for a solid century, and for a solid century he lied to us. I understand our actions were seen by some as . . . extreme." Brett snorted, but Eva went on calmly. "Especially you five. Considering what the Dawn—what *we*—put you through. But please, try to understand. We believed we were acting for the right reasons. All we wanted was to harness Arcadia's magick to turn Earth into a perfect society. No war. No poverty. No disease. It was all we lived for."

Kaz glanced at his friends. "That's what Ms. Willis told us."

"But Thorne *never* wanted that!" Eva clenched her fists. "Ever! He used us all. Played us for pawns. For *fools*. All in his quest for power."

Brett's dark eyes flashed blue-green. "So what? What does it matter! Everything we've been through is your fault! And now our grandma is out there in your nightmare of a city, surrounded by freaking eyeless ooze monsters, thanks to you! She might even be right outside your stupid dome, right now!"

Quietly, Lily asked, "What do you want from us?"

Eva folded her hands, her eyes downcast. "Your help. We have some limited command of magick now. You've seen our glyphs. Those have become much more potent since the convergence. But they're still nothing compared with what you five can accomplish. You're the only ones who stand a chance of undoing this."

Brett half turned away and threw his hands up. "Unbelievable."

Lily nodded. "Seriously. After all this, we're supposed to

just blindly accept that you've switched sides now?"

Kaz considered his words carefully before he spoke. "I don't think they've switched sides. I think they just finally realized they got betrayed. Thorne tricked them, just like he tricked us."

"Well at least it didn't take *us* a century to figure that out," Brett said.

"Indeed." Eva sighed. Kaz couldn't tell if she sounded exasperated or just tired. Finally she spread her hands. "How can I prove we're on the same side? How can we earn your trust?"

Immediately, Kaz pointed out the nearest window. "You've got a bajillion refugees out there. Innocent people, getting eaten alive. Let them in."

"And if our grandmother's not out there, then you have to get us to her apartment to look for her," Lily added.

"There's no chance we'll open the dome!" The voice came from outside the room, but Kaz recognized it as Norton's. The scar-faced null draak rider burst around the corner. "Forgive me, Primus. I know you wanted to speak to them alone, but what the boy suggests is absurd! The barrier is the only thing keeping us safe! If we lower it, even for a minute, we expose ourselves—expose *you*—to mortal danger! Not to mention, what if we let these snot-noses go out into the city and one of them gets himself killed?"

Watching Norton, Eva slowly nodded. "You're right. That's a . . . that's a chance we probably shouldn't take."

Kaz was about to reach out for earth to drop his voice to

argue his point. It had worked pretty well last time, but Brett beat him to it.

"Then none of what you're saying matters!" Brett boomed. "You only care about yourselves—forget everybody else, right? *Right?* You were gonna make the world a better place, huh? And what were you all gonna do when it happened? Just step out of the way? Let the world run itself?"

Eva's eyes dropped again.

"No!" Brett's words grew louder and louder, and when Norton took a threatening step toward him, Kaz did reach for earth enough to make the stone floor around the rider's feet tremble and waver. The man froze in his tracks. "No, you were gonna be in charge! Kings and queens of the new utopia! *Weren't you?*"

Eva nodded and covered her face with her hands. "I'm sorry. I'm . . . I'm sorry. Yes. We wanted the power. The power and the wealth. It was greed borne of a century of Jonathan Thorne's lies." She dropped her hands to her sides, straightened her shoulders, and nodded once. Firmly. "But that's who we *were*. Now we must be different. We must be better." She looked each of them in the eye. "You're right. We'll let the refugees in. It's the right thing to do."

Norton snarled, "Primus, your mother would never have even considered this!"

"My mother is dead!"

The words echoed and rang around the room. Eva went on, her volume lower but her tone just as intense. "Loyalty to a lie killed her! The Dawn was *wrong*, Norton! You must see that now. The proof is all around us. *Thorne was lying to us the whole time!* We can't keep thinking the way we used to!" Norton sputtered, but Eva cut him off. "I am Primus now. You swore your allegiance to *me*. And if you want to survive this, this *eternal dawn*, you will do as I say! *Do you hear me?*"

Norton stared at her for a long moment before he bowed his head. "Yes, Primus. I obey."

"Good." Eva seemed to be trying to calm her breathing. "Lower the barrier in sections. Make sure it goes right back up as soon as the civilians in each area make it inside."

"Yes, Primus." Norton gave her a brief, respectful bow and left the room.

Brett exchanged a look with Lily. She gestured toward the door with her chin. Brett said, "We're going out to look for Abuela in the crowd."

"And help hold off the sawjaws," Lily added. "Coming, Kaz?"

"He'll catch up," Eva answered for him, to everyone's surprise.

Lily looked at Kaz, who nodded shakily. He wasn't sure how he felt about being left alone in Dawn HQ, but something about Eva made him want to trust her.

Both Hernandez twins spun on their heels and rushed out the door.

Eva's gaze settled on Kaz, and her clear, hazel eyes startled him. "Gabe's mom," Eva began. "How bad is it?"

Kaz shrugged uncomfortably. "Aria—she's, uh . . ." He wondered if he should be saying this, but he was sure Eva would be told all the details eventually. "She's not doing too well. Since the, uh, the convergence? Most of our powers are kind of unpredictable, and Aria . . ." *How do I put this?* "Aria's having a hard time keeping control of hers."

Eva strode toward the door. "Come on, then. Let's go find them first. It's about to get a lot more crowded around here, and an out-of-control elementalist won't make things any easier."

Kaz followed. "So, um. If you don't mind me asking. Your mom was the old Primus? Did she, like— I mean, were you *raised* in the Dawn?"

"Hardly. I grew up in boarding schools. Up until age sixteen I had no clue about any of this. Arcadia, magick, the elements. But on my birthday, Mom came to my school and . . . well, she told me everything. I thought she was crazy, of course. Then she proved it was all real."

"What'd she do?"

Eva's expression darkened. She just gave her head a tiny shake. Kaz recalled the things he'd seen Eva's mother do himself—transforming stray dogs into hunters, commanding giant monsters, and performing ritual sacrifices—and decided he didn't really want to know.

They exited the building just as a wedge-shaped section of the dome winked out of existence. Shouting and cheering, civilians poured inside. Eva stopped near the doorway and just stood, watching them. Kaz couldn't tell what she was thinking. He said, "This is right, you know. You're doing the right thing."

A tiny line appeared between her eyebrows. "I should've done it sooner. This is . . . it's compassion. It's basic human decency. You were right. We'd been thinking only of ourselves for so long . . . it was a habit that needed breaking."

"Glad we could give you the nudge you needed."

Almost all the nearby civilians had made it inside the dome when a dozen sawjaws came diving through the gap. The cheers turned to screams as people scattered, and Kaz heard Norton's voice bellow, *"Archers!"*

A series of sharp snaps sounded out from overhead. A volley of violet-glowing arrows blazed from rooftops to pick the creatures out of the sky. Kaz saw one, pinned against a wall, leaking golden ichor and bristling with arrows as the gap in the dome slid closed again beyond them.

Kaz took a few steps out and looked up to see a line of Dawn members spread out along the roof, every one holding a glyph-inscribed compound bow. He gave a low whistle. "Your guys are pretty good shots." *Glad you're on our side now!*

"They have to be. Any technology more advanced than a crossbow has quit working." Eva scanned the crowd. Thirty yards along the perimeter, another gap opened, and a few hundred more civilians scrambled inside the barrier. "We'll keep these people safe," she said. "Or at least, we'll do our best. I promise you that."

Kaz gazed out beyond the barrier, at the bizarre, horribly altered skyline. "There must be more survivors out there in the city. I hope there are. If they can make it here, will you let them in, too?"

Eva gave him a smile laced with fatigue. "I guess we'll see how many people can fit." Her smile faded. "And how long our supplies will last."

5

Gabe held his mother's hand. At least she looked like his mother for the moment. But under her skin? Just out of sight? Something lurked there. Now Gabe knew that beyond any question. Whatever was there, whatever dark magick had grown within her in the decade she'd spent in Arcadia—the Dawn and everyone else had good reason to be terrified of it.

Her eyes were closed now, and for that Gabe was immensely grateful. With her eyes closed he felt as if she was safe from whatever was inside her.

And everyone else is safe from her.

"I thought she'd be better here," he said softly to Uncle Steve, who braced Aria as she dozed. Jackson sat right beside him. The rest of the courtyard buzzed with activity—Dawn members moving supplies, civilians flooding in, null draaks flapping their wings, archers patrolling—but for a moment the four of them inhabited their own quiet pocket of the yard. "I thought, once she was out of Arcadia, there'd be a chance that she'd go back to normal."

"I told you when we were in Arcadia that that was unlikely," Uncle Steve said. Gabe had heard about a million I-told-you-so's from Uncle Steve over the years but none so sad as this one. In this case, he knew Steve wished nothing more than to be wrong.

"But I was allowed to hope, wasn't I?"

"Hope?" Uncle Steve asked. He loosened his embrace of Aria to give Gabe an affectionate pat on the head. "Yes, I'm told we're all allowed some of that from time to time."

Gabe let his uncle ruffle his hair and thought, maybe it wasn't that bad, sitting here on the ground with his mom's hand clasped in his own and his uncle affectionately patting his head. Maybe it was the best Gabe could reasonably expect.

"Although," Jackson said after a moment, "she's not really out of Arcadia, is she?"

"What do you mean?" Uncle Steve asked.

"Arcadia is all around us. She hasn't escaped magick any more than the rest of us have. To really free her from its pull, we have to—"

"Undo the merging of the worlds," Gabe finished. "Undo our mistake."

Uncle Steve mulled this over for a few moments. "If Arcadia and its influences were truly destroyed, then theoretically magick would return to how it was before Jonathan Thorne created Arcadia back in 1906."

"Back before buildings ate people."

"Before 1906, there wasn't even enough power for elementalists like us to do a fraction of the things we do," Uncle Steve said. "Of course, we don't yet have any idea of how to actually reverse—"

Aria sat bolt upright, her wide eyes wild and already gone gray.

Her sudden movement just about scared the life out of Gabe.

"The Dawn!" she whispered. Her eyes frantically took in the banners and cloaked cultists all around them "They have us!"

Oh God, she's going to go on another rampage!

"Mom, no!" We're safe here!" Which Gabe knew wasn't strictly true, but here with the Dawn was a heck of a lot better than any other place he could think of. The important thing was to try to calm her down. Another epic freak-out like the one where she exploded the behemoth, and Gabe was sure that nothing in this world or any other would convince the Dawn to let Aria stay here.

"They did all this, Gabe!" Aria said. "Your father and I worked so hard to try to protect you from this! We tried to remake the worlds themselves to save you, and now they have all of us!"

"Aria," Uncle Steve said soothingly. "Try to remember. Jonathan Thorne is our enemy, but he's the Dawn's enemy as well. Together, we might be able to—"

"No, NO!" Aria began to shout. An ominous shudder passed through the ground around them. "This *world*! There is something wrong with it! It's broken! And—and I think I'm broken, too."

Gabe could feel her pain, her confusion, and her terror. And as much as he wanted to help his mom, for a moment, it was all he could do to keep tears from over-spilling his eyes. He couldn't remember ever feeling so utterly helpless.

She's still in there. She's still my mother! Not some monster!

"Aria, it's all right," Jackson said. The pale boy gripped her shoulder. "You're all right."

She turned to look at Jackson, and Gabe saw his mother's tear-stained face, so full of fear and sadness. But also maybe . . . shame?

Jackson went on. "I know what it's like to be trapped. I know how hard it is, and how difficult it can be to adjust when you finally escape." Jackson moved his hand to her forearm. Gabe watched a soft, gentle, golden glow spread out from the touch and envelop Aria's body. It wasn't like the times when Jackson touched him or Kaz or Brett or Lily, when he used his magick to supercharge their own elemental powers. This seemed more like something . . . therapeutic.

Since when can he do that?

After a while, Aria sat up straight, carefully pulling away from Uncle Steve's support. She sniffled and dried her face, and finally gave Jackson a tiny smile. To Gabe's relief, her teeth still looked entirely human. "Thank you," she murmured. "It *is* difficult. I guess that's obvious, considering the display I just made. But yes. Thank you."

Jackson ducked his head and took his hand away. The golden glow lingered around Aria for a few moments before gently dissipating. Gabe sighed, relieved that she had calmed down, but frowned at an unwelcome thought—a thought that pinched his heart.

Ghost Boy can help my mom, so why can't I?

"Is everything all right here?"

Gabe sprang to his feet at the sound of the new voice. He whirled to see Kaz standing alongside a young woman wrapped in the cloak of the Dawn. He quickly glanced back at his mom, who was glaring at the woman with frightening intensity. Uncle Steve nodded to Gabe, which Gabe took to mean that he should handle this lady while Steve and Jackson kept Aria calm. They were the best at this. While she was calm for the moment, there was no telling what would set her off.

"So I guess you're the new Primus, huh?" Gabe asked sourly.

"I am. Welcome to the Presidio."

Gabe heard Jackson make a rude noise behind him.

Kaz ignored this and went on to make introductions, giving them the highlights of how the Dawn had been tricked by Thorne to do his bidding, and how Eva had given the order to let the civilians through the shield in order to demonstrate that the Dawn wanted to do the right thing now.

"So what's the deal, *Primus*?" Gabe wasn't inclined to trust any of these people, but he also couldn't ignore the evidence all around him that San Arcadia wasn't exactly what the Dawn had signed up for. And he had to admit that, when he took the time to think about it, if he dug really deep, he had a little sympathy for them. Maybe even empathy. After all, he and his friends had all been duped by Thorne more than once. And as for Thorne murdering Eva's mom, well, his friends had witnessed that firsthand.

"I know you don't want to trust us, but we genuinely want to help fix this disaster. We want to stop Thorne, and we want Arcadia and San Francisco separated. It only makes sense that we work together to figure out how to do that."

"You mean this is only happening to San Francisco?" Gabe asked. "The whole world isn't like this?"

She cocked an eyebrow. "No. At least not yet. Here, take a look." Eva pulled a collapsible telescope from inside her robe and handed it to him. She pointed west. "You'll see what I mean."

This nightmare isn't happening everywhere?

Gabe felt as if he could take a deep breath for the first time in days, the relief was so great.

He expanded the telescope, raised it to his eye, and looked where Eva had indicated. At first he wasn't sure what she wanted him to see, but then it sprang out at him: a glowing red line that ran across land and ocean both. It was hard to get a handle on how far away it was. A few miles?

He lowered the telescope. "What *is* that thing?"

Eva said, "It's some kind of barrier. We haven't been able to investigate it. But what we do know is that it seems to be keeping the convergence effect confined to just the Bay Area."

"So maybe we can get some help! Have you seen the military? Maybe they can do something?"

Eva's expression darkened. "Look more closely."

He did. After about five seconds Gabe saw why she wanted him to look. On the other side of the weird red band, a flock of birds wheeled in formation. Not Arcadian freak shows, either, just regular California birds. Except they weren't moving. It was like looking at a beautifully detailed landscape painting, or a perfectly focused snapshot; the birds simply hung there, in mid-air, frozen. "Why aren't they moving? What happened to them?"

"It's not just that flock." Eva showed him how to zoom in even further. "Keep looking."

"I don't see what you— Oh. *Oh.*"

The birds actually *were* moving . . . incredibly, impossibly slowly. Gabe had to stare long and hard to make sure it wasn't his eyes playing tricks on him, but he could clearly see a wing begin the stroke of a down beat. Gabe handed the telescope back to Eva, and immediately Kaz said, "I wanna see! Can I look? I mean, may I, uh, may I use the telescope? Please?"

A tiny, sad smile curved the corners of Eva's mouth as she handed Kaz the spyglass. "As far as we can tell, time beyond that barrier has slowed to a near standstill. Or time here has sped up. It amounts to the same thing. I doubt the outside world has any idea what's going on in here. And that means no, I'm afraid the cavalry is not coming. We're on our own."

"Thorne won't stop with this city." Aria spoke calmly, which Gabe took as an encouraging sign. She stared across the water toward the barrier. "He wants the world."

The words hung in the air like the sad tolling of a bell.

"Hey! Guys!"

Gabe turned to see Brett and Lily jogging toward them, both of them sweaty and breathing hard. Lily pulled out her asthma inhaler and took a puff from it. Gabe realized that was the first time he'd seen her use it in . . . he wasn't sure how long. *Since the day we first got our powers?* After that, her bond with air had made it unnecessary.

It must be another way San Arcadia is messing with us.

Uncle Steve said, "Did you find your grandmother?"

Brett shook his head, panting. "No. She's not here."

Lily put her inhaler away. "We looked everywhere. Twice. She's not here, and nobody's seen her. Which means she's still out there. In the city."

Brett made a vague gesture toward the south. "She might still be in her apartment."

Lily nodded hard. "Right. We have to bring her back here."

Eva furrowed her eyebrows and said, "You realize your grandmother could be *anywhere* in the city."

Brett shot her a nasty look. "Yeah, thanks for being so positive. But we can *start* with her apartment."

Kaz handed the telescope back to Eva. "I'll help you guys. I already got my family out of town. I can't let Mrs. Hernandez stay out there and maybe get hurt."

Brett said, "Castellanos. Her last name. It's not Hernandez. It's Castellanos."

Kaz ducked his head. "Sorry. I've only ever heard you call her 'Abuela.'"

Uncle Steve shifted right into one of his classic Uncle Steve Tones. "I know you're worried about your grandmother, but going out there is a terrible idea. This reality is at *least* as dangerous as Arcadia! You don't know what you'll run up against!"

Anxiously, Eva said, "I have to agree with Dr. Conway. We rescued the five of you so you could help us defeat Thorne. You can't do that if you're getting gnawed apart by some eyeless abomination."

"You say you need our help, but what you need is our powers, right?" Gabe asked Eva. "Do you have any clue how hard it is for us to control the elements here? It's hard."

"Like really. Freaking. Hard," Brett added.

"Practically impossible, you might say," Kaz chimed in.

"So think of it this way," Gabe continued, "we need total concentration to keep our powers in check. We can't be distracted, not by anything, and we *definitely* can't be worried about the people we love." He glanced at Aria and Uncle Steve. "Lily and Brett need to know their grandmother is safe, and that means that you need to let them find her."

Eva thought this over, and as she did, Aria approached Gabe.

"But Gabe . . . you've said it yourself—the elements are so wild here. Even if you can focus, who knows if you will be able to control them when it matters?" Aria said gently. When she spoke, she sounded for the first time like a regular, ordinary mom. "Going out there . . . it's so dangerous."

Gabe looked from Aria to Uncle Steve to Eva in turn. "But I just *did* control the fire, though. You saw me do it. It's a lot harder than it was before, but I could still do it. We all can. We just have to learn how, and maybe practice some." He looked over at Brett and Lily. "Nothing's going to stop you guys from going out there, right?" he asked.

"No way," Lily said.

"Not even an army of null draaks," Brett said.

"Uncle Steve . . . Mom. What if that were one of you out there? You think I'd let anything keep me from coming for you? They have to look for their grandmother, and we have to help them."

Eva groaned. "If you *insist* on leaving the Presidio, at least let me send a squad of my people with you."

Gabe thought about it but finally shook his head. "You need all the help you can get here. Better if it's just the five of us." He glanced at Jackson. "Or will it just be us four?"

Jackson narrowed his eyes and managed to pack a gallon of dripping sarcasm into his every word. "Yes, the only elemental-ist here who is in complete control of himself is going to leave you four to stumble around a hellscape and get slaughtered."

Lily said, "Jackson! *Tone!*"

Jackson's eyes flashed, but after staring at the sky for a moment, he said, "No, Gabriel, I will not be abandoning you." The sarcasm had disappeared, replaced by somberness. "The five of us should go and locate Lily and Brett's grandmother."

Aria pulled away from Uncle Steve and came to Gabe. "Honey . . . may I talk to you for a moment? In private?" She put a hand on his shoulder and steered him away from the rest of the group.

The word "honey" rang in his ears. Gabe wondered if she'd called him that when he was a baby. "What's up, Mom?"

It felt so good to call her that. To be *able* to call her that. Despite the mess the city was in. Despite what she turned into when she lost control. *Mom.* He savored it.

Aria raked her fingers through her hair. She said, "First off, I'm sorry. I'm sorry for all the trouble I'm causing. I never thought I'd make it back to this world at all, and now, with things all mixed up the way they are . . ." She paused. Her voice sounded strained. "Gabe, you know, or at least I *hope* you know, that the elements have their own desires. They're willful. If you're not careful, they can . . . they can take you over."

For a moment Gabe found it hard to concentrate on what she was saying because of the *way* she was saying it. *She's so clear! This is the real her. My real mom.* He wished she could be this way all the time.

"Yeah. I've felt it. Heard the fire talking to me."

"Gabe, the earth is rising inside me. In my soul. I hear its voice all the time now, not just when I'm connected to it. It wants me to give in to it completely, and it's getting harder to resist."

Gabe let those words sink in. *What happens if your element takes over?* He couldn't look his mother in the eye, not at that moment, and instead cast his gaze out at the civilian survivors around them. Not far away, a cluster of little kids stood near the corner of the closest building, and Gabe realized they were all staring at Aria. *They look scared.* Aria followed Gabe's line of sight, and a small, haunted smile touched her lips. She murmured, "So small . . ."

Aria's blue eyes flickered to slate gray and back. "Your dad and I wanted you to grow up in a world that was free from things like . . ." She waved a hand. "All of this. That's why we tried the ritual ten years ago. That's why we tried to destroy Arcadia." Her laugh was bitter, like the tinkling of cracked bells.

"But we didn't know we needed *five* elements, did we? And when it went wrong, when I . . . when I started getting pulled through, to Arcadia, your father fought *so hard*. He was bound to fire, just like you. He did everything he could, used every bit of power he had to keep me here. It just wasn't enough. And it cost him . . ." She grabbed Gabe by the shoulders. "It cost him *everything*, Gabe, and I don't want that to happen to you."

"It won't, Mom." Gabe wrapped his arms around his mother and held her tight. *Her hair still smells like blueberries.* "I promise it won't. I have my friends with me, and I'll be careful. But you have to be careful, too." Gabe was sure finding Mrs. Castellanos was the right thing to do, but a part of him also felt like he was abandoning his mom.

Gently, Aria pushed him back far enough to look into his eyes. "You're lucky to have such good friends, and I think . . . I think you're right to help them. They're your family, too, you know." Aria kissed him on the forehead. "And as for me being careful, well, I plan to be."

She sighed and called out to Eva. "Excuse me? Miss? Could you come here, please?"

Eva walked over to them with a tiny line of puzzlement between her eyebrows. "Yes?"

"Those shackles your men were going to put on me before. They dampen elemental magick, correct?"

"That's right."

"While my son and his friends go and do what they need to

do . . . I think it might be best if I wore them."

Gabe's mouth dropped open. "What? Mom, *no*! Don't let them put you in chains!"

Aria smoothed Gabe's hair back from his forehead. "It's all right, honey. Considering the, ah, the state that I'm in, it would probably be best to make sure I'm no danger to anyone. Or to myself. The last thing I want to do is hurt anyone."

Gabe looked around for Uncle Steve—*Maybe he can talk some sense into her!*—but his uncle stood in the nearest doorway, speaking with Norton Scar-Face and two other robed Dawn members. Steve saw Gabe looking at him, said something else to Norton, and came over to join them.

"I'm coming with you," Uncle Steve said without preamble. Aria nodded at once, but Gabe wasn't so sure.

"Shouldn't you stay here? With Mom? We can't just take off and leave her alone!"

Uncle Steve glanced at Norton. "I've made sure your mother will be safe. Mr. Norton and I came to an understanding." Steve's eyes flickered silver. "I can't stop you from helping Brett and Lily look for their grandmother, but I also can't let you do it on your own. I'd never be able to live with myself."

Aria took Gabe's hand and squeezed it. "It's fine, honey. I'll be fine. But you must take care, too."

"I've got his back," Brett said.

"Me too," Lily piped up as she joined them.

Kaz slung an arm around Gabe's shoulders.

"Indeed, we will all look out for Gabe," Jackson said. "As we will also look out for one another."

Tears rose in Gabe's eyes, and he couldn't tell if they were happy or sad ones. He had to swallow to keep his voice steady.

"All right. Okay. We go into the city, we find Mrs. Castellanos, we get back here as soon as possible—" Gabe's jaw set. "And then we figure out how to take the world back from Jonathan Thorne."

They'd decided to travel across the water to get to Grandma Castellanos's place. It seemed like the most direct way to get there, at least until Uncle Steve or Lily regained enough control to fly them safely. Eva had offered to take them there via null draak, but while Kaz didn't seem to mind that option, Gabe had zero desire to climb aboard another of those armor-plated monstrosities. So the Dawn opened a section of the dome just long enough for the six of them to leave, and now Gabe stared out at the bay and tried not to shiver as sprays of ice-cold, salty water settled on his skin.

Gabe was supposed to be watching the water for more spike seals. They all were; stationed around the perimeter of the broad, golden disk, they made up a five-person lookout team as Jackson maintained the magickal construct. But as they skimmed across the tops of the waves, in spite of his best efforts, Gabe's thoughts wandered.

The occasional lone sawjaw winged past, high overhead. Always headed toward the dome. It was like the magickal barrier was a flame, luring in hideous, reptilian moths.

"We've got to check out that red-perimeter thing," Gabe said, mostly to himself.

Kaz, standing closest to him, nodded emphatically. "I know, right? The sooner we understand the rules of San Arcadia, the sooner we can fix it!"

Gabe didn't respond. Aria's words wouldn't leave him.

"The earth is rising inside me. In my soul."

The thought of the earth taking his mother away struck him like a physical pain. He knew exactly how he'd felt when fire had tried to overcome him. How powerless and hopeless and small.

The only way to save Mom is to get San Francisco back to normal.

San Arcadia had only existed for a short time, but it was awful and wrong and . . . what was the right word? *Grotesque.* The place was a horrible mistake. Unfit for anyone.

Off to the west, the radiant red line of the strange border around San Arcadia had grown larger, more visible. Gabe couldn't tell exactly how far away from it they were, but at this distance, he thought the red barrier might actually be solid, instead of just a crimson glow.

"You said that the district your grandmother lives in is

called Sunset?" Jackson asked.

"Yeah." Lily stared toward the shore. "I've never seen it from this angle before, but . . . that's it." She pointed. "I recognize those row houses. . . . Wait, what's that stuff covering them?"

Gabe looked where Lily was pointing. "Oh," he said. And then, "Oh . . . no."

"What?" Kaz abandoned his lookout post as Jackson guided the golden disk in to the shore. "What 'oh no'? *Why* 'oh no'? Tell me!"

But Gabe didn't need to explain once they walked out onto the rocky ground, the disk fading away behind them. It was obvious: most of the houses in the neighborhood were draped with what at first looked like heavy, white silk ropes. Gabe knew what they really were, because he had seen them before. "Those are spiderwebs."

With a tremble in his voice, Kaz asked, "And how far away is your grandma's place?"

Brett's face had gone a little pale. "A block that way, and half a block to the left." He swallowed. "Over the river and through the woods, huh? Huh?" He gave everyone a grin, but no one returned it.

Uncle Steve's eyes flickered from blue to silver-white and back. "Listen, everyone. Gabe and I saw webs like these when we were trapped in Arcadia."

A sudden stiff wind ruffled Lily's hair, and only with a

visible effort did she make it stop. "Did you ever see the spiders that *spun* the webs?"

Uncle Steve said, "No. We were lucky. And maybe we'll be lucky now, too. But everyone—*please*—keep your eyes open. And for God's sake, don't touch them."

Carefully, slowly, making as little noise as possible, they entered the neighborhood. The thick, heavy webbing lay across the road here and there, and reminded Gabe of photos he'd seen of the aftermath of a tornado, with ripped-loose power lines all over the ground. In a couple of spots the web lay especially heavy, covering a patch of pavement so densely they couldn't see through it. Uncle Steve pointed and whispered, "Watch out for these. Some kinds of spiders have been known to set traps like this for their prey. One step and their victims fall through the webs and are ensnared by them."

They all skirted those places. On tiptoe.

They got through the first block without incident, which actually made Gabe more nervous than if they'd seen a few Arcadian creatures here or there. *Where are they? What are they waiting for?*

"Okay," Lily breathed. "We'll be able to see her building from around this corner."

She and Brett were in the lead, and when they rounded the corner she'd indicated, both twins stopped dead in their tracks. Lily's eyes flared silver. Brett's mouth simply fell open.

Gabe came up behind them and peered over their shoulders.

"Uh . . . is that, um." He wasn't sure how to phrase the question. "Is that your grandma's apartment building?"

"It was only two stories!" Brett's voice went high with shock. "There were only four apartments! *Four!*"

Gabe stared. What had once been a very modest building, according to Lily and Brett, was now dozens of stories high, as if the original building had been duplicated and stacked on top of itself . . . but not in any way that made sense. Not even in any way that obeyed the laws of physics. Now Gabe thought it looked more like a half-finished game of Jenga on a planet where gravity was reversed.

Lily's shoulders slumped. "It's like it . . . *multiplied.*"

From behind them, Kaz chirped, "Well, hey, at least it doesn't have any webs on it. That's something. Right?"

Gabe got the impression that Kaz might burst into hysterical giggles at any moment. He looked up at Uncle Steve. "What do we do now?"

Uncle Steve only shook his head.

"How're we supposed to find her in there?" Brett asked. "Where are we even supposed to look? What if she's all the way at the top? Will there be stairs?" His voice got louder and more shrill. "What if there aren't any stairs?"

Lily faced her brother and put her hands on his shoulders. "Brett. *Brett.* You've got to calm down. Remember why we were being quiet? Spiders?"

Eventually Brett's breathing grew less ragged.

To Uncle Steve, Gabe said, "This is gonna be a lot harder than we thought, isn't it?"

Uncle Steve studied the building. "I wish I could say I was surprised. Everyone—listen. There's only one entrance. Once we're in there, the only way out will be back through the front door."

Jackson said, "Indeed. What do you propose?"

Uncle Steve's eyebrows twitched. "I hate to say it, but we should have someone stand guard on the bottom level. While the rest of us go up."

Jackson nodded. "I should do that. Perhaps there aren't any creatures inside, but the webs suggest there are ample numbers of them on the streets. I am most in control of my element, but still, I would not mind a bit of . . . what is the term? 'Backup'?" He looked pointedly at Kaz.

Kaz blinked. It made him look sort of owlish. "Me? Why me? The only thing I've been able to do since the worlds merged was spray everyone with superhot mud!"

"If we are to be on the ground, I would think an earth elementalist would be perfectly suited." Jackson showed his teeth in another of his rare smiles. "And while everyone else goes up, you can practice control. Yes?"

Kaz exhaled, long and slowly. "If it's an earth guy you need, it's an earth guy you'll get." He shuffled his feet. "Just don't blame me if a bunch of spike seals show up and all I can do is yell mean things at them in a deep voice."

"Okay," Lily said, tapping her foot. "Jackson and Kaz stay below, and the rest of us go and get Abuela. Ready? Brett? You good to go?" Her brother gave her a thumbs-up. His hand only shook a little. Lily's mouth tightened into a thin line. Gabe had only seen that expression once, right before she ran a race at a track meet. She said, "Then let's do this."

6

Kaz knew he was supposed to be keeping watch over the street in general, but he found it next to impossible to stop staring at the webs draped across the nearby buildings. Apart from the obvious ways in which the massive webs were super-disturbing, something else was bothering Kaz. "Square-cube law," he muttered.

Jackson, leaning against the doorframe of the bizarrely morphed building's front entrance, turned his head. "Did you say something?"

"I said, 'Square-cube law.' There's a reason why you only see giant ants or cockroaches in, like, fantasy and science fiction, okay? It's the square-cube law. Basically, every time something gets bigger, its volume increases by a lot more than its surface area. So if you double an insect in size, its surface area doubles—"

Jackson nodded, frowning. "But its volume triples."

"Right! So we *can't* have dog-size ants. Since they have exoskeletons and not bones, they'd collapse under their own weight."

One of Jackson's eyebrows quirked up as he cast a glance at all the webs. "So the conclusion at which you have arrived is that those webs could not have been spun by giant spiders."

"Exactly." Kaz grinned. "That's why we haven't seen any. There *aren't* any."

Jackson's eyes shimmered gold. "Of course, the laws of physics do not allow for magick, either. Yet we cannot deny that it exists."

Kaz threw up his hands. "Can't you just for one second let me think that I have something about this crazy life figured out?"

Jackson opened his mouth as if he was about to say something, then stopped. To Kaz, with his mouth agape, he looked sort of hilariously like the goldfish his sister June had won at some school fund-raiser. *RIP, Swimmy.*

"Did you . . . Kazuo, do you hear that?" Jackson finally asked.

Kaz's attention darted back to the huge webs. "What? More spike seals? Sawjaws? Something else ripped straight from my worst nightmares?"

"No, it . . ." Jackson stepped out from the doorway, slowly turning his head. He closed his eyes. *"There."* He beckoned. "Come here. Come, listen."

Kaz walked over to Jackson and listened. He was about to say "Dude, I think you're imagining things" when to his shock he *did* hear something. "Holy crap."

Kaz couldn't tell if the sound carried through the air to his ears or traveled through the earth to his bones, and the more he narrowed his focus on it, the more he thought it might be both. He felt it, too—as if wasps had built a nest beside his heart. "It's kind of like that thing you use when you're fixing a piano." Kaz shook his head. "A tuning fork! Right?"

Jackson nodded. "Can you *feel* it?" He tapped his chest. "I do not merely hear it. It vibrates—here."

Kaz swallowed hard. "Yeah, I feel it, too. But . . . what is it? Where's it coming from?"

Jackson's eyes flew open, flashing between pale blue and solid shining gold. He gasped and took an uncertain half step and bumped into Kaz, but righted himself before Kaz could even raise a hand to steady him. "Wait. I have heard this before!" The gold took over the pale blue completely, and sparks of pure magick popped and crackled around Jackson's eyes. "But it is *impossible*." Kaz didn't think he'd ever seen Jackson this upset before. "I fled . . . I escaped! *No!*"

Without even a glance at Kaz, Jackson bolted down the street.

"Jackson!" Kaz's voice echoed around the empty street, and he flinched at the sound. Who knew what weird San Arcadian monsters were nearby? More softly, he called, "Jackson! *Jackson!* Get back here! Jackson, *we're on guard duty!*"

But Jackson kept going.

Kaz flashed through a dozen different scenarios, all of which boiled down to, *If I let him run off by himself, he's likely to get killed.* Kaz went and leaned inside the apartment building's main entrance. All he saw was an empty lobby, about a million ancient-looking mailboxes, a couple of giant flowered plants that Kaz was pretty sure were *blinking* at him, and a staircase leading upstairs.

"Guys! Guys, can you hear me?" His words echoed just as much as they had on the street, and produced exactly the same result: nothing. "Guys, I'm really sorry, but Jackson's running off toward something, and I'm going after him! We'll be back ASAP! Okay?"

No response. Gritting his teeth, Kaz took off after Jackson.

It wasn't hard to follow his trail. He hadn't bothered avoiding any of the massive, ultracreepy webs lying all over the place, so Kaz could pick out his footprints with zero trouble. *Right. I'll follow Ghost Boy into a city filled with monsters and giant spiders and giant spider monsters.* Kaz's eyes watered. He couldn't tell if that was from fear or hysteria. *I wonder if Jackson's got big strands of web hanging off his feet now? Like if he came out of the men's room and had a long thing of toilet paper stuck to his shoe?* He couldn't help giggling.

The footprints took Kaz two blocks from the apartment building before they turned right. As soon as he rounded the corner, Kaz saw Jackson, standing in the middle of the street, his arms hanging loose at his sides. Then he saw what had caused Jackson to stop, and it became the only thing he *could* see.

The red barrier around the city was not a construct, or a force field, or anything else that Kaz would ever have guessed.

It was an immense, ruby-red serpent.

Kaz's jaw went slack as he stared. Brett's words during the ritual on Alcatraz came to him: *"Red snake! Red snake!"*

Kaz walked up beside Jackson and, in a tiny voice, said, "So forget the square-cube law, huh?"

The serpent was at least thirty feet thick, and its incredible mass continued out of sight beyond the demolished buildings to their left and right. Kaz remembered the maps he'd seen at the Presidio marked with a giant red circle. *This is it. This thing is so big, it surrounds the entire city!* And directly in front of them was the massive serpent's head, bigger than a commercial jetliner, swallowing its own tail.

"Ouroboros," Jackson whispered.

Kaz nodded. He knew the word: an ancient symbol of a snake eating its tail, meant to indicate eternity, the cycle of life. As they watched, the great red serpent opened its massive reptilian eye—and looked directly at him and Jackson.

The serpent's eye glowed the blue of a welding torch's flame. No—deeper than that. The blue of the ocean. *The blue of Earth itself.* But it burned just as brightly as the flame, and though the serpent had barely moved, Kaz felt rooted to the spot in sheer, unbridled terror.

"I hear them," Jackson murmured.

"Wh-what?" Kaz tore his eyes from the serpent, relieved to look at something as nonthreatening as Jackson.

"The words. I hear them now." Jackson gripped Kaz's shoulder. "Listen. *Listen.*"

Kaz realized the noise he had heard back at the apartment building, the tuning fork–like rumble, had indeed grown much, much louder. He'd just been too distracted by the *giant freaking horror snake* to pay it any attention. But Jackson seemed really intent on it, and the serpent had made no move to hurt them other than just to look at them. So Kaz closed his eyes and tried to focus.

"Five . . . elements," Jackson whispered. Kaz could barely hear him over the now-thunderous wash of noise from the serpent. "Do you hear? *Five . . . elements . . . for . . . one.*"

Kaz scowled. Trying to tune in to the buzz emitted by the snake was a little bit like listening to the "electronic voice phenomenon" recordings on those stupid "ghost-hunting" TV shows he and his dad liked to make fun of. The sound was a ton of static, and maybe a part here or there that might kind of sound like a word.

And unlike those dumb shows, the noise from the snake is actually real.

Except that the more Kaz concentrated, the more he *could* hear words.

"Five elements for one," Kaz repeated. "You're right, that's what it's saying. But wait — Jackson, there's more."

Jackson nodded furiously. When he said the words, Kaz moved his lips, repeating them as well: "Five-elements-for-one-act-across-all-worlds-with-five-elements-for-one-act-across-all-worlds-with . . ."

The words kept going. Endlessly looping. Kaz felt them burrowing into his brain. He wondered if he'd ever stop hearing them. "Wait, wait. Wait. What does it mean? Where's the beginning of the sentence? Is it 'One act across all worlds with five elements?' Or is it 'With five elements for one, act across all worlds?' Or 'Across all worlds with five elements, for one act?' Or what? Jackson?" The smaller boy was just squinting at the snake, either dumbstruck or listening with every fiber of his being. *"Hey, Jackson?"*

Jackson snapped out of it and scowled. "What does the order of words matter right now? Is it not saying the same thing either way?"

"I'm just trying to make sense of this. Like, okay, you said you'd heard it before, right? Where?"

Jackson folded his arms across his chest. Kaz thought he might have been sort of hugging himself. "In the Umbra."

". . . Oh. That's where you were stuck before you . . . uh . . . found us?"

That was what Kaz said—what he meant was: is the Umbra the place where you were trapped before you infiltrated Brett's dreams through your family ring, conned him into binding us to the elements, and set into motion a series of events that got yourself sent back to San Francisco but imprisoned Dr. Conway and Brett in Arcadia in the process?

Jackson turned to him with an unreadable expression. "That's a very polite way of phrasing it, Kazuo."

Kaz couldn't really imagine what it must have been like for Jackson, a boy of eleven, to be trapped in a shadow dimension for over a hundred years. If he understood correctly, the "Umbra" wasn't Earth and wasn't Arcadia, but sort of its own dimension somewhere in between. From there, Jackson had sometimes been able to get brief glimpses of both worlds. It had also kept him from aging.

Jackson stared at the colossal serpent. "In any event, yes, that was where I was. It was like . . . like being trapped in a lightless labyrinth . . . but one where you knew the outside world was just on the other side of the walls. They were thick walls. Sturdy. Proof against sound. So that no matter how loudly you screamed, or how hard you slammed your body against them, no one on the other side could know you were there." He pulled his eyes from the serpent and met Kaz's gaze. They were normal eyes, just the pale blue of a normal human boy . . . except there was nothing normal about Jackson. His eyes held so much pain and loneliness and sadness. *Too much. Too much for anyone to relate to.*

Kaz was starting to understand why Lily seemed to have a soft spot for the Ghost Boy.

"But every so often, at random, something like a window would open," Jackson continued. "No, not a window—a crack. A tiny opening in the wall, something I could rush to and press my face against and *see through.* I never knew when or where they would appear, these cracks, or how long they would last. But they never gave me more than just a glimpse of the life, of the *world* I had left behind. Then Brett found my family's old ring. Then I was able to communicate with him through his dreams. That's when everything began to change. *Finally.*" Jackson swallowed hard.

Kaz shuddered. Once, a couple of years ago, he and his little sisters had been playing hide-and-seek. Kaz had climbed into an old footlocker of his dad's, and before he realized it was a bad idea, the lid had closed and latched. That was the first time Kaz had felt claustrophobic. It came over him in a rush, curled up there in the trunk, practically folded in half, barely able to move. The only light he could see was a tiny ray, as narrow as a needle, coming through the keyhole . . . and when he couldn't stand it any longer and banged on the trunk's lid to get his sisters' attention, none of them had been able to figure out how to open the clasp.

By the time Kaz's mother got home half an hour later, Kaz had shouted himself hoarse. And when she opened the footlocker, he flung himself into her arms, his heart hammering and his light-dazzled eyes filled with tears.

What would've happened to me if I'd been stuck in there for a century?

Jackson continued, "But while I could seldom see anything in the Umbra, there was *sound*. One sound."

Kaz rubbed a hand over his scalp. "*This?* This is what you heard in the Umbra?"

"I did not know what it was. I only knew that I heard it. Much more faintly than here."

Kaz shook his head. Horrible as it was, he knew his memory of being stuck in the footlocker didn't even scratch the surface of what Jackson had gone through.

He gave the pale boy a few moments before asking him, "So are you ready?"

"Ready? For what?"

"There's a giant snake encircling San Francisco. It's somehow keeping magick from infecting the whole planet, and it's making a sound you've only heard while imprisoned in another dimension." Kaz threw his arms toward the snake. "We can't just take a selfie in front of it and call it a day, can we? We've got to find out what's going on!"

Jackson sighed. "I don't know what a 'selfie' is, but . . . I suppose you're right."

Kaz climbed onto a wrecked car and took a deep breath. "Hey! Excuse me, uh, Mr. Serpent?" he shouted. "Could you please tell us what the words mean? The ones you keep chanting at us?"

The serpent's great blue eye moved. Its pupil narrowed as it focused on Kaz.

It said nothing.

"Maybe if we get closer?" Kaz asked, looking down at Jackson.

Jackson looked from Kaz to the serpent and back. "Seriously? You want to get cl—" He cut himself off. "Of course. Why not. That makes as little sense as anything else."

Kaz climbed down off the car and, with Jackson falling into step beside him, began creeping toward the red serpent. Kaz's instinct was to appear as unthreatening to the snake as possible. That's how you were supposed to approach a strange animal, right? But he soon realized that was sort of ridiculous—him freaking out this snake would be like a mosquito startling the Empire State Building.

They'd halved their distance to the massive reptile when a strange shadow on the ground nearby caught Kaz's attention. He craned his head over his shoulder in an effort to pinpoint what had thrown the shadow. . . .

With a squeaking sound in the back of his throat, he grabbed Jackson's arm and dragged him forcibly toward a large pile of rubble.

Jackson tried to pull away. "What are you— Kazuo! What are you doing? Let go of me!"

But Kaz didn't let go, and when it felt as if Jackson might wriggle free, Kaz used just the barest touch of earth magick to strengthen his grip. He wasn't sure it would work, but it definitely did; Jackson yelped in pain. But by then Kaz had him behind the rubble pile, crouched down out of sight, and clapped a hand over Jackson's mouth. "Look back the way we came," he whispered. "But don't stick your head up! Just take a peek!"

Raising their heads *just* high enough to peer over the jumble of twisted metal and concrete, both boys stared at the two figures rapidly drawing closer. Kaz wasn't touching Jackson now, but he could feel Jackson's trembling through the earth itself and was pretty sure he could hear Ghost Boy's jackhammer heartbeat. His own beat just as frantically.

One of the figures appeared to be female, and wore long, silken purple robes. The other—with his shock of white hair and unmistakable, malevolent green eyes—was Jonathan Thorne himself, dressed in an old-fashioned three-piece suit. They came walking toward the serpent on legs stretched impossibly, hideously long, moving with inhuman grace and speed over the rubble-strewn city. As they drew closer, Kaz saw that it wasn't that their legs themselves had lengthened. Instead, they had created shadow projections, extensions of their bodies made of horrifying, vile black energy, like twisted parodies of carnival workers' stilts.

"Down there," Kaz heard Thorne say, and the shadow-stilts shortened, shrinking down to nothing as the pair set their own feet on the broken pavement.

Kaz had never seen the woman before. Only her face and her hands were visible, since the robe and hood covered everything else . . . but Kaz was glad he couldn't see any more of her. She had bronze skin and dark eyes, and her hands appeared to be the normal hands of a woman in her thirties. . . . .

But the robe was *moving*.

Kaz's stomach clenched. *There's something under there. Something that shouldn't be.*

Bulges pressed and shifted beneath the fabric. Sharp spikes protruded, threatened to punch through, and receded. Something large and . . . and *coiled* . . . inched outward from her back, moved around to her side, and disappeared again.

"Here, Madam Kureshi. The serpent's head. Just as I predicted."

Kureshi. That's Persian. And he's superpolite to her. That's not how he talked to the other Dawn members!

He's acting like they're old friends, and if she's as inhuman as the writhing shapes beneath her robe suggest . . . What if she's one of the cult's original members? What if she's been trapped in Arcadia for over a century, like Thorne? No wonder she's not human anymore!

"Yes, Lord Thorne," Madam Kureshi purred. The sound of her voice washed over Kaz like the sonic equivalent of a heady perfume. "Shall we test your other theory?"

Except for the vivid, glowing green eyes in Thorne's gaunt, sunken, sallow face, he looked very much like a corpse. The eyes ruined that illusion . . . and when his mouth widened in a grin, the illusion that he was even remotely human vanished completely. His teeth shifted every few seconds, crunching and squelching as new and different sets of horrifying, predatory fangs filled his ravenous jaws. "We shall."

Thorne and Madam Kureshi faced the serpent, raised their hands, and unleashed a blistering torrent of purest, blackest fire on the vast creature's head. Kaz lost sight of the enormous creature as clouds of smoke billowed out from the point of impact.

Kaz risked a glance over at Jackson. The other boy had gone as pale as a piano key, and greasy sweat ran from his hairline down his cheeks. Jackson stared at Jonathan Thorne the way someone might stare at a wildfire sweeping toward the house in which they had grown up.

As abruptly as it had started, the barrage of black fire vanished. Madam Kureshi simply crossed her wrists, hid her hands inside the sleeves of her robe, and bowed her head; but Jonathan Thorne threw his head back and screamed—a horrible, brittle sound like distant, crackling thunder.

"It was a good thought," Madam Kureshi said quietly.

The fabric of her robe rose as two large lumps appeared on her shoulder and slid down her back. "Reason would indicate that the head would be more vulnerable than the body."

"And yet this proved no more effective than our earlier attack!" Thorne spat.

Kaz wondered where else along the snake's body they had tried to do this.

"No matter," Thorne went on. "The Crimson Serpent confines our magick to this city, and therefore must die. It remains only a matter of discovering how to effect its demise."

"Perhaps . . ." Madam Kureshi's voice trailed off, until Thorne snapped his head around to spear her with a look. "Perhaps the Crimson Serpent cannot *be* killed."

Thorne made a noise of disgust. "No. The Serpent was documented extensively in the pages of the Emerald Tablet. And I learned every word of *every page* of that book before its destruction. This colossus"—he glared at the massive snake—"exists in some form across many, many realities, but it is *not* immortal. It can be killed. And when it dies, the magick of Arcadia will blossom forth across the globe. Unimpeded. Glorious!"

Madam Kureshi's head turned, still mostly hidden by the hood of her robe. "I am not so sure, Lord Thorne. I can think of one impediment."

Kaz had time to think *Oh crap* before Madam Kureshi threw out one hand and blasted the pile of rubble he and Jackson hid behind with a storm of black fire. The strike turned the rubble to a smoking crater; and if Jackson hadn't generated a broad, circular, golden shield, Kaz was sure he and Jackson would both have been incinerated. As it was, the impact knocked both of them sprawling, exposed for the world to see.

Kaz couldn't remember the last meal he'd eaten, but whatever it was, he came very close to puking it up.

Jonathan Thorne stalked toward them, his disgusting mouth twisting and cycling through set after set of fangs. "Impediment indeed, Madam Kureshi. Do you know, the other members implored me not to admit you, back in '05? No foreigner could be useful, they said. How happy I am that I made an exception."

Kaz scrambled backward, scuttling on his butt, pushing with his heels and hands. *Do something do something DO SOMETHING!* As scared as he was to do it, he had no choice but to reach for earth. The ground beneath him began to rumble.

Then it collapsed, dropping him into a depression that felt exactly like a shallow grave. Thorne towered over him, a terrifying scarecrow built from bones and long-dead skin. "Mr. Smith, is it?"

Kaz tried to shout for Jackson, but he couldn't get enough breath, and the sides of the hole he'd created only crumbled under his fingers the more he tried to claw his way up. Thorne raised one hand in a calm, casual gesture, and Kaz's heart almost stopped.

But Thorne didn't get the chance to unleash another

shadow-blast, because a broad, rectangular barrier of golden magickal light sprang up between Thorne and Kaz. Jackson grabbed the back of Kaz's collar and hauled him up out of the hole. "Run," Jackson grunted. "Run as fast and as far as your legs will carry you!"

Kaz spun, taking no more than a tenth of a second to decide which way to go, but that was long enough. A spiraling cloud of black fire *curved* around Jackson's barrier and swept both boys off their feet.

It's not hot! That thought had just enough time to register before a wave of ripping, shrieking pain tore through his body, as if the black fire were made of needles that passed through his skin and pierced his soul.

The air rushed from his lungs when he slammed into the ground. Things went hazy for a long moment. Kaz thought he saw more flashes of golden light and knew he felt the foul, unclean rushes as more shadow-blasts swept past him, but when the world finally came back into focus, one thing and one thing only filled his vision: Madam Kureshi's face.

More hideous lumps and ridges moved under her robe as she bent over, putting the two of them almost nose to nose. She smiled, and when she spoke, it made Kaz's guts tighten and harden into a ball of ice. "There's no point in running, Jackson," Kureshi said, in *Kaz's own voice*. The mimicry was perfect. "There's nowhere we could hide where they couldn't find us."

Madam Kureshi smiled just as slick purple tentacles burst

from her robe and wrapped themselves sickeningly around his ankles and wrists. This time, Kaz actually did throw up a little. Madam Kureshi laughed and he tried to turn away from her, desperate to look at something, *anything* besides her.

A few yards away, Jonathan Thorne was moving slowly, steadily closer to Jackson. Jackson kept trying different defensive tactics—shields, barriers, domes—but Thorne either bent his horrid black flames around them or aimed them at the ground beneath Jackson's feet, causing him to stumble. Finally Jackson abandoned defense and went on pure offense, thrusting magickal golden spears and spinning blades at Thorne. These Thorne simply pushed away, a field of black flames and dense shadows dancing about him. Thorne's laughter rolled out along the ground to Kaz's ears, low and filled with insane menace.

He's just messing with us! Madam Squidbody is right—we can't take them on! What's he doing? Are we just a warm-up?

Jackson bellowed and seemed to dig his fingers into the very air, and one last massive golden spear rocketed straight at Thorne's head. This time Thorne didn't bat it aside. He simply moved, allowing the spear to pass over his left shoulder . . .

. . . where it struck the Crimson Serpent.

The tuning fork keen rang out so loudly Kaz thought his ears would bleed. The Serpent twitched, and a ripple of golden energy sprang out from the point where the spear had struck it, traveling along its body in both directions out of sight.

For several seconds, it appeared that Jonathan Thorne had

forgotten about Jackson. He stood, staring at the Serpent, his eyes wide and his mouth slack . . . but then noxious green fire roared and crackled from both his eyes and his mouth, and he spun around to face Jackson again. "My dear boy! Do you realize what you have just done? You have shown me the *way*! Little wonder we could not affect the Serpent—it must be made of magick itself!" Thorne's blazing gaze narrowed, and it looked as if all the blood had left Jackson's head. Even his hair looked paler. Thorne went on, his voice rising in pitch: "This changes the game! And it makes you, my little temporal outcast, very valuable indeed. . . ."

He may have looked too scared to breathe, but when Jackson spoke he sounded fearless. "I would see you destroyed, Thorne. But I shall see *myself* destroyed before I help you."

Thorne laughed. Kaz had never heard a sound like it before. *It's like the air's tearing apart.* "This strange new world is both perilous and fragile," Thorne said, never taking those poisonous eyes off Jackson. "And tenfold so for those bound to the Art. The terrestrial elements are wildly out of balance. The only way to stabilize this newborn reality is to kill this red-hued monstrosity. You are remarkably unique; no human is supposed to be able to wield pure magick. If I may be so presumptuous, it seems you were specifically made to slay this beast."

Jackson generated another dome-shaped shield and tried to back away, but Thorne hammered it with such an intense, sudden barrage of black flame that it cracked and collapsed.

Jackson fell, panting, but instead of pouncing for a kill, Thorne knelt in front of him. "You were made for this world, Jackson Wright. Join me. Free magick to roam this planet as it was intended. Stand by my side."

Jackson's eyes were wild. "Never. You imprisoned me. You *sacrificed* me. I would never join you."

"And yet I understand you better than anyone else alive. We are two of a kind, Jackson Wright. Harnessers of magick. Men of another century. I have done you a great wrong, I know. Please, allow me to make it right."

Jackson didn't say anything. He just looked up at Thorne . . . and Kaz had a bad feeling about the expression on the smaller boy's face.

Jackson seemed to be *thinking about it.*

Kaz growled and reached for earth, and a gigantic fist made of dirt and rocks and broken pavement exploded out of the ground beside him and punched Madam Kureshi so hard it was as if she vanished. The fist was as big as her entire body, and Kaz knew the impact had just flung her off somewhere, not destroyed her outright. But he didn't care. He just wanted her out of his way so that he could focus on Thorne.

"Get away from him," Kaz rumbled as he rose from the shallow grave on a broad column of rock. Green light flashed and shimmered around his hands, and when he spoke, the words seemed to thunder up from the collisions of tectonic plates far, far beneath the earth's surface. *"Get away from him!"*

Jackson stared at him, bug-eyed. Even Jonathan Thorne seemed mildly taken aback. Kaz didn't know what he must have looked like, but he knew exactly what he felt like, perched atop his rocky throne.

I feel like a god!

A voice rushed through his ears. Not a whisper. A *shout*.

"Crush . . . bury . . . shatter . . . erupt!"

Kaz's body swelled. He roared as he felt his bones lengthen and thicken as his muscles grew. As his skin turned the same slate gray as his eyes, he screamed, but not a scream of pain. He wanted this. He *needed* this. The cry of exultation blasted up from the roots of the planet below him, and the earth around the column on which he stood cracked open as fire and molten magma spewed forth.

"I will bury you!" Kaz thundered, and the earth split beneath Thorne's feet. "I will take you down, and down, and down, where no one will ever find you."

But Thorne flickered like a shadow and slid sideways, away from the hungry fissure, and his air-shredding laughter rang out. "Have a care, Kazuo Smith."

Kaz bellowed in frustration, but Thorne flickered again, avoiding another fissure like the first one. "You move too close to the edge! Do you know what happens to elementalists when their element consumes them?"

Suddenly Jackson rose to Kaz's side, buoyed on a floating golden disk. "Kazuo! Kazuo, you must maintain control!"

"Crush! Bury! Shatter! Erupt!"

More fissures opened around them. Magma spewed in the air, and Jonathan Thorne flickered out of sight. For a split second Kaz thought Thorne might have retreated entirely, but his gut-churning laughter rolled out again, coming from everywhere and nowhere.

Kaz gritted his teeth. His mouth felt filled with sand.

Jackson shouted, "You cannot let the earth overpower you! You are in control, Kazuo! *You*, not it!"

"Crush . . . bury . . . shatter . . . erupt . . ."

Kaz forced his grit-filled mouth and lungs to work. "I . . . I am in control. . . ." He pictured himself. Kaz Smith. Good-natured nerd. Not this, this *rock monster. What am I doing?*

He felt himself begin to shed mass. His limbs returned to their normal sizes. His skin lost its rocky texture.

Jackson kept on. "That's it! Keep going, Kazuo! Exert control!"

But the earth wasn't done with him. The strength of soil and rock surged through his body. Teasing him with its power. Green light flared all around him as he looked up at Jackson, and the voice of the earth spoke through Kaz's lips. *"Crush! Bury! Shatter! Erupt!"*

Jackson's face filled with pain. He floated backward a few feet, his eyes crackling with golden magick, and with deft motions of his hands he sent loop after loop of blazing golden energy around Kaz's body, like a series of lassoes. Kaz felt the earth loosen its grip on him. He was able to muster his strength just enough to ask, "Jackson, what're you—"

Kaz's words cut off, along with his connection to the earth, as Jackson lifted him off the ground. "Sorry, Kazuo. I must prevent this."

"I can fight it," Kaz panted. "I can help you against Thorne!"

"It is I who must help you, my friend." Jackson made a sideways whipping motion with one arm. Kaz's stomach lurched with the sudden motion as the lassoes flung him up and away, far over the city's distorted rooftops. Far above the hungry earth. Far away from Jonathan Thorne.

7

Gabe had never considered himself claustrophobic. Tight places didn't bother him, and he'd actually felt sort of comforted the few times Uncle Steve had taken him camping, both of them snugged down in individual pup tents. But walking through the monstrosity Grandma Castellanos's apartment building had become, Gabe felt himself getting more and more freaked out. He remembered Kaz once telling him that it felt as if the walls were closing in on him whenever he was in a tight space. As he, the Hernandez twins, and Uncle Steve made their way along the hallways and up the staircases, Gabe wasn't convinced the walls *weren't* closing in.

Brett said, "Worst. Fun house. Ever."

Gabe thought that was a good description, though there was nothing fun about this place at all. The inside of the building made no sense. Hallways meandered and curved and turned corners where they shouldn't have. The stairs made even less sense, as some of them climbed steep, straight flights, while others corkscrewed and bent in S-shaped arcs.

Worst of all, half the place was draped and strung with the same kind of massive spiderwebs they'd seen outdoors. They all took great pains not to touch them.

Uncle Steve, who'd taken the lead, looked back at Brett and Lily. "Does any of this look familiar at all? Can you tell if we're anywhere near your grandmother's apartment?"

Brett nodded, and Lily said, "Believe it or not, yeah. I mean, I've never seen most of this place before, but some of these details are familiar."

Brett pointed at a welcome mat half covered in webs. It displayed a cartoon cat, along with the words PLEASE WIPE YOUR PAWS! "That's Mrs. Morrison's welcome mat."

Lily said, "It's like this *is* still Abuela's building, it's just gotten all stretched out." She nudged the welcome mat with her foot.

A chiming sound traveled out along the web connected to it. Just one of the weird, thick strands vibrated with the sound, but it made Gabe's skin pucker with goose bumps.

Lily's expression tightened. The sound quickly died away, and she let out a soft exhale. "Sorry about that."

"Okay, new rule." Uncle Steve gestured at the webs around them. "No one touches these things."

Gabe, Lily, and Brett all nodded in assent.

When they turned the next corner, Gabe had to clap a hand over his mouth to keep from making a noise a lot louder than the web-chime.

A cocoon the size of a grown man lay propped against a wall. It didn't look like the kind of blood cocoons in which Jonathan Thorne had encased people when he was preparing to merge Earth and Arcadia. This one was composed entirely of webbing and fit around the shape inside it much more snugly.

The four of them stood there for a long moment. Gabe didn't breathe. He didn't think anyone else did, either. Finally Brett said, "Oh, man, that's a person, isn't it?"

Moving carefully, clearly intent on not touching any of the webs that led away from the cocoon, Uncle Steve knelt and pressed two fingers into the webbing where the throat would be. He grimaced and shook his head. "Not anymore. No." He met Gabe's eyes. "Whoever this was, they've been dead for a while. Should we . . . uncover the face?" Steve's gaze switched over to Brett and Lily. "See if, um. See if you recognize who it is?"

Brett let out a long, shuddering breath, but Lily spoke up. "No. It's not Abuela. She's way smaller than that. Let's just . . . let's just go find her as quick as we can, okay?"

Uncle Steve straightened up. "All right. Let's go."

Gabe was *sure* the walls were moving closer to him now. Plus he kept imagining things moving underneath the webs. He almost said "Finally!" when Lily pointed at a door ahead of them.

"There. That's our grandmother's door."

When they reached it, Uncle Steve knocked softly. "Mrs. Castellanos?"

Brett said, "You might need to knock louder."

Lily softly cleared her throat and, stepping between Gabe and Brett, held up a key. "No need to knock at all."

The lock disengaged with a soft click, and the door swung open.

Gabe peered over Lily's shoulder as they all edged into the apartment. He saw no webs, no weirdness, nothing. Just lots of little ceramic figurines, alongside heavy, old-fashioned furniture fitted with plastic covers.

Softly, Lily called out, "Hello? Abuelita? *¿Estás aquí?*"

Silence. Behind them, Brett quietly closed the door. Uncle Steve stepped forward and, slightly louder, called out, "Mrs. Castellanos? Are you here?"

Gabe heard a very distinct *click*, and then threw himself sideways and shouted, "Get down!" as a column of flame blasted down the entry hall from the kitchen door ahead on their left.

A shrill voice screamed, "*¡Déjame solo!*" and Mrs. Castellanos stepped out from the kitchen, a lighter and a can of hair spray in her hands. "You leave me alone, you hear? Go! Get out!" She clicked the lighter again, ready to fire another stream of burning aerosol at them.

Brett shouted, "Abuelita! *¡Somos nosotros!* Grandma, it's us!"

Mrs. Castellanos paused, squinting, and finally lowered the lighter. "Brett?"

Brett and Lily's grandmother had the carefully styled white hair of a woman in her sixties but the same athletic build as Lily. She was decked out in a magenta velour tracksuit, and from the stories Brett and Lily had told him, Gabe knew that she was not to be messed with. Once, armed only with an umbrella and some forceful language, she had overpowered two teenage boys trying to break into her car and kept them there on the sidewalk until the cops arrived.

Now Mrs. Castellanos dropped the lighter and hair spray can, pulled Brett and Lily up off the floor, and enveloped them both in the grandmotherliest of hugs. "*¡Mis bebés! ¡Mis angeles!* Praise *Dios* you're all right!" She pulled back from them to look Gabe and Uncle Steve over. "Who are your friends?"

Lily said, "This is our friend Gabe. You met him once, remember? Last year? And this is his uncle. Steve."

Uncle Steve stepped forward with his hand extended, and Mrs. Castellanos shook it. "Steven Conway, ma'am. Under the circumstance, that is a rather ingenious use of hair spray. But, if you don't mind me asking—who were you expecting?"

Mrs. Castellanos's face went a little gray. She hugged herself.

"Not *who*. It's a *what*. A bunch of whats." Her voice dropped. "*Las arañas*. The spiders! They're all over the place! First the earthquake happens, and those awful red cocoon things show up all over the place, then my building has this"—she made a wide gesture—"this *growth spurt*. Then these spiders show up! One hour to the next, and the webs are everywhere! I didn't dare go outside!"

Gabe tried for a hopeful tone. "Well . . . we didn't see any when we came in. We didn't even see any on the way here. Maybe they all left the area?"

From the hall, faint but easily identified, came another chime.

Then another. And another.

Lily said, "Oh no."

Mrs. Castellanos grabbed the lighter and the hair spray can back up. "They are coming! You didn't see them before? Now's your chance!"

Gabe went to the door and looked through the peephole. Down at the far end of the hall, the webs were vibrating like crazy, and he saw multiple shadows cast from around the corner. Shadows with lots and lots and *lots* of legs. He said, "We need to get out of here. Right now."

Mrs. Castellanos scoffed. "Go out there? Are you insane? We have to stay here! Barricade the door!"

From one of the bedrooms behind them came the high,

brittle crash of breaking glass, followed by more web-chimes.

Lily choked out, "They're coming in through the windows, too!"

"Change of plans!" Mrs. Castellanos started pushing Brett and Lily toward the door. "Go! Out in the hall! We can't stay here!"

Uncle Steve put his hand on the doorknob, and Gabe came up to stand beside him. Gabe tried to keep his voice low so only his uncle would hear, but he wasn't sure how successful he was. "Listen, the only way out is all the way back down. If there's spiders all over the place, and we can't control our powers, how're we gonna get out?"

Uncle Steve paused for a second as the chimes outside grew louder and louder. He threw a look over his shoulder at Mrs. Castellanos. "Ma'am? How fast can you move?"

More broken glass crashed from the living room. Mrs. Castellanos said, "Faster than you, blondie! Now open that door before we get chewed on!"

"Chewed on . . . yes . . ."

Gabe spun around, and Lily screamed, as a spider the size of a horse moved from the living room into the hallway. Except it wasn't a spider. Not really. It had eight legs, yes, and eight eyes. But a normal spider would have had a shell, an exoskeleton. Gabe knew that from science class. And this one didn't. It was just as skinless as the hunters, abyssal bats, and spike seals they'd seen. And as its many long, horrible legs moved, wiry muscles clenched and rolled all over its body. It also had a pair of fangs as long as Gabe's hand, from which dripped gobbets of golden Arcadian slime.

And behind those fangs was a mouth.

A *human* mouth.

The octuple eyes narrowed as the mouth curved into a vicious, cruel parody of a human grin. *"Wrap you up . . . keep you fresh . . . chew and drink and gnaw for days and days . . ."*

The not-a-spider slowly advanced. Gabe felt his eyes ignite, and waves of heat danced around his hands. "Stay away from us. You stay away from us, and you tell all the other spiders to stay away, too!"

In his ear, Lily whispered, "Gabe, you can't use your fire in here! If it goes wrong you'll cook us!"

"Fire?" Mrs. Castellanos said. "That's exactly what we need." She stepped past Gabe, raised the lighter and hair spray can, and blasted a column of flame straight into the spider's face. The creature screamed and thrashed, and tried to knock the can out of her hand. But she dodged its grotesque legs and kept pouring on the fire until the spider scuttled backward, all the way to the far end of the living room.

"Your fates . . . are sealed . . . vermin!" The spider used four of its legs to swat out the flames dancing along its body, and for the first time Gabe realized that its legs ended in golden,

skinless, but undeniably *human hands*.

"We've got to run!" Uncle Steve bellowed. "It's our only chance!"

The five of them bolted down the hall away from Mrs. Castellanos's apartment, but Gabe heard the revolting clicks and scuffle of the spider chasing them.

"Here!" the spider barked out. *"A taste of things to come!"* Gabe glanced back just in time to see the creature's throat ripple and contort. With a sound like a cat bringing up a hair ball, it spat a slimy glob down the hall. The glob landed squarely on the back of Brett's neck.

Brett screamed and faltered and would have fallen if Gabe and Lily hadn't supported him. He clawed frantically at his neck. "Get it off! *Get it off!* It burns! *Dios mio,* it's burning me!"

Another spider scuttled out in front of them, but Uncle Steve didn't waste a second: he drew back a foot and kicked the creature squarely between its fangs. The spider's head snapped backward with a horrible crunch, and Steve stepped on its collapsing body as they rushed past.

From behind Gabe, Lily retched in disgust. She had pulled a crumpled napkin from one of her pockets and was using it to swipe at the glob on Brett's neck as they ran. And while the glob was mostly gone, Gabe saw Lily shaking the kerchief like a madwoman. She finally threw it down. "Gabe!" Her eyes had gone wild. "Gabe, it's *tiny spiders*! The big one spat a bunch of tiny spiders on Brett! They were *biting him!*"

Gabe shuddered. "Did everybody hear that? Don't let them spit that glop on you!"

"We heard, *chico*, we heard!" Mrs. Castellanos wasn't even breathing hard yet. The lady had about five decades on Gabe but might have been in better shape. "You want to tell us something useful? Figure out how we're going to get out of here!"

They ducked down a stairwell, past the cocooned corpse they'd passed earlier, and for a moment or two Gabe believed they might be able to get out of the building ahead of the spiders. Then he risked a glance over his shoulder, and almost fell over his own feet.

A mob of spiders scuttled after them down the hall. A horde. A *tsunami*.

There must be a whole nest on the top floor!

One of the spiders hissed, *"Make haste, brothers and sisters! Do not let them escape!"*

As they hurled themselves down another flight of stairs, Gabe heard that hocking–hair ball sound again, and a glob of slime sailed past his head and smacked into the side of Uncle Steve's face.

His uncle screamed and stumbled, then crashed down the last two steps and slammed hard into the wall, clawing at his face.

"Somebody help Uncle Steve!" Gabe shouted. He stopped and turned, facing the oncoming mass of spiders. "I'll keep these freaks off of us!"

Lily grabbed his arm, her eyes shining silver-white. "Gabe, no! Let me! I can slow them down!"

Gabe felt the heat building inside of him and shook his head. "That won't be good enough. They'll just come after us again. I've got to fry them."

She tried to get in front of him, and he heard her say *"No!"* but it was too late. Roaring like a wildfire, Gabe thrust both hands up at the oncoming spiders to unleash the full fury of his fire. Twin blowtorches erupted from his palm.

But when a gust of wind tore through his hair a moment later, he knew something was wrong. A split second too late, he realized that Lily had tried to beat him to the punch by funneling a tornado up the stairs. Lily's air radiated a pulse of silver energy, and its coiled power hit Gabe's fire.

Gabe gasped. Earth meeting water had been dangerous, but air *feeds* fire.

This new thing, this impossible thing that was somehow both air and fire, *ignited*. Gabe knew fire didn't ignite, but that was the only word he could think of to describe what happened. A reaction a thousand times more destructive than flame alone. And it burst across the floors and walls ahead of them almost like a liquid.

It's going to destroy everything!

Desperately, Gabe tried to disconnect from fire, to stop this before it got any worse, but he couldn't.

"Pull back, Lily!" he yelled. In his peripheral vision he could

see her, hair waving and eyes shining silver.

Through gritted teeth, Lily ground out, "I can't!"

The voice of the fire hissed in his own mind. *"Burn . . . burn . . . burn!"*

Gabe was trying to control his element as the hall ahead of him was consumed by a firestorm like nothing he'd ever seen. It roared and burned blue-white with the heat of a captive star, and as the fire poured out of him, fueled by Lily's relentless, unstoppable flow of air, the inferno they had unleashed destroyed the spiders, the walls, and the stairs, and exploded up through the top of the impossible building, revealing the sky overhead. He and Lily had cored the building like an apple.

Gabe heard Brett's voice. It sounded distant. Faint. "Gabe! Lil! Stop! You're going to kill us!"

But Gabe didn't know how. The fire and the air were combining, bonding, growing. And as the voice of the fire cheered inside him, Gabe realized that he had the solution to the problem of San Arcadia.

I'll burn it all. I'll burn it all to the ground.

Gabe felt the heat in his eyes intensify. He imagined them going from red-orange to the blue-white of the firestorm above them. Then something struck him in the side and drove him against the nearest wall.

"That is quite enough out of you."

Dazed, Gabe stared up into eight glowing red eyes as a spider easily twice the size of the others they had seen pinned him to the floor with two of its vile human hands. He didn't know where his friends or his uncle or Mrs. Castellanos had gone. All Gabe knew for sure was that he lay in a stairwell in a burning building, and that he was about to die.

The spider bit him.

Its fangs sank into the space between his neck and his shoulder, and Gabe almost blacked out from the pain. The agony was so blinding that he barely felt it when a blast of air like the eye wall of a hurricane took hold of the colossal spider and sent it spinning into the inferno consuming the building. It was chaos. The world around him turned hazy and warped, a kaleidoscope of crumbling walls and burning beams, as Brett dragged him down more stairs and into the main entryway. Lily took his other arm, and Mrs. Castellanos was close behind as they stumbled out onto the street.

The pain. Oh God, the *pain*. Gabe had to time his words to come between the waves of it that crashed into him like tides of acid. "Uncle Steve? Where's . . . *unh* . . . Uncle Steve?"

No one answered him.

"Where is he? Hey—*hey*. Where's my uncle?"

Lily said, "Gabe . . . he's still in there. He told us to get you out. . . ."

Gabe hesitated. "What?"

Lily couldn't seem to look at him. "The walls were coming down, the spiders were everywhere, and the fire was . . ."

Gabe's heart thudded against his ribs. It wasn't real. It

couldn't be real. The world swam and distorted around him.

Uncle Steve—we've got to go back—we've got to—

The apartment building collapsed.

Even over the smashing, thunderous crash of the structure falling in on itself, Gabe could hear the web-chimes ringing up and down the street, growing louder and louder. He fell, rolling onto his side, and was sure he had begun hallucinating, because he saw Kaz, also lying in the middle of the street. Except Kaz had glowing golden hoops around him, and was flopping around like a fish, and kept shouting at them.

Uncle Steve. Gabe shuddered as the fear hit him. *Is he really gone?* That would tear Gabe's life in half. The waves of pain from the spider bite crashed and crashed against him, over and over, and he let them, because every time his body shook with agony, he could forget the terrible feeling of loss.

Gabe watched Lily rush to Kaz. She helped him sit up, and as she did, the golden hoops faded away. He scrambled to his feet, and a wild rush of words tumbled out: "Guys, guys, Jackson ran off and I followed him and that red-snake thing that came out of the ring in the ritual, it's *huge* now, like *circling-the-entire-city* huge. It's what's keeping Thorne's magick in, and then Thorne showed up and we tried to fight him and he wants to kill the snake so he can take over the rest of the planet and Jackson saved my life, but—but, like, Thorne says he *needs* Jackson, so I don't think he'll kill him, and— Oh my God, what happened to Gabe's neck?"

"Here." Mrs. Castellanos knelt next to Gabe, and he watched in dull horror as she opened a small pocketknife. "I don't know what kind of nastiness that critter put in you, *chico*, but we've got to try to get some of it out." Gabe felt the pressure as she made a small, X-shaped cut at the place where the spider had bitten him, but he couldn't figure out what she meant to accomplish.

Then she *squeezed*.

From nearby, Kaz said, "Whoa. Dude. *Dude*. That is, like, the grossest pimple in the history of gross pimples."

Gabe felt the spider's venom spurt out of the wound. Some of it landed on the ground in front of him, and he stared at it in a detached kind of way, because he was much more interested in the immediate, profound, altogether *life-changing* relief it brought him.

After a few seconds, Gabe sat up, and Mrs. Castellanos eyed him critically. "Your color's a little better. You feel better? Hmm?"

Gabe knew there was no way she could have gotten *all* the venom out of him. But now, thanks to her first aid, he no longer expected to die in the next five minutes. Instead, his shoulder simply hurt really, really bad. That he could deal with.

Except now that the waves of pain had stopped crashing into him, he remembered all the other things that were wrong. Across the street, the burning rubble of the apartment building popped and cracked, and another wall collapsed as a support beam gave way.

Could *anyone* have survived that?

He didn't want to consider the answer. "We have to go and look for my uncle."

Mrs. Castellanos said, "Gabe . . . I don't think—"

"I have to know. If Uncle Steve is in there, if he's alive. And he's . . . if he's not. *I have to know!*"

"I get it, Gabe," Lily said. "I'd feel the same way. I'm with you."

"Yeah, we don't leave anybody behind," Kaz said.

Brett said, "Uh . . . guys, I think that's gonna have to wait." He pointed.

Gabe realized the collapsing building hadn't killed all the spiders. It had only stirred up the nest.

8

Kaz watched in horror as countless spiders swarmed out from around the burning wreckage and scuttled toward them, shrieking in fury.

There's got to be somewhere we can go, somewhere we can hide!

Gabe said he felt better, but he looked worse with every passing second. Terrible acid-green lines had begun creeping out from the ghastly spider bite between his neck and shoulder, his skin had gone even paler than usual, and he was *drenched* in sweat.

Brett shouted, "Come on, come on, everybody *move!*" They all followed him down the street as fast as they could, away from the rapidly approaching spiders. Gabe's breathing sounded terrible.

Kaz moved to Gabe's side as they ran. "Are you okay? Can you keep this up?"

Gabe gave him a ragged grin. "Don't worry, Kaz. It looks a lot worse than it is."

But Kaz did worry. *That's one of the things I do best.*

"If we can't outrun them, we need to find someplace they can't get to us," Lily called out. "A door we can barricade, or *something*!"

Kaz spotted a florist shop on the other side of the street and pointed at it. "There! In there!"

The creatures were gaining on them. Kaz ducked as another slime-glob whipped past his head. Lily led the group toward the florist shop, but just as they were about to reach the door, the glass shattered outward as a spider jumped through it to greet them.

"Square-cube law," Kaz whispered. It was the first time he'd seen one of these monstrosities up close. *It's got muscles and . . . and bones! No wonder they get so big!*

The spider hissed at them. The hiss became a scream as a gout of flame sent the spider fleeing back inside the shop. Kaz turned to see Mrs. Castellanos with a can of hair spray.

Holy homemade flamethrowers!

"Empty," Mrs. Castellanos said, dropping the can.

"We need to keep going!" Brett barked, and as the group ran down the sidewalk, Mrs. Castellanos scooped up a stray length of rebar instead.

"Kaz!" Lily dropped back beside him. "Can't you do anything here? Magick up a big wall or something? We could at least slow them down!"

Kaz swallowed hard. He pretended to be more out of breath than he was to give himself time to answer. His fight against Thorne and Madam Creepy for Days had left him shaken. *I almost lost control. I almost let the earth take me over.* He shuddered. *And what was that Thorne said? Something about what happens to elementalists who lose themselves in their element?* The very thought of calling to the earth made him nauseated.

"Uh . . ." He scanned the scene around them. "Brett, how about that fire hydrant up there?" He pointed just ahead toward a half-collapsed automatic car wash. "Do that spike ice stabby stabby you're so good at?"

"I'll give it a shot!" Brett slowed down. "All of you head for that car wash! Let me try something!"

They sped past Brett, and Kaz turned halfway to look back. Brett stood in front of the fire hydrant, and as the wave of spiders got closer, he raised his hands, ripples of blue-green power shimmering around them. One side of the hydrant exploded toward the spiders—Kaz saw a chunk of metal shrapnel punch all the way through one—and a fan of water shot out of it like the thrust of a jet engine. It tore the closest of the spiders in half and swept the rest of them far down the street in a mangled jumble of slime-covered limbs.

Kaz thought that might have done it, that Brett might have bought them a chance to get away . . . until he saw more waves of spiders emerge from the tops of nearby buildings. *Oh God. More nests.*

The hissing of the spiders echoed up and down the street. Brett turned and sprinted to catch up with the group, and he grabbed Kaz's shoulder. "Come on! No time to stop and gawk, buddy!"

Kaz and Brett caught up with Lily and Gabe and Mrs. Castellanos right inside the car wash. The wash bay had a huge, rusted, roll-up metal door, and Mrs. Castellanos shouted, "Somebody give me a hand! We need to pull this down!"

Kaz *loved* that idea.

They all worked to lower the door—the thing *did not* want to move—and they were almost there until a spider ran, as fast as a galloping horse, and threw itself against it. The metal buckled, and the huge door got stuck a few feet from the ground. The spider scrambled up off the floor, wobbly from the impact, and Mrs. Castellanos put it down for good with a two-handed grip on the length of rebar.

Kaz heard the hisses of more spiders, and he knew they'd be inside the car wash in moments.

His voice weak and breathy, Gabe said, "Well, I for one am open to suggestions. . . ."

An idea hit Kaz like the proverbial bolt from the blue. *Maybe I need to be scared to death for my brain to work at full capacity?* He yanked off his backpack and dug into it with both hands. *"Guys!* The Mirror Book! I used it earlier to trap a spike seal! Its pages are like a portal!"

"A portal to where?" Lily asked.

The hissing of the spiders grew louder. "Somewhere without spiders?" Kaz laid the open book on the floor.

Please don't let this be a frying-pan-fire thing!

"Come on, guys, we've got to go! I don't know where it'll take us, but it's got to be better than here, right?"

Lily took Mrs. Castellanos's hand. "Abuelita, we need to go, all right? And this is gonna be weird."

"Things passed 'weird' a long time ago, *mi ángel.*" Mrs. Castellanos shook her head. Now just tell me what to do."

Kaz watched Lily take her grandmother's hand. The pair approached the Book, closed their eyes, and stepped into it. In the instant before the Book swallowed them, they both appeared to become two-dimensional, mirrored versions of themselves. The effect was bizarre. But then they were gone. And when Kaz leaned over and looked, he could see them within the Book, the same way he'd seen the spike seal in its pages.

"Brett, help Gabe through, okay?"

The shadow of a spider fell across the ground outside the car wash. Brett nodded, put a shoulder under Gabe's arm, and the two of them stepped into the Book.

A twisted, humanlike hand grasped the edge of the rolling door's frame. Then another. And another and another.

Kaz jumped feetfirst into the Book.

The transition itself almost knocked the breath out of him, and the ungraceful pile in which he landed did the rest of the job. When he got some air back into his lungs, he said, "Sorry, sorry," while Brett rubbed his head where Kaz's foot had struck him.

"Don't worry about it," Brett said, wincing. "It's not like it's my first magickal portal. I should've gotten out of the way faster."

Kaz got to his feet and turned slowly in place. The word escaped him involuntarily: *"Whoa."*

They stood in a cave with walls composed entirely of broken mirrors. Thousands of mirror fragments, tens of thousands, maybe even millions, all of them reflecting jagged, distorted images of Kaz back at himself.

On the wall behind him, at roughly head height, hung a window—except it wasn't a window. It was the Mirror Book, still lying on the floor of the ruined car wash in San Arcadia.

And as an eight-legged shadow fell across it, Kaz realized there was no way to close the window from this side.

9

Jackson fought down a wave of nausea as he dangled above the city, dragged by Madam Kureshi.

Thorne and Kureshi had both sprouted the impossibly long, spindly shadow-legs Jackson had seen them using when they'd arrived. And without a word, Kureshi had uncoiled a purple, sucker-covered, ooze-dripping tentacle from somewhere beneath her robe and wrapped Jackson up in it. Now he wobbled in the tentacle's grip as his two captors strode across roofs and over hills, the city sliding by beneath them.

Jackson had taken a breath to shout "What is our destination?" but seconds later the question answered itself. They were headed straight for the Golden Gate Bridge.

Or what had become of it. Jackson had seen the towering, twisted trees while approaching the Presidio on the back of Myra Willis's null draak, but he hadn't realized the full extent to which the bridge had changed. The towers were trees now, yes . . . but trees being eaten alive by repulsive Arcadian fungus. The closer they drew to the nearer tree-tower, the more horrible the sight grew.

He had never seen a fungus actively writhing and squirming and burrowing into its host before. And where the fungus met the tree's bark—bark as thick and dense as stone—he was fairly sure he could see *teeth* gnashing and tearing. A faint sound seemed to reach him, borne by a stray current of air. Was that . . .

Is the tree . . . screaming?

Jackson wasn't sure, and before he could observe any further, they reached the trunk, where his captors' shadow-stilts hooked into the bark and propelled all three of them upward. Jackson craned his head back, trying to twist his body in the grip of Kureshi's tentacle to get a look at what awaited them, but the top of the tree-tower disappeared inside a low-hanging cloud.

Jackson held his breath as water droplets from the cloud accumulated on his cheeks. It seemed reasonable that any vapor this close to the heart of evil itself would be poisonous.

"Relax, boy," Thorne said as Jackson felt their momentum slow. "Breathe."

They came to rest on a broad, half-circle-shaped deck, and Jackson finally released the air from his lungs and gulped in more. If he hadn't been in dire need of oxygen, he might have forgotten to breathe altogether.

The top of the tree, shrouded in the low-hanging, misty clouds, was a kind of wooden fortress. Not the kind any architect or carpenter had ever built—instead, the tree itself seemed to have created the place, weaving branches and carpets of leaves together to form a vast warren of rooms and chambers. *Three . . . four . . . five . . .* Jackson wasn't sure how many levels above him the fortress stretched, some of them walled off, others open, revealing hundreds of rooms like cells in a wasp's nest.

The deck where they stood led directly into a massive, oblong room, at the far end of which branches and vines had woven together to form something like a throne.

Of course. The king must have a place from which to survey his kingdom.

Three figures moved out of the throne room's shadows, and Jackson's blood turned as cold as frigid ocean water.

He recognized them. All three of them.

No. No no no . . .

Three of Jackson's most vivid nightmares were striding toward him. He had glimpsed their faces from the Umbra. Through the tiny cracks in the veil that separated him from the living realms, he had seen these men—if they could still be called men—serving Jonathan Thorne in Arcadia, by his side the entire time. *Original members of the Eternal Dawn. Corrupted and transformed by Arcadia's magick.*

All three of them bowed, and the nearest one spoke. "We celebrate your return, Lord Thorne."

Jackson knew the speaker's name was Grillion.

The Umbra was fickle in what it let Jackson see and hear. Only now could he fully understand the monsters these followers of Thorne had become.

Like the other two, Grillion wore Victorian clothing, though the trousers and waistcoat fit him more snugly than they should have, and—Jackson couldn't help but stare—a patchy layer of *mold* covered him. With every breath, a fine cloud of spores escaped Grillion's nostrils, and when he spoke, the air around his head turned a faint, noxious green.

Next to Grillion stood Humboldt, a man as broad and massive as Jonathan Thorne was tall and gaunt. Humboldt might have passed as an average, over-large human, except that his solid black, unblinking eyes were faceted, like those of a fly. Humboldt twitched and jerked with every movement, and he took too many steps for such a big man when he walked. Jackson had heard him speak in years past, and the memory of it—the way every word formed with a horrid clicking, like the mandibles of a great insect—made him shudder.

Jackson had long ago lost the ability to guess a human's age with any accuracy, but if he had to try, he would have put the third man at twenty. Perhaps even younger. "Kretschmar," Jackson breathed. The bronze skin, the long, fine nose, the sculpted cheekbones, the wavy auburn hair. *Unmistakable.* The young man looked like something out of a Renaissance painting—until, hearing his name whispered, Kretschmar shifted his gaze from Jonathan Thorne to Jackson, and Jackson thought for a moment that he would lose control of his bowels entirely.

Worms writhed and shifted inside Kretschmar's eyes.

Jackson became convinced, utterly convinced at that moment, that every one of those millions upon millions of worms, the worms he knew occupied every cubic inch beneath Kretschmar's skin, knew his name.

So thoroughly petrified had Jackson become that he didn't even flinch when Jonathan Thorne stepped close, blocking Kretschmar from his sight and lifting Jackson's face with a finger under his chin.

"The rest of you. Leave us." The piercing green of Thorne's gaze bore into Jackson's skull.

Jackson had long feared nothing more than Thorne's inhuman green eyes, but after seeing Kretschmar's worms, they were almost a relief. *Anything is better than the worms.*

Jackson couldn't look away from Thorne and only heard footsteps—shuffling, sliding, clicking footsteps—as Grillion, Humboldt, Kretschmar, and Madam Kureshi took their leave. Finally Thorne put a gentle hand on Jackson's shoulder and turned him to look back at the edge of the platform where they had arrived.

"The city lies below us," Thorne said. Jackson ground his teeth together to keep from jerking away from the man's touch. "Would you like to see?"

Jackson stared out at nothing but solid gray mist, and was preparing to come up with some acidic quip about how there was nothing *to* see, but Thorne waved a languid hand. The clouds parted and whiffed away into nothingness.

San Arcadia stretched out beneath them. Every corrupted, malformed, soot-black part of it, laid out like a piece of a board game. Towering gothic towers pierced the sky of downtown, the Mission District seemed to throb like a beating heart, and practically at their feet, the glowing, glyph-covered dome of the Presidio shined. A series of glyphs surged in brightness as a flock of sawjaws threw themselves against the dome.

Jackson looked away. "Why have you brought me here? What do you want from me?"

"Nothing for which you were not destined, Master Wright." Thorne made another gesture, and a chair rose from the wood of the platform, creaking and groaning as it grew. He motioned for Jackson to sit.

"No, thank you. I prefer to stand."

The green of Thorne's eyes grew harder, more vivid, and Jackson caught a stomach-churning glimpse of the horror inside Thorne's mouth as the man said, "Please. *Sit.*"

Jackson sat.

Thorne moved as he talked. Slowly circling him.

"It is almost as if you have been made to order for our purposes, Master Wright. As you are the sole wielder of pure magick, your abilities should be precisely what we need to slay that accursed Crimson Serpent and remove the barrier that prevents Arcadia from expanding."

Jackson swallowed and chose his words carefully. "You expect me to do this for you?"

"No, no. Not you by yourself. Your power is but one ingredient. But with the proper finesse, the correct reagents, the necessary incantation . . . we shall hone your abilities, Jackson. Sharpen them. Sharpen *you*. I shall make you into the perfect weapon. *My* weapon."

"Why would you believe, for even the barest second, that I would assist you?"

Another chair grew from the platform, facing Jackson, and Thorne perched on its edge. It put his face almost even with Jackson's. "Because you were made for *this* world! Not . . ." He waved at the land beyond the Crimson Serpent's barrier. "Not *that* one. What do you have in common with the humans of today? Nothing. You brim with power, Jackson. Power that *we* understand. Power we *respect*. Your place is with us. Not with those . . . insects."

Jackson allowed his expression to soften. Just a hair. Just a degree. "And what . . . what would be my part in this incantation? What role would I serve, exactly?"

Thorne sprang up again, and the chair on which he had sat crumbled to dust. "All shall be revealed in due time, Master Wright. The barrier will fall, and we shall watch as our kingdom and its might and majesty roll forth across the mountains and valleys and seas of this world." Thorne fixed his terrible eyes on Jackson's again. "Your place is with us. Not with them. Or have you forgotten Gabriel Conway's attempt on your life?"

Jackson looked away. The painful memory stabbed at his mind. Gabe, back on Alcatraz Island, trying to trade Jackson for the life of Dr. Conway, shoving him toward the blood cocoon that would have shunted him from Earth into Arcadia. It might not have killed him, but being trapped there? Trapped *again*, in a place every bit as horrible or more so than the Umbra? Jackson would have preferred death.

"Come." Thorne held out a hand. "Walk with me. Let us discuss the new world. And your place within it."

Slowly, Jackson lifted his hand and placed it in Thorne's. It felt as dangerous as thrusting his hand into a bag of vipers.

"Very good," Thorne purred as Jackson stood up from the chair. "Now. Matters of priority. I could use your assistance with a certain issue . . . but first, are you hungry?"

Jackson's stomach felt as dust-dry as the fist of a skeleton, but as he walked beside Thorne into the wooden fortress, he nodded his head.

10

Inside the pages of the Mirror Book, Gabe and his friends watched the portal nervously for some time before they were sure the spiders didn't follow them into—well, wherever it was that they were.

Gabe's eyelids felt like five-pound weights. He closed them and let them stay shut, but he did wince at the pain in his shoulder. His brain felt slow, as if his thoughts were stuck in hardening concrete. He gradually became aware of two different conversations going on, one to his left, one to his right.

To his left, Brett spoke in quiet tones to Mrs. Castellanos. ". . . kind of impressed you're taking all this so well, Abuelita."

Mrs. Castellanos made a sound halfway between a chuckle

and a snort. "I've been trapped in a building overrun by giant spiders, *nieto*. I'm not going to be surprised by much." Gabe heard a sound as if someone was shifting positions on the floor. "So you and Lily and your other friends . . . you are all, *cómo se dice*, 'elementalists'?"

"Yeah. I'm water, Lily's air, Kaz is earth, and Gabe is fire. Jackson's magick."

"Magick? Magick is an element?"

"Turns out, yeah."

Gabe was propped against a rough, raw, stone wall and tried to shift to get more comfortable. When he did, the pain from his spider bite became blinding. A scent filled his nostrils, the damp smell of *cold*.

On his right, Kaz was talking to Lily. "So Thorne mentioned the red snake, only he called it the Crimson Serpent, and— Hey, Gabe, are you awake?"

Gabe groaned and opened his eyes. "I'm awake, I'm awake."

He almost wished he'd left his eyes shut. A faint greenish haze lingered around the edges of his vision, and the effort it took to focus on his surroundings made the spider bite in his shoulder throb. Lily came and crouched next to him, and put the back of her hand on his forehead. "You've got a fever."

"I'll be fine." Gabe hitched himself up a little farther on the wall but didn't try to make his legs work. "Thanks to your grandmother."

Mrs. Castellanos got up and knelt on Gabe's other side. She

pulled the collar of his shirt down to look at the bite. "Basic first aid," she said. "Nothing to get excited about. Gabriel, you need a doctor."

Gabe sighed and glanced around. He wanted to say "Great. Where's the nearest hospital?"

They all sat in the irregularly shaped chamber Gabe had come to think of as the Mirror Cave, staring at thousands upon thousands of their own reflections in the shards of mirrors lining the walls and ceiling and ground as the cold lingered in his nose and permeated his clothing and hair. High up on one wall, the portal still showed part of the car wash, and as he watched, the shadow of a spider's leg passed over it.

Are we ever going to be able to climb back out of this place?

Gabe blearily tried to focus on the source of the cave's light, and just as blearily realized he couldn't pinpoint it. It seemed to come from the stone walls, glowing weakly out from between the mirrors, but he wouldn't swear to that.

Gabe cleared his throat and turned his head toward Kaz. "So, what happened to you and Jackson?"

"Oh. Right." As quickly as he could—with only a few shuddering detours about one of Thorne's lieutenants, a woman named Madam Kureshi, whom he described as "aggressively creepy"—Kaz related everything he had heard Thorne say before Jackson had roped him up and flung him into the sky.

"How did you land?" Lily asked. "Weren't you, y'know, *falling from the sky?*"

Kaz nodded. "Yeah, for about ten seconds. Then I felt Jackson's bonds slowing me down. He was trying to save me from Thorne, not kill me. Plus, uh, I had a little trouble with, uh . . . with the earth. It kind of tried to, y'know, like. Take over. And Jackson snapped me out of it. Anyway! So, yeah, Thorne thinks the Crimson Serpent exists in, like, every reality at once? I guess? And he wants to kill it. So the whole planet can get turned into . . . whatever San Arcadia is."

Gabe tried to pay attention to what Kaz was saying, but he kept flashing to images of his mother and Uncle Steve. Aria was supposed to be safe back at the Presidio, but what if she lost control again? What if that glyph-dome barrier failed? What if the Dawn decided she was too dangerous to let live?

If Uncle Steve is really gone . . . if Mom is all the family I have left now . . .

It was too hard to think about. He closed his eyes and shifted, which made his bite hurt worse. He tried to distract himself with what Kaz had said.

The Crimson Serpent exists in all realities? What does that even mean?

The constant hum grating in his eardrums wasn't helping him collect his thoughts.

Wait. What is *that sound?*

He tried to focus on the hum the way he had on the conversations he'd heard when he woke up. It wasn't just a hum, there was . . . *texture* to it. Regular breaks in the sound, like . . .

. . . like words. The voice seemed to come from inside his head and chest, similar to the way fire spoke to him. But he didn't think it was fire.

"Am I the only one who— Can any of you hear that?" he asked.

Kaz said, "Oh! Right! The sound! That's the Serpent! Jackson said he'd heard it before, when he was stuck in the Umbra."

Lily cocked her head to one side. "Holy crap, I *do* hear something. I mean, I didn't at first, but it's . . . it's like when there's a ticking clock in a room, and you don't realize you can hear it until all of a sudden you can't *not* hear it."

Brett walked slowly around the chamber, turning his head this way and that. "Where's it coming from? And what's it saying?"

Kaz rose to his feet. "'With five elements for one act across all worlds.' And you're right, Lily. Now I can't help but hear it. It's even louder now than it was right next to the Serpent!"

Mrs. Castellanos shook her head. "I believe you, but I don't hear anything. Maybe you have to be an elementum."

Brett said, "Elementalist," and when his grandmother shrugged, he went on: "Okay, but what does that mean? What did you say it was?"

Kaz repeated, "With five elements for one act across all worlds."

Brett rolled his eyes to the ceiling. "What is that, a riddle?"

Lily's brows drew together. "Five elements for one. We're

supposed to combine all our powers."

Kaz kicked one toe at the mirrored floor. "I thought that, too, but mixing powers hasn't worked out too well for us so far. And, besides, the last time we got mysterious advice about a red snake we kind of broke reality. I think we need to be really careful."

"Agreed," Gabe said.

"So, instead of combining the elements, what if it means we all have to do one thing, like we did with the ritual?" Kaz continued.

Brett snapped his fingers. "Exactly! The Crimson Serpent is what screwed up the ritual last time, right? That's the part Thorne tricked us into including! So what if we get rid of the Serpent? That might undo this whole San Arcadia mess!"

"Dude! Brett! *Dude!*" Kaz sputtered for a couple seconds. "No way! Killing the Serpent is exactly what Thorne wants! I heard him *say so*!"

Lily stepped between Kaz and Brett. "We don't know what would happen if we killed the Serpent. And that's what you're talking about, right, *hermano*? Killing it? You really want to kill some gigantic multidimensional being and just see what happens?"

As Brett grumbled, Gabe's eyes drifted out of focus. He peered at one of the countless reflections of himself, and winced at how bad he looked. *Probably for the best I can't see too clearly.* The sounds of his friends' voices grew fuzzy. Muffled. He struggled to focus again . . .

. . . and realized one of the many reflections of himself that spanned the cavern wall was different from the others. Directly across from him, a larger-than-average shard of mirror showed Gabe his own face—but the reflection was *smiling* at him.

I'm hallucinating. My brain's soaked in spider venom and I'm seeing things.

He blinked. Blinked again. The other-Gabe stayed the same, smiling, staring back at him. The smile didn't waver as the Gabe in the mirror caught fire. Red-gold flames licked up from his shirt, scorched the skin of his face, lit his eyebrows and his hair.

This is just like the Library of Mirrors. Now I know I'm hallucinating.

But he couldn't stop watching. The other-Gabe's face burned, melted, and reformed into a new face altogether.

The face of his father.

"Gaaabe!"

The room jerked back into perfect clarity as Gabe lurched away from the wall, scrambling to get to his feet, the feminine scream ringing in his ears. His legs didn't want to cooperate. The scream came again: *"Gaaabe! Help me! Help me, Gabe!"*

Kaz said, "Holy cats, is that *Aria*?"

Gabe grabbed hold of Brett and tried to pull himself upright. As he did, the room spun violently and turned solid green. He lurched, but Brett caught him, and Lily jumped to help. She said, "Gabe, you need to stay down! You're sick!"

The green faded, and he slowly regained his balance. "But that's my *mom*! She's calling me!" The scream came again, pouring through the portal back to San Arcadia. "She's out there, and she needs us! She needs *me*! Come on, let's go, let's go!"

Brett moved to just below the portal. "Well . . . I don't see any spiders anymore."

Kaz said, "But what if it's a trick? What if this is just them trying to get us to come out of hiding?"

The scream echoed out once more. *"Gabe! Please! You've got to help me!"*

Gabe turned pleading eyes on his friends. "Guys . . . come on. What if it was *your* mom, Kaz?"

A tense silence stretched out. Finally Brett said, "He's right. We've got to at least take a look."

Kaz said, "I'm not going."

"Gaaabe!" The scream made the entire Mirror Cave vibrate it was so loud.

Gabe scowled at Kaz. "What? How can you—?"

Kaz shook his head. "You should go and help your mom. Absolutely. But listen. The Serpent is the key to all this, right? And Thorne's obsessed with it, which means he's probably got creeps in robes watching its every scale—*in San Arcadia*. But if it's also *here* . . . I might be able to get a better look at it. A closer look, I mean, and not get interrupted? Back in San Arcadia, I started talking to it, and I could tell it heard me. Maybe here

I can get it to respond! So I'll stay here and try to get some, y'know. Knowledge."

As soon as Gabe said the words "No way. It's out of the question," he realized who he sounded exactly like: Uncle Steve. Kaz tried to protest, but Gabe waved away his objections. "You've never spent time in a place like this. I have. If *this*,"—he gestured to the mirrored cavern all around them—"is like the Library of Mirrors where Uncle Steve and I went in Arcadia, it's not all peace and quiet. It'll try to trick you and show you things that aren't real. Things that you fear, like your inner demons. Then it'll show you *worse* things that actually *are* real. In the library we got attacked by these *elemental* things. Like, mine was basically living fire. And it looked like me, which was really freaking creepy. So no, you—" Gabe faltered as his vision went green around the edges. "You . . . uh . . ."

What was I saying?

Lily came to him and put a hand on his uninjured shoulder. "Look. Gabe. You're in no state to be making decisions. Okay? I think Kaz is right. So I'm gonna stay here with him. He shouldn't try to find this Serpent on his own, and this way I can watch his back."

Mrs. Castellanos shook her head and waved her hands at the same time. "*No!* You are coming with us, *nieta*! You maybe don't know what is in here, but we *all* know what is out there! We need strength in numbers!"

Gabe's vision had blurred again, and his friends' voices

sounded as if they were coming from the other end of a tunnel. He thought he should probably say something. Probably protest. But somewhere along the way he had lost the strength. Suddenly, it was all he could do to keep standing.

Brett looked from Lily to Gabe to his grandmother. "It's all right, Abuelita. Lily's right. Kaz shouldn't be alone in here. And I can protect you and Gabe. We'll look for Aria, and then we'll all meet back at the Presidio, okay?" Lily moved over to Brett, and he held up his hands. "I know what you're gonna say, okay? I've messed up, and I've been messing up for a long time. I messed up with Charlie, he wouldn't have died if I hadn't screwed up on the bay that day, but I can *do* this, I swear to you, I—"

He cut off as Lily gave him a hug. She let him go and stepped back. "That wasn't what I was going to say. And we didn't lose our brother because of you, Brett. Okay? I know that—and you should, too. I was going to tell you that I know you can do this. I have faith in you."

Brett looked surprised for a few seconds, then his face broke into a grin. "Thanks . . . thanks, Lil. That, uh . . . that means a lot."

She hugged him again.

Lily and Kaz helped Brett climb through the window of the open Mirror Book. Gabe hadn't been a hundred percent sure they even *could* get back to San Arcadia from here. The Mirror Book might have been a one-way trip, like the freaky water toilet-portal that had taken them to Argent Court. But Brett clambered through, took a look around, and poked his head and shoulders back into the Mirror Cave. "All clear. No spiders. I don't see your mother anywhere, either, though."

Kaz handed Brett his backpack. "Here. To carry the Book in." Lily and Mrs. Castellanos lifted Gabe up and through the window. He had a moment of dizzying disorientation as his body slid through the portal and he found himself back in San Arcadia, the smell of soap and gasoline in the air. He watched the distinctly weird sight of Mrs. Castellanos wriggling out of the book after him. Then Brett carefully closed the Book and opened it back up, and Gabe let out a sigh of relief when they saw Kaz and Lily, still there on the other side, waving at them.

Gabe waved back, and swallowed a surge of nausea. He tried to ignore the brighter and brighter green tinge at the edges of his vision. "All right. Let's go find my mom."

11

Kaz watched the window back into San Arcadia fold in half and disappear as Brett closed the Mirror Book. Like so much associated with Arcadian magick, it made his brain hurt with its sheer *wrongness*. Reality wasn't supposed to behave this way!

He turned to Lily. "Ready to get moving?"

"Yeah," Lily said, but her gaze lingered on the spot where the portal had been.

"They're going to be okay, Lil," Kaz said. "Brett's got this handled."

"I know," Lily nodded. "I know he does." She sighed, and Kaz knew just how she felt. Yeah, he wasn't the one who'd just watched his brother and grandmother step into the mortal danger of San Arcadia, but it still felt wrong to be separated from the others. The ritual that had bound them to the elements had also bound them to *one another*. Kaz only really felt *right* when he and his friends were together.

"So we should just follow the sound?" Lily asked. She pointed behind Kaz. "Because I think it's louder that way."

They left the chamber, moving slowly down a mirror-lined passageway, concentrating on the hum and the words hidden within it. It took Kaz several minutes to get used to the sight of Lily and himself reflected endlessly across the shards that covered the walls, ceiling, and ground. It was making his peripheral vision go a little nuts.

The tunnel branched, and branched again, and it took most of Kaz's brainpower to keep track of which way they'd come. Then a terrible thought struck him.

What happens if we can't find our way back to the Mirror Cave?

For that matter, Kaz had been assuming that when the Mirror Book opened again, the portal would pop back into existence in the Mirror Cave. But he realized now that this was a big assumption. Even if it was true, what if it opened while he and Lily were somewhere else in the maze? How would they ever get out of this labyrinth?

Kaz considered saying something about this to Lily, and maybe something about leaving a trail, too—*except we don't* have anything like bread crumbs, and the closest we could get to string or yarn would be if one of us unraveled their shirt, and I'm not gonna ask Lily to do that, and I don't really want to unravel mine 'cause that would be superembarrassing, plus I bet I'd get cold, and why didn't I pack a can of spray paint so we could've been spraying arrows on the wall this whole time—when he noticed something new about the fractured reflections in the mirror-lined walls.

Just like every other surface they'd seen, every facet of the passage they walked down reflected Kaz and Lily as they walked past. Except . . . were some of those reflections moving out of sync? Kaz tried to find one in particular, tried to watch it happening, but looking straight at the mirrors seemed to prevent the effect. If he stared directly at one of the mirrors, the reflection within it seemed totally benign.

Kaz rubbed his arms to combat a sudden chill.

"It's getting louder," Lily said. "Definitely. We're going the right way."

Kaz thought so, too. He tried to figure out just what he was going to say to the Serpent, if and when they found the creature in a conversational mood. He figured he'd ask it to quit encircling the city and to go back to being a ring—hopefully that would pull all the magick from San Francisco. But how exactly do you ask a fifty-mile-long snake something like that? *Really politely,* Kaz guessed.

The tunnel before them forked again, and when they took

the side from which the hum emanated most strongly, it led them around a gentle curve to the right and then dead-ended at a broad, tall, unbroken mirror. Nothing seemed out of step with this one; Kaz lifted a hand and waved, and his reflection followed him perfectly. *Just like a normal mirror.*

"Dead end. So what are we supposed to do?" Lily took a step closer to the reflective surface. "Try to break it? So it looks like all the other broken mirrors in here?"

The hum had gotten loud enough that Kaz expected the surface of the mirror to be vibrating. Which it wasn't. "Hang on." He walked up to it.

"What're you doing?"

"Trying something. I don't think this is actually a mirror."

He pushed a hand toward the surface and yelped when it passed straight through it. No ripples, no distortion, nothing to indicate any kind of physical presence at all. "Holy pancakes! Lily, it's like a hologram!" He pulled his hand back out and wiggled his fingers. "And my hand's okay."

She came up beside him. "It's an illusion. So we need to walk through it?"

It wasn't really a question. "I don't think we have a choice," Kaz said. "I mean, it's either that or just keep wandering around this maze."

"And the hum is definitely coming from this direction."

"Yeah. All right, here goes nothing," Kaz said, and began to step forward.

"Wait!" Lily cried. "What if we get separated?"

"Okay, good point," Kaz said. "Getting separated would be bad."

Lily took his hand. "Okay, so, on three?"

He gulped. "One. Two. . . . Three."

Kaz and Lily stepped through their own reflections and found themselves standing in a corridor. Not a rough, natural-looking tunnel anymore, but an actual corridor like anybody would encounter in a school or an office building . . . except that its walls and floor and ceiling were all perfect, seamless, endless mirrors. A glance to the left or right showed endless reflections of themselves, dwindling to tiny, distant points.

At least these reflections are only moving when we move and not on their own.

Lily glanced behind them and gripped Kaz's shoulder. "The illusion."

He turned. The mirror hallway stretched out behind them, unbroken, and Kaz's shoulders slumped. "It's like it was never there. Like the *caves* were never there."

"So how are we supposed to get out of here?" Lily asked. "How are we supposed to get back to Gabe and Brett and Abuela?" Her voice rose with each word, and Kaz knew exactly what she was feeling, because he could feel it rising in his own guts. He balled up his fists as tightly as he could and fought down the approaching panic.

Are we trapped here? Because I really, really, really don't want to be trapped here!

Lily dug out her asthma inhaler and took a puff from it.

"Okay, so I admit that's not great." He squeezed his eyes shut. "But it doesn't change what we need to do." He opened his eyes again and saw Lily. Her face had gone a little gray, but she nodded as she stared back at him.

"We still need to find the Serpent," Lily said.

"Right."

"So we keep going."

"Right. We keep going." Kaz surprised himself by chuckling. "You know, I was wishing earlier we had some spray paint so we could mark the way we came with arrows—or at least some bread crumbs. Wouldn't do us any good now, would it?"

"I guess not. Well, if we're gonna do it, let's do it," Lily said. "I don't think the Serpent's gonna come to us."

Now we're in a proper labyrinth.

They had been following the Serpent's song for what felt like at least an hour. They hadn't seen any doors. Only more hallways, and the mirrors threw off their depth perception so that Kaz had banged into walls and corners more than once. It was impossible to tell if they were making any progress because every hallway looked exactly alike, and he had no idea whether they were covering new ground or just moving in mirrored circles.

At least the Serpent's song keeps getting louder. We must be going in sort of the right direction!

"The air feels weird," Lily said. "I mean, not just the weird smell. It *feels* weird. Like, in my lungs."

Kaz couldn't help but agree. "Yeah. It's *thin*. . . . It feels like we're way up high. On the ridge of some huge mountain or something. Like you said, *weird*."

As they turned another corner, Lily threw out a hand and stopped Kaz short.

"We definitely haven't been here before," Lily said.

She was totally right. Golden ooze had been sprayed up and down the length of the hallway and lay in a thick, congealing pool beneath some creature's ruined body. It looked familiar. Then he figured it out: *The spike seal I trapped in the Book, the one that was just about to rip me and Gabe to shreds . . . it's been ripped to shreds itself!*

Kaz covered his nose as an odor like week-old roadkill washed over them. "That is *so* gross."

Tiny ripples moved across the pool's slimy surface in time with the Serpent's pulsing hum.

"Well, I guess it answers one question," Lily declared.

He glanced at Lily. "Huh? What?"

"Unless the seal tore *itself* apart, we're not alone in here." She looked at him, eyes wide.

A part of Kaz really, *really* wished he and Lily had gone with Brett and Gabe and Mrs. Castellanos. But it was too late for that. They couldn't go back. They had to go forward.

With a running start, Kaz jumped over the spike seal carnage and only got gold-colored slime on the heel of one shoe. Lily sailed over the awfulness easily and didn't get any on her at all.

"Always making me look bad, Lil," he muttered, which earned him a little smile from his friend.

They kept walking, neither of them looking back. Kaz tried not to think about what could have done that kind of damage to such a frightening creature.

Two hallways later, he turned to say something to Lily, and thought his heart might stop.

Lily wasn't there anymore.

Right behind Kaz was a brand-new wall, just as perfectly mirrored as all the others.

Please be another illusion, please be another illusion!

But cold, hard glass met his fingers when he tried to pass his hand through it. His stomach felt as if it had just dropped completely out of his body. And maybe through the floor, too. *No! What was I thinking before when I offered to stay here alone? I can't do this by myself!* Kaz knocked against the wall, slammed his fists against it, threw his whole body against it. "Lily!" He no longer cared who or what might hear him. *"Lily!"*

Only silence answered him. Silence, and his own reflection.

Except, he suddenly realized, it wasn't his. The Kaz facing him stared back with slate gray eyes and a smile that sent chills all over his body.

I'm not smiling.

Kaz whipped his head left and right, checking the mirrored walls on either side of him, and no matter where he looked, he saw the same eerie stare and malevolent grin reflected endlessly.

That's not me!

He spun and bolted down the hall, but his twisted, grinning reflections just kept perfect pace with him as his breathing came faster and faster, until he spotted a door ahead, a normal, brown, wooden, ordinary door. It was the greatest thing he'd ever seen. Kaz dashed to it, twisted the knob, and flung himself through . . .

. . . into his own dining room. In his own house.

His own normal, ordinary, back-before-San Arcadia house.

No way. No way is this real!

But his mother sat in her usual seat, and his father stood, a platter of steaks in his hands, serving one each to June, Kira, and Carlie. His father paused, steak skewered on a large metal serving fork. Kaz's entire family turned to look at him.

This is impossible! You all left town! You got out! You're safe!

"Kaz!" His mother gave him her warmest, sunniest smile and pulled back an empty chair. "You're just in time to join us for dinner!"

12

His mother's scream seemed to cut out the moment Gabe stepped through the portal back into San Arcadia.

There were about a thousand things to worry about in this twisted city, but his mother was just about the only thing Gabe could think of. He moved as quietly as he could to what remained of the battered roll-down door of the car wash. Waves of pain slid up into the side of his skull and down his arm from the spider bite, and he wondered if the venom was causing nerve damage. He choked back the urge to vomit.

The street outside appeared to be empty. Fresh webs were strewn around, but nothing moved, and he beckoned for Brett and Mrs. Castellanos to follow him.

Brett's grandmother squinted and tilted her head when she reached him. "I don't hear the spiders anymore."

There was still no trace of his mother's screams, either. The street outside was unnaturally quiet.

"I hope they're not just out there waiting to ambush us," Brett said as he slipped the Mirror Book into Kaz's backpack.

Gabe felt his friend's eyes on him.

"Hey. Gabe. Look at me."

Gabe leaned against the wall. Brett wobbled out of focus, but only for a few seconds. "What?"

"Dude. You're pouring sweat and as white as snow. Plus . . ." He leaned closer. "Holy crap. One of your pupils is crazy big."

No worries. That only means I've got brain damage, right?

Gabe scowled and looked away. "Thanks for the update. So, can we get moving now?"

Brett swapped a glance with Mrs. Castellanos. "Yeah . . . back to the Presidio."

The world pulsed green around the edges as Gabe's heartbeat sped up. "What? No! You heard Mom's screams! She needs us! We have to find her!"

Without even asking, Brett tugged Gabe's collar to one side, exposing the spider bite. Gabe couldn't turn his head far enough to get a good look at it, but Brett went a little pale, and Mrs. Castellanos gasped at the sight of it. From the corner of his eye Gabe could see that his skin had gone a sort of splotchy red and green.

Brett shook his head. "Gabe . . . listen, man. I know we got some of the venom out, but I don't think it was enough. You need to get a doctor to look at that."

Gabe wanted to laugh but was afraid he'd puke. "A doctor? Brett, look around you! There are no doctors here!"

"There might be . . . back at the Presidio, like I said."

Gabe felt his knees start to give way and pressed his back harder against the door track, steadying himself. "No. Just *no*." *She's— She might be all I've got left! I can't just leave her out here!* "We've got to look for Mom. We've got to find her!"

"Look where?" Brett waved his arms, taking in the whole city. "We have no way of knowing where those screams came from, and you can't do her any good if you're dead. Right?"

Gabe tried to answer, but his knees felt as if they'd suddenly turned to water, and on his way down he doubled over and heaved out the contents of his stomach.

Which was empty. *When was the last time I ate anything?* He heaved again, wishing he had something in there to bring up.

"Okay, buddy, no more arguing. Time to go. Abuela? *Ayudame?*"

Gabe felt Brett and Mrs. Castellanos hoist him back to his feet. He couldn't do much to resist. "You can't . . . take me through the whole city . . . like this. How're you gonna get me back . . . to the Presidio?"

Brett nodded off down one street. "The shore's not that far away. It's time to see if I can get water to listen again."

The salty spray of the bay waters felt good on Gabe's skin. He didn't even mind how numb his butt was getting, sitting in the middle of the ice floe Brett had conjured. He'd begun to feel an odd sort of calm. The ever-increasing green flashes in his vision didn't even bother him much anymore.

He wondered if he should be bothered that he wasn't bothered.

Brett had rooted himself to a spot on the ice a couple of feet away from him, his whole body shaking and his jaw clenched. Mrs. Castellanos stood beside Brett, her head pivoting constantly as they skimmed across the waves.

"This is amazing, *nieto*!"

Brett didn't move. "Please . . . don't talk to me . . . right now, Abuelita. I really . . . have to . . . concentrate!"

She held out her arms. "But it *is* amazing! Like a speedboat made of ice!"

Brett grumbled. The ice floe kept moving.

Gabe narrowed his eyes and focused on the Presidio, dead ahead. The closer they got, the less he liked the looks of it. One of the buildings had been halfway destroyed, and the sight of it snapped him out of the calm he'd been feeling.

It looks like a bomb went off. Did something get through the dome? Surely those sawjaw things couldn't have caused that much damage?

There were so many sawjaws flinging themselves against

the barrier. It looked like the attacks had tripled—maybe qua-drupled. The glyphs flared constantly as they repelled attack after attack. As Gabe watched, one of the magickal symbols flickered and went dark, like a burned-out lightbulb. Then another.

Oh my God. The dome is failing!

A massive shadow fell across them, and Gabe looked up to see a null draak, carrying an Eternal Dawn member, robe and all. The null draak swept low enough for the rider to get a good look at them, and Gabe caught a fragment of the rider's shout as it glided past, heading for the dome. ". . . coming in!"

With a grunt, Brett guided the ice floe out of the water and across the ground, where a wedge-shaped section of the dome vibrated and vanished. Mrs. Castellanos helped Gabe get up, and two robed Dawn members rushed out and practically dragged him inside. Once Mrs. Castellanos and a sweating, panting Brett had followed them, the dome closed behind them.

Between one flash of green and the next, Gabe was taken inside one of the fort's buildings, and someone laid him down on what felt like a table.

"What's wrong with him? Where's everyone else?"

Whose voice is that? I know I know that voice. . . .

It came to him. Eva. The new Primus. He turned his head and saw her as she bent over him. Her cool hand rested against his forehead, and she almost jerked it back, as if she'd touched a hot stove.

"It looks worse than it is," Gabe whispered.

Eva gave him a skeptical look before turning back to Brett. "What happened out there? Tell me everything."

Brett and Mrs. Castellanos talked over each other, filling in Eva on their encounter with the huge spiders, how they'd lost Uncle Steve in the collapsing building, and how they'd left Kaz and Lily in the Mirror Cave. Gabe tried to say "What happened to the fort?" but it seemed like an awful lot of effort, so he was glad to hear Brett ask the question instead.

Eva cast another glance at Gabe. "What happened is that Aria heard her son calling to her."

Gabe frowned. "Me? But I never . . . called to her."

"Uh, not to contradict you, kid, but we all heard you. It echoed all over the city."

Gabe closed his eyes. He was so tired, but he knew he had to try to stay awake. He heard Brett say, "No, he didn't. We *did* hear his mom calling to *him*, though."

"Well, be that as it may, the second Aria heard Gabe, she turned her shackles into shiny dust and basically went berserk. Did you see the blown-out building? Yeah, that was her. We couldn't stop her. Nothing could have. She blew a hole in the dome on her way out, and now it's sort of . . . unraveling."

Mom. She's out there. Alone. I have to find her!

He tried to sit up, but Mrs. Castellanos gently pushed him down. There was no strength left in him.

"I don't know how much longer we're going to be able to

hold this place," Eva continued. "But first things first. What's wrong with Gabe?" Eva asked. "He looks terrible."

Gabe mustered enough energy to reach up and pull his collar aside.

Eva said, "Oh my *God*. What is that? What *did* that?"

"One of the spiders!" Mrs. Castellanos said. "Bigger than all the others! It bit him very hard."

Gabe couldn't see well, but he had the sense of people coming over to look at his bite wound. Brett was trying to keep his voice low, but the words reached Gabe's ears just fine: "I didn't want to say anything till we got here, but I'm afraid that bite might be . . . full of little baby spiders?"

Eva made a sound like *eeugh*. "Why would you think that?"

"Well, the globs they were spitting at us *were* filled with tiny spiders. But also, I think that's what happens in, like, *every* monster movie, right? That's gotta be why Gabe's so sick!"

Lying there on the table, the green threatening to take over his vision, Gabe knew Brett was wrong. He hadn't been willing to acknowledge it to himself before, but now he knew the truth and could no longer deny it.

The spider bite *had* implanted some kind of creature inside him. But it wasn't baby spiders. Gabe couldn't resist it any longer.

He was dimly aware of screams around him, and a moment later, he felt an oily, black tendril slide out of the bite wound and writhe against his face.

13

The scent of juicy steak filled Kaz's nostrils, and his mouth watered as he took in the big serving bowl full of mashed potatoes and the platter heaped with ears of corn on the cob. His stomach gave out what sounded like a low roar.

It was all so familiar. The glasses slipping down his father's nose, his mother's nail-bitten hands, the scab on Kira's knee that he was sure she'd gotten in another skateboarding mishap. The doll tucked into the chair at June's side. Carlie's pigtails.

No. No. I'm in the Mirror Labyrinth.

"What're you waiting for, Kaz?" his mother asked. She patted the empty chair next to her. "I know you must be hungry. Come and sit!"

Kaz shifted his weight from one foot to the other. *Don't listen to her. Don't look at them!* There was no way this was actually his family's dining room. This was definitely a messed-up mind game like the ones Gabe said that he and Dr. Conway had faced in the Library of Mirrors back in Arcadia. This was exactly the kind of thing Gabe had warned him would happen here.

And yet . . .

When Kaz took a half step sideways, the floor squeaked under his foot exactly as he expected it to because the nail in that floor joist had squeaked for as long as he could remember. He glanced up and saw the crack in the ceiling shaped sort of like the coast of Maryland—the same crack that he'd stared at every day of his life, every time he'd ever sat at the dining-room table. The table that, yes, had the two sugar packets under one leg to keep it level.

It looks real. It feels real. But it isn't. This isn't real. You know this isn't real!

Rain began to fall outside. He recognized the sound it made on the roof. Careful not to look at his mother or father or sisters, he turned his head and peered out of the dining room, down the hallway to the front door, beside which leaned a pair of sawhorses, next to a couple of buckets of paint and some brushes and rollers. *Dad still hasn't finished painting the front porch.*

No! What are you thinking? This isn't real.

"Come on, Kaz, sit down." His father set the plate of steaks on the table. "Your food's getting cold."

June piped up. "*Eww*! Cold mashed potatoes! *Gross!*"

Kira and Carlie both giggled.

The steaks *did* look good. Kaz's stomach rumbled again. *It's not real, it's not real, it's not real.* He kept repeating the words to himself, even as he crossed the dining room and sat down next to his mother. She immediately plopped a steak onto his empty plate and reached for the potatoes.

"Guys . . ." Kaz's voice wavered. "Guys, this is nice and all, but . . . I'm not supposed to be here. This isn't . . . it isn't right."

Taylor Smith pulled back his own chair and sat down. "Isn't right? How could it not be right? You're with your family, aren't you?"

His mother, Noriko, playfully and affectionately tugged at his ear. The way she had since he was a tiny baby. "Exactly right. All the problems you've been dealing with . . . you need a break, son. Just let it all go for a while. Relax."

"Mom and Dad say you've got too much responsibility." Kira, only a couple of years younger than Kaz, had always sounded like a miniature adult when she talked. "You're only twelve, you know! And we haven't seen you in *forever*. Just stay with us. That wouldn't be so hard, would it?"

Kaz balled up his fists in his lap and stared at the tabletop. "This is just some kind of illusion. My real family got out of the city. They're far away from here. They're safe."

His mother grinned. "What are you talking about? We

never went anywhere! We've been right here the whole time! Waiting for you, silly!"

"Ooohh." Kaz's dad nudged his mom with his elbow. "This is all that 'San Arcadia' stuff. You remember."

His mother's eyes widened with comprehension. She laughed. "Right! When you came over with your friends and that odd, pale boy. I swear, Kaz, you have always had just the *richest* imagination."

His father leaned toward him across the table. "And don't get me wrong. The last thing we want to do, your mother and I, is to discourage active imaginations. Magick, and other dimensions, and monsters and cultists and whatnot. We know you and your friends are very creative and like to pretend a lot, but you still have to sit down for dinner."

"But . . ."

Kaz had to admit, it did sound pretty far-fetched. Especially hearing the words in his father's voice. *Monsters and cultists and whatnot.* How awesome would it be if that's all it was? Just . . . make-believe?

"Yes, honey," his mother said. "Stories are well and good, but you're home now, with us. It's time to come back to real life, at least during dinner."

Kira kicked him under the table and giggled. June played with a glob of mashed potatoes on her plate. Carlie pulled at one of her pigtails. It couldn't be any more *normal*.

"Now, come on, I didn't spend all that time working on

these steaks to let them go to waste." His father used his own steak knife to point to the one lying on Kaz's plate. "Dig in!"

Kaz could feel the lifting of the weight off his shoulders. If none of it were true . . . if magick wasn't real, and Jonathan Thorne didn't really exist, and there was no San Arcadia . . . He picked up his steak knife, held his steak in place, and cut off a bite-size chunk. It looked perfect. It smelled perfect. His dad was terrible at home improvement, but he'd always been a master on the grill.

Kaz remembered bad dreams he'd had before. Where he'd been lost in a cave, trapped, alone . . . and another one where he had a pet dog that had gone missing and he couldn't find anywhere . . . and another one where he'd failed all his classes and had to go back and repeat the same year at school. Every time, when he'd finally awakened, he'd been flooded with immense, overwhelming *relief.*

Could he do that now? Could he let go of all the "monsters and whatnot"? And just *wake up*?

I wish I could. I want to.

But he couldn't let go of Gabe, with his supergross, giant spider bite.

Or Jackson, and how he was kinda starting to like him, and how he talked like a cranky professor.

Or Brett and Lily, who were trying to rescue their grandmother—

Lily.

Lily's still in the labyrinth!

Kaz set his uneaten bite of steak back on his plate, pushed his chair away from the table, and stood up. "I'm sorry." His voice broke, and he used his sleeve to wipe his face. He didn't know when the tears had sprung up, but they were there. "I'm sorry, I can't."

Kira stopped giggling. His father frowned. His mother set down her own utensils and, in a tone that came close to breaking Kaz's heart, asked, "But why? Don't you want to be with us?"

Kaz groaned. "Of *course* I do. More than anything! But . . . guys, please try and understand this, okay? It's *not* a dream. San Arcadia *is* real. And . . . and I have to find the Crimson Serpent. I have to save my friends!"

Kaz's father favored him with a patient smile. "Are you *sure*, son? Wouldn't it be so much easier just to stay? Stay here with us?"

His sisters joined in a chorus of "Stay! Stay! Stay!" and Kaz had to grit his teeth as hard as he could and turn away from them before he could answer.

"I do want to stay. More than just about anything. But I can't. This isn't right. And I need to help my friends. I need to leave! *I need to leave!*"

The words echoed around the dining room.

And Kaz's family, along with the dining room and the rest of the house and the rain outside, evaporated and blew away like steam in a sudden wind. Between one heartbeat and the next, Kaz found himself standing in a large, square, perfectly mirrored room, staring at Lily.

She almost took him off his feet with the force of her hug. "Kaz! Thank God!"

With his face mashed into her shoulder, he said, "Where've you been?"

Lily pushed him back to arm's length but didn't let go of him. "I've been right here! The whole time, stuck behind, like, a two-way mirror! I saw that whole thing. Kaz, I'm so sorry you had to go through that! Letting your family go again."

He stepped away from her. "Yeah. Me too."

"But . . . what was the *point*?"

"Huh?"

Lily mimed cutting a steak. "Making you think you were back with your family. Why? Is that what this place is? Like a psychological torture chamber or something?"

Kaz folded his arms, his brow creasing. "I know one thing. If this is anything like what Gabe and Dr. Conway went through in that library place, no wonder Gabe told us to be careful."

"Yeah, but he said they just had to face evil versions of themselves. Not like this. Not this . . . Well, like I said. Torture."

Kaz shook his head. "No. No, it didn't feel like torture."

"Uh . . . okay. What'd it feel like?"

"It felt like I was being *tested*."

Lily started moving around the edge of the room. Kaz guessed she was looking for a way out. She said, "Well, that's better than torture, I guess, but then—who was testing you? And what for?"

"Dunno. But, I mean, I guess I passed, right?" He rapped his knuckles lightly against his temple. "Maybe I don't have enough emotional baggage for this place to take advantage of."

"Ah-*ha*!" Lily pressed against a section of the wall, and it swung open soundlessly, an almost perfectly concealed door. "There it is! I'm very good at finding secret doors. Have you noticed that?"

Kaz let himself smile. "I had, yeah." He followed her out of the room and into yet another long, mirrored hallway.

As they walked, Lily said, "Gabe told us he and his uncle had to, sort of, face their inner demons? But you're right, that doesn't seem like what you saw. Wonder why?"

Kaz shrugged. "Maybe I'm kind of inner-demon-free?"

Lily gasped, and froze stock-still. Kaz almost bumped into her. "What? What is it?"

She pointed. Ahead of them, the hallway turned a corner, but thanks to the mirrors, they could see someone standing just on the other side of the bend.

Is that—Brett?

Kaz shouted, "Brett! Brett, how'd you get here?"

The figure turned so that they could see his face, and Lily grabbed Kaz's forearm so hard that he had to bite back a scream.

"That's not Brett," Lily breathed. "Kaz, *that's Charlie.*"

14

"Oh God." Gabe kept his head turned the other way, his eyes squeezed shut as tightly as he could get them. "Oh *God*. Is it . . . is it working?"

He heard Eva grunt and felt another terrible, wrenching pressure, as if all the bones in his shoulder were being pulled out through that too-gross-for-words spider bite. "Yes," Eva snapped. "But I really need to concentrate!" From somewhere off to his left, past Eva, Gabe caught the sound of Brett gagging.

Against his better judgment, Gabe slowly turned his head and opened his left eye, just a crack.

He wished he hadn't.

Somewhere in the rapidly crumbling fort, Eva had found a broom handle, and was—she was using it to pull the shadow-creature out of his body. Eva had grabbed hold of the tendril that had slapped against Gabe's cheek like an eel out of water and pinned it to the broom handle. Now she turned the handle, slowly and steadily, winding the creature onto it like a winch coiling up a chain.

"Is there anything I can do?" Mrs. Castellanos asked for maybe the fortieth time.

"Not really," Eva gritted out. "It's sort of a one-person job. I just need Gabe to hold still. . . ."

"Holding," Gabe gasped. He was hurting and afraid, but even more than that, he was impatient. The sooner this was over, the sooner he could look for his mom.

". . . and Brett not to puke on me."

Brett said, "Can't make any promises."

Another inch of horrible, slimy blackness slid out of Gabe's shoulder, and now he couldn't stop staring at it. "Where . . ." He took a deep breath and tried not to envision so vividly how far into his body this thing must have burrowed. "Where did you learn how to . . . uh . . . do this?"

Eva didn't look up at him as she answered. She just kept turning the handle. Enough of the creature had gathered on it that now it looked like a pulsing, slimy black football. On a stick. Gabe fought down the urge to hurl. "A friend of mine did a stint in the Peace Corps." Eva's mouth twisted in a grimace as she exerted more pressure on the broom handle. A knot of something hard and gristly—Gabe thought it looked sort of like a knuckle—popped free of the wound on his shoulder. He almost passed out. Eva went on. "My friend wound up treating a man who'd been bitten by this nasty bug called a botfly." This time she did glance up at him, just for a second. "Do yourself a favor. If we ever get the internet back, don't google 'botfly.' Anyway, if you tangle with one of them, you wind up with, uh, basically with a big giant maggot under your skin. So you get one end out, and you start rolling it up, like on a Popsicle stick. And if you're not supercareful, the worm will tear, and then you're stuck with what's left inside you."

Gabe felt his face turning green as she spoke. "I am truly sorry I asked."

"Come on . . ." Eva's eyes narrowed to slits as she stared at the grisly bite wound. "Come on . . . *come on* . . ."

Gabe had felt sudden, profound relief before. Once he'd developed an ingrown toenail that turned into an abscess so painful he could barely walk. He'd suffered through an entire day of school with it, struggling not to cry out with every step. That night Uncle Steve had taken him to a minute clinic, where the nurse had said, "Oh yeah, we need to lance that." He clearly remembered how she'd unwrapped the scalpel, swabbed his agony-filled big toe with alcohol, and made the tiniest little cut—followed by the immediate, total vanishing of the pain.

That sense of relief was *nothing* compared with how he felt when the shadow-creature came loose.

Eva fell over backward, the broom handle flew out of her hands, and as Brett finally did puke and Mrs. Castellanos screamed, the shadow-creature started whipping and flailing and unwinding itself from the broom handle, which made the shaft of wood clatter against the floor and the walls like a demented drumstick.

"Stop it!" Eva shouted. "Don't let it get loose!" She leaned against the wall, rubbing the back of her head and wincing. Gabe tried to get up from the table, but his head went light, and he decided it would be better to stay horizontal for a minute. Dimly he was aware that the shadow-creature, which looked like the world's most nausea-inducing starfish, had wrenched itself free of the broom handle and was now skittering around the room.

"It's looking for a way out!" Brett bellowed, and the creature pivoted and streaked toward him. Brett screamed, "No *no* keep it off me keep it off me Abuelita *help!*"

Gabe had made it up to one elbow at that point and stared, fascinated, as Mrs. Castellanos picked up the broom handle, broke it across one knee to give it a pointy end, and nailed the shadow-creature to the floor with it. Golden ooze streaked with what looked like ink splashed across Mrs. Castellanos's face.

She ground the handle deeper into the creature's body. "You do *not* mess with my *nieto.*"

The relief flooding Gabe's body turned into a kind of euphoria. It was over.

Now I can look for my mom.

Then he finally passed out.

"So, you just let her walk out?" Gabe lurched to his feet, caught his balance, and turned to face Eva. "You were supposed to keep her safe!" He scratched at the skin around the bandage covering his wound. It didn't hurt anymore, but it itched horribly, like the world's worst mosquito bite.

Eva leaned against the biggest table in the middle of the room. She'd set aside her Dawn robes for the moment and was now dressed in sneakers, jeans, and a Princeton T-shirt. She held up her hands. "I *tried* to stop her, Gabe! Everyone *tried* to stop her. But it was no use! Do you know how powerful your mother is? Once she heard you calling for help, that was it. There was nothing anyone could do. We're lucky she didn't destroy the entire Presidio."

Gabe turned his back to her. Brett and Mrs. Castellanos stood by the door, both of them looking uncertain of what to do, or if they should even be there.

Of course I know how powerful my mother is. I never should've left her alone here.

The only person Gabe was angry with was himself.

"I've got to find her."

Eva shook her head. "Just slow down and think for a moment, Gabe. If that wasn't you calling to her—"

"I already said it wasn't," Gabe snapped.

"Then who was it?" she asked.

Gabe drummed his fingers on his elbow. "Does it matter? These magickal freak monsters make the weirdest sounds I've ever heard. So one of them can sound like me? So what?"

"If someone used your voice to lure your mom out, and if someone used her voice to lure you . . ."

He faced Eva again. "I know, okay. You're going to tell me it's a trap, but what else am I supposed to do? All I know is this: she's missing. She's probably scared, and lost, and in danger. No matter whose voice you heard or we heard—it doesn't change any of that." He thrust out his jaw defiantly. *I'm not about to lose her when I just got her back!* "I have to go. I'm gonna find her. And Uncle Steve, too, if he's still alive. And maybe Jackson, if Thorne hasn't turned him into a footstool or something."

Eva sighed. "I suppose there's no point in trying to talk you out of this?"

From near the door, Brett spoke up. "Gabe, are you even well enough to go out there? I mean, you *did* just have that magickal shadow-squid thing all . . . y'know . . ." He gestured toward his own neck. "*Inside* you. And stuff."

"I'm fine. And, Eva, I know I've said this already, but . . . thanks. I'm pretty sure you saved my life, but . . . that doesn't change what I've gotta do."

Eva sighed and closed her eyes. "All right, *fine*. I'd offer to send people with you, but the dome is already failing. I don't know how long we have left and—" As if to emphasize her words, a bone-shaking impact slammed against the dome outside, and through the window, Gabe saw another glyph flare, then go dark.

He moved toward her, stepping around the maps still scattered around the floor.

"You need to protect your people. I get it, Eva. Because I need to protect my people, too. I'm getting a handle on my connection to fire again. I'll be fine."

"Especially if I come with you," Brett said, and turned to his grandmother before she could speak. "Abuelita, I know what you're going to say, but Gabe needs my help, all right? And I'm even better with water now than he is with fire. We'll be fine."

Mrs. Castellanos shook her head, then smiled and grabbed Brett by the shoulders. "What I was going to say, *nieto*, is for you to go out there and kick some monster butt and bring Gabe's mama home."

Then she folded Brett up in her arms.

"Thanks, Abuelita," Brett muttered into her neck.

When she finally let her grandson go, Gabe walked over to him and held out a fist, which Brett readily bumped. Red-orange fire danced around Gabe's eyes. "Let's do this."

Gabe didn't recognize the city at all.

It wasn't just that San Francisco had lost its distinctive

character. It was that the cityscape had changed so drastically, with the black, twisted buildings and rampant destruction and ever-increasing amounts of giant spiderwebs, that Gabe had literally gotten lost. He might as well have been in Siberia, or Australia, or Ghana for all the connection he felt to this place.

And for all the horrors that he could see, he was afraid this was just a taste of the darkness that was growing around them. Along the streets, eerie golden light streamed up from the drains and sewers. Every once in a while, the pale fog rolling down from the mountains seemed to crease into thousands of reaching, grasping hands.

San Arcadia is just waking up. This is only the beginning.

"There's another one," Brett said quietly, pointing.

Ahead of them lay the corpse of a giant spider. It had been crushed flat as if by a massive pile driver. He and Brett had been following this trail of obliterated San Arcadian "wildlife" since they'd left the protection of the dome, starting with what had appeared to be an entire swarm of sawjaws crushed against a concrete wall.

Brett said, "Are we sure it's your mom doing all the . . . squashing . . . here?"

Gabe nodded. "Pretty sure. Remember those bug things that lived in the walls at the Alcatraz Citadel? In Arcadia?"

Brett shuddered. "I wish I could forget."

"Well, the first time I saw Mom, she had just crushed, like, five hundred of those things. They looked just like that spider."

"Good enough for me, I guess."

Gabe glanced at the sky. "Let's try and hurry. I think it's starting to get dark."

They picked their way over the crumbled, buckled sidewalks, skirted piles of rubble from collapsed structures and wrecked cars, and gave an even wider berth to the gaping mouth-holes of living, hungry buildings. Gabe was not quite as confident about fire as he'd pretended to be with Eva. He needed to practice but was afraid to draw any unwanted attention.

Their pace was agonizing. Every minute that passed increased the likelihood that Mom had run into something she couldn't squash as easily as these spiders.

And if something happens to her, that will be my fault, too. She ran out here looking for me.

He and Brett had been traveling for what could have been an hour, maybe more, when Gabe heard something that wasn't the wind or the creaking metal from the city changing around them. He stopped and turned his head. Listening hard.

"There! Did you hear that?"

Brett frowned. "Hear what?" He readjusted the straps on the backpack with the Mirror Book in it.

Gabe pointed. "Over that way! I think I just heard my mom's voice! Come on!"

"Hey, hey, Gabe—dude, hang on."

Gabe had already taken a couple of running steps, and he

all but stomped his feet as he stopped and turned. *"What?"*

"Um, the whole thing about this probably being a trap? Aria busted out of the Presidio following your voice, which obviously *wasn't* your voice. Her voice might be a fake, too, so let's, like, not rush into anything."

Gabe was going to snap back at Brett that he didn't *understand*. That he didn't know what it was like to have this kind of guilt, to feel this body-racking dread that someone you love might be in trouble and that you could have prevented it.

This surge of irritation was replaced by the heat of shame a moment later, because Gabe realized that Brett in fact knew this feeling all too well.

Lily and Brett's older brother, Charlie, had died in a sailboating accident last summer. Brett had been there and blamed himself ever since it happened. *That's what started all this. Jackson reached out from the Umbra and lied to Brett and said Charlie wasn't dead.* If Brett hadn't wanted to get Charlie back so badly, he wouldn't have cooperated with Jackson, the four of them wouldn't have performed the friendship ritual down in the tunnels beneath the city, and none of them would be bound to the elements now.

And none of us would have ever even heard of Arcadia.

So that's how guilty Brett felt about losing Charlie: he'd crossed worlds and broken every law in reality to try to fix what had happened.

In fact, maybe that was why Brett was here with Gabe

right now. He was trying to save his friend from those relentless regrets.

"Sorry, Brett. You're right." Gabe nodded his head. Shadows had begun to grow longer around them. "Can we pick up the pace, though?"

But a minute later, they heard a crystal clear cry from ahead—"Gabe! Gabe, where are you?"—and Gabe broke into a flat-out sprint. Following his mom's voice, he turned left, and right. Brett kept up with him, but just barely. Once they crested a small rise, Brett called for him to stop, then grabbed Gabe's arm and *made* him stop.

"Let go of me! What're you doing?"

Brett gestured around them. "Don't you see where we are?"

Gabe sighed and looked around . . . and almost laughed.

Holy crap. We're back at Argent Court.

The once-grand house was little more than crumbled, charred ruins now, a wispy ghost of the proud ancestral home of Jackson Wright's family. The place where Gabe had once lived, as a tiny child. The place where Uncle Steve and Greta Jaeger had worked, trying to figure out some way to destroy Arcadia.

"See, this makes sense, Brett! It would make sense that Mom would come back here!"

Barely louder than a whisper, Brett said, "Last time we were here, we almost got killed by a leviathan. So if we're going to do this, can we at least do it slowly and carefully? *Please?*"

Gabe nodded. He couldn't argue with that. He and Brett kept to cover, darting from shadow to shadow as they approached the house. Nothing stirred in the ruins themselves, but in the garden area out back Gabe caught a glimpse of movement—and heard his mother's voice, clear as a bell.

"Gabe!" Aria moved from one corner of the garden to another. Looking for something, or seeming to. "Gabe!"

Gabe's heart surged with relief at the sight of his mother.

It's really her! She's looking for me!

Gabe and Brett huddled beside a broken brick archway that led into the garden. He had tensed his muscles to step out into the open, to reveal his presence to her. But just then, Gabe heard a sound in addition to his mother's voice. Something distorted, a bit lower.

"Mom! *Mom!*" is what the voice said.

It almost sounded like . . .

"Dude," Brett whispered. "That's you! That's your voice!"

And it *was* Gabe's voice. Every time it sounded, Aria chased it to another part of the garden. She was following his voice in exactly the same way he'd been following hers.

"What *is* this?" Gabe demanded.

A dramatic sigh floated down from above. Gabe and Brett spun around, and found Jackson Wright standing on the roof of the house next door. "Well, it's a *trap*," Jackson said. He rolled his eyes. "Obviously."

Five more figures joined Jackson at the edge of the roof. A bronze-skinned woman in robes, three pale men in Victorian clothing, and . . .

Gabe's heart nearly stopped dead.

Jonathan Thorne.

15

Kaz took hold of Lily's upper arm. "You know that's not your brother. Right? Lily, you *know* that, right?"

She wouldn't look at him, but Kaz caught her reflection in the corridor's mirrored wall. And as her eyes flickered silver-white, Kaz's hand suddenly closed on nothing but air where Lily's arm had been. Lily dashed down the hallway toward the thing that looked like her dead older brother.

Panicking, Kaz rushed forward and put himself between Lily and the false Charlie. "Stop! Lily, *stop*! It's an illusion! Like my family was! This isn't real!"

But Lily's eyes flickered again and looked past Kaz, and

she smiled a smile so sweet and sad that Kaz thought his heart would break.

Oh God, this is bad. This is so bad.

"Lil! There you are!"

Kaz looked over his shoulder and saw Charlie waving at them. His voice sounded so much like Brett's. "We've been waiting for you! Come on!"

Lily pivoted out of Kaz's grip and glided past him, heading straight for the fake Charlie.

Don't do it!

Kaz took a quick step to follow her and rammed nose first into something that felt like a pane of glass. He yelped and stumbled backward. "Lily! Lily, stop!" He thrust his hands out, but they came up short, stopped by a transparent force field.

This must be the two-way mirror Lily talked about, when she saw me with my family!

"Lily! Lily, c'mon, don't do this!" Kaz desperately pounded on the mirror, but if Lily could hear him, she didn't acknowledge it.

As he smashed his fist into the barrier again and again, the scene in front of him changed. Instead of being inside a mirror corridor, Lily and Charlie now stood on the end of a dock at a marina, in front of a small, fast-looking sailboat. Beyond the marina, the Golden Gate Bridge spanned the horizon, looking the way it used to, the way it was *supposed* to, before Jonathan

Thorne brought Arcadia crashing down on Earth. The tops of the bridge's lofty towers were shrouded in fog, even though it seemed to be midafternoon. The whole view looked like something on a postcard.

Brett waited for Lily and Charlie on the boat, checking the ropes. *That's not Brett. Not the real Brett, not any more than that's the real Charlie.* Kaz pounded on the barrier again, harder and harder. "Lily! Lily, turn around and look at me! *Lily!*"

"Ready to go, *hermana*?" Brett grinned and made a sweeping gesture with one arm. "Welcome aboard!"

Kaz could hear every word of their conversation. He might as well have been standing right next to them, yet they were totally unaware of him. *Is this what it's like to be a ghost? If it is, I really hope for their sake they're not real, because this is a nightmare!*

Lily shifted her weight from one foot to the other. "I thought this trip was just for you and Charlie. Y'know, bro time, or whatever."

"It'll be better with you here, Lil, like Mom and Dad wanted. Y'know, get all the kids out of the house for the day, let them have some peace?" Charlie gave her a quick one-armed hug. "Besides, it's supposed to be kind of windy today. And wind's your specialty, right?" He winked at her.

Lily took a half step backward. "Um . . . I . . ."

"C'mon!" Brett leaned against the mast, grinning at her. "If all three of us go, there's nothing we can't handle! Isn't that right, Charlie?"

Kaz's stomach tightened and sank. *The maze . . . it's trying to give her a do-over! Let her change things. Let her save Charlie.* He knew it was what both twins wanted more than anything.

"Well." Lily hopped aboard the boat. "It won't hurt to have six hands instead of four."

"That's the spirit!" Charlie freed a heavy rope from a cleat on the dock, tossed it on the deck, and jumped on board after Lily. "Let's get going!"

A moment of vertigo swept over Kaz as the scene before him changed again. The three Hernandez siblings were still on the boat, but now the small craft rode the choppy waves in the middle of the bay. Lily and Brett and Charlie scurried about the deck, adjusting the riggings, ducking the boom as the tall sail swung on the mast.

"Lil!" Kaz bellowed as loudly as he could and pounded on the invisible barrier with both hands. Then he paused and took a step back. "Okay, okay," he said to himself. "Think, Kaz. Let's say your friend is on the ghost ship of doom with her brothers. Is that so bad? A little cruise to break up all this labyrinth wandering. Get a little sun, take in the scenery. None of this is *real*, so—"

A horrible fear gripped Kaz and made his guts tighten. What would happen if Lily didn't resist the way he had during his experience with his family? What would happen if she gave in to the illusion?

If this was some kind of a test, what would happen to Lily if she failed?

It was hard to say good-bye to my family, but at least I know they're safe outside the city limits. Charlie is anything but safe. Will Lily be able to walk away from the chance to save him?

Kaz didn't know, but he also wasn't just going to stand around and find out.

The sailboat skimmed across the waves. Farther and farther from shore. And farther and farther from Kaz.

He reached out for the earth. Opened the pathways in his mind and his heart that let the energy of the stone and dirt and minerals flow through him. He remembered the last time he'd done this, when he'd fought Jonathan Thorne, and his body had grown larger and stronger and as tough as rock.

He concentrated every bit of that power into his fist as he brought it pistoning forward into the barrier. He both heard and felt a *crack*, along with a jolt of pain so intense that for a second he thought his hand had exploded, and realized he'd broken a bone. But more amazingly . . . Lily stopped what she was doing, raised her head, and stared back.

A jagged crack a foot long had appeared in the barrier. Lily's gaze focused on it—and then, to Kaz's inexpressible relief, focused on *him*. She met his eyes squarely and, in a tiny voice filled with confusion, said, "Kaz?"

Before Kaz could even draw a breath to answer her, the sailboat gave a crazy lurch, throwing Lily and her two brothers to the deck. The sail snapped taut with sudden wind. Kaz heard the boat's rigging pop and creak with strain, and his breath caught hard in his throat.

A translucent, silver-white mass descended on the sailboat, half fog bank, half cyclone. Currents of destructive wind roared out from it, every one of them centered on the boat and the three siblings aboard it, and Kaz screamed as the mass battered and lifted and tossed the sailboat as if it were a toy.

A realization chilled Kaz's blood in his veins. *That's not just some freak wind. That's . . . that's air! That's the air itself! Just like Gabe warned us about, from the Library of Mirrors. Our elements are attacking us.* "Lily! *Lily!*" Kaz renewed his attack on the crack in the barrier, smashing it with his good fist and with both elbows, the adrenaline of panic lending him new strength—

—until something moved in the corner of his eye.

Something reflected in the walls to his left and right.

Kaz turned, slowly, aware that on this side of the barrier, he was no longer alone.

16

Gabe's jaw dropped open as he stared up at Jackson and the personifications of evil that stood with him. "J-Jackson? What're you *doing*?"

The woman in the robes spoke, and Gabe's exact voice, every tone and inflection, emerged from her mocking lips: "What're you *doing*?"

"Allow me to introduce everyone," Jackson said. "Gabriel Conway, Brett Hernandez, this is Madam Kureshi, along with Mr. Grillion, Mr. Humboldt, and Mr. Kretschmar. You already know Lord Jonathan Thorne."

Gabe felt a hand on his shoulder and almost screamed. He turned and looked up at Aria. She didn't seem like his mother in that moment. She didn't even seem like a grown woman. She was more like a little girl, lost in the wilderness, frightened and confused and alone. "Gabe?"

Madam Kureshi did it again, projecting Aria's voice just as effortlessly as she had done with Gabe's. Only this time she howled his name in just the same way as she had the scream that had drawn Gabe back to San Arcadia through the Mirror Book.

Brett hadn't taken his eyes off Jackson. "Ghost Boy, ¿qué pasó? Are you on *his* side now?"

Jackson cocked one eyebrow. "My word, you two are thick. Is it not clear by now that Lord Thorne cannot be defeated?"

At that, Thorne's lips parted in what would have been, on a normal human, a satisfied grin. Gabe caught a glimpse of the growing and moving fangs inside Thorne's mouth and quickly looked away. Jackson went on. "It was not a difficult choice on my part. Lord Thorne actually wants me on his side, unlike *you*, Gabriel. Do not tell me you have forgotten how eager you were to shove me through the portal into Arcadia, back on Alcatraz?"

Thorne made a subtle gesture with one hand and glanced toward the three pale men. "Secure them."

"With pleasure, my lord," said the biggest of the three— Humboldt—and Gabe recoiled from the clicking, alien sound of his voice. The three men stepped off the roof, and long tendrils of shadow sprouted from their feet, spiking into the ground. Then the tendrils shortened, lowering the three until they stood facing Gabe and Brett and Aria.

"*No!*" Aria shrieked, so loud and so close to Gabe's ear that he flinched away. Aria glided forward, putting herself between Gabe and the three men, and threw her arms wide as if to become a wall. "You won't touch my son! I won't let you! I'll destroy you all first!"

As soon as she said this, Grillion, the thin man who looked as if he was covered in mildew, turned yellow and just . . . *dispersed*, becoming little more than a stream of vapor that poured off to Gabe's left. Simultaneously, Kretschmar, who seemed more like a male model than an instrument of corruption, became—Gabe's guts roiled and churned at the sight—a column of tens of thousands of *worms* and slithered straight down into the ground.

Unlike his associates, Humboldt didn't go anywhere. As the sound of Aria's scream echoed off the ruined walls of Argent Court, Humboldt put his head down and charged straight at her like a bloodthirsty bull. Aria brought her hands together, and a shock wave of power rushed out to meet him.

Gabe had seen this before. Twice now: once in Arcadia, when Aria had taken on a telepathic monstrosity that had tried its best to eat Gabe alive, and again back at the Presidio, when she attacked the behemoth. He knew what would happen. This "Mr. Humboldt" was about to detonate into a billion little specks.

Instead, Humboldt's mouth opened. No, not opened, not like a normal mouth . . . it unhinged from his face, yawning wider and wider, a great black pit, and Humboldt *ate* the wave of power that Aria had thrown at him. All that energy, all that undeniable, final destruction, just . . . *vanished*.

Gabe didn't have time to absorb this before Humboldt closed his creepy maw and charged Aria, crashing into her with the force of a wrecking ball. Gabe screamed and rushed to her as she slammed against a blackened segment of Argent Court's foundation and slid bonelessly to the ground.

Or rather, Gabe *tried* to rush to her. Before he could reach her side, the air turned noxious yellow, and Mr. Grillion materialized in front of him. "Leave her," Grillion hissed. His voice sounded like sand slithering down a sloping piece of metal. "She is of no further concern to you."

"Burn . . . burn . . . burn!"

The voice of the fire leaped into Gabe's mind, more suddenly and more forcefully than it ever had before, and white-hot flames blasted from his eyes and his mouth. He wanted to see Grillion burn alive, see him become a man-shaped bonfire, wanted to hear his screams as the fire took him apart atom by atom.

"Oh, we'll have none of that now," Grillion said, and blew a stream of yellow spores directly into Gabe's face.

Gabe couldn't breathe. He staggered, choking, coughing, his sinuses and lungs starting to *close up*. The fire snuffed out.

He could feel the poisonous cloud moving inside his body, growing, festering, a million times worse than the shadow-creature left in him by the giant spider. Gabe only vaguely registered falling to his knees.

Wet. The ground is wet. Struggling to pull oxygen into his lungs, Gabe looked over and saw Brett, tendrils of water flailing around his body—which was *covered with worms*. Gabe would have vomited if his throat hadn't closed up. He watched as Brett gave up on the water and started clawing at his face, his eyes, his ears, tearing away huge gobbets of wriggling worms, only to have even greater masses swarm over him again. Brett's movements slowed . . . his arms fell to his sides . . . and he collapsed.

Only then did the worms slide off Brett, collect into a disgusting, twisting pile, and reform into Mr. Kretschmar. Gabe's lungs convulsed, and he heaved out a huge cloud of the microscopic yellow particles, which wafted through the air and reabsorbed into Mr. Grillion's outstretched hand. Grillion leaned close to Gabe. "Be a good boy now. I haven't withdrawn from you completely. Just enough so that you won't die . . . yet." He straightened up and turned his head. "Master Wright, if you will?"

Gabe closed his eyes, but through them he could see the radiance of Jackson's magick, and opened them enough to witness Jackson descending slowly toward him on one of his golden disks. Jackson's eyes shimmered solid yellow-gold, and orbs of magick surrounded his hands. He stepped off the disk and crouched next to Gabe.

The words barely made it out, Gabe's lungs and windpipe were still so choked with Grillion's spores. "What're you . . . waiting for . . . traitor? Go ahead . . . kill me."

Jackson didn't speak very loudly, but his words carried every bit of his trademark haughtiness. "I certainly could if I wanted to, couldn't I?" Jackson picked up Kaz's backpack from where it had fallen near Brett.

The Mirror Book! Gabe just had time to think before he felt himself jerked upright as bands of golden light clamped around his body. Gabe watched Jackson give Brett the same treatment. Soon they were both bound in shackles of pure magick. Neither of them was able to resist, or even move. Gabe had to strain to see that Brett was even still breathing.

A sound like a tremendous clap of thunder exploded all around them, and Humboldt crashed to the ground right in front of Gabe, so hard his body left a crater a foot deep. Jackson stumbled, and might have fallen, but the golden disk reappeared beneath his feet and restored his balance.

What's happening?

"Let them go." Aria stalked toward Jackson, her eyes solid slate gray and throwing off streams of green fire. Her skin had taken on the stony texture Gabe had seen before, and her voice was pitched deeper than normal. "Or I'll dispatch you the same way I did your friend."

Grillion didn't move. Kretschmar merely poked Humboldt with a toe and said, "Get up. No shirking." Humboldt made a small sound, and shifted an inch or two, but stayed where he was. Kretschmar sighed and fixed his eyes on Aria. "Dear Aria, consider your actions. You know the power it will take to fight us. Are you willing to risk your mind, your very *self*, in this endeavor? What would become of your son *then*?"

Aria stopped. Her teeth ground together with a sound like a glacier splintering.

"Well said, Mr. Kretschmar." Jonathan Thorne and Madam Kureshi descended from the roof and strode toward them. No—Thorne walked. Kureshi seemed to *glide*.

Gabe's attention snapped back to his mother as a long, agonized moan ground out from her throat. The moan grew louder and deepened as if the earth itself were crying out in pain. Deep cracks appeared along her arms, up her neck, and on the sides of her face. And as her skin returned to human, the cracks began to bleed. Aria dropped to her knees, then to all fours, and moaned again.

"Mom," Gabe whispered. He struggled against his bonds, but the magick restraints felt stronger than steel.

Rocky outcrops burst through Aria's skin on the backs of her hands and her forearms. She reared up, teeth bared and gritted, and screamed. The largest of the rock shards that pierced her skin receded, but the effort seemed to take what strength she had left, and she fell over on her side, gasping. Her skin changed, pulsing from normal to rocklike and back again in time with her breath. Gabe's heart pounded frantically, helplessly, as he watched her blood run out onto the ground. *It's like she's turning into the earth itself!*

She was no longer a threat to Thorne or his monstrous friends. It seemed to take every ounce of strength Aria had to keep herself together, to keep the earth at bay.

"Oh, Aria." Thorne moved to stand a few paces away from her and folded his arms. "How painful this must be. And how . . . inevitable it feels. You know the path to becoming an Incandati is quite the slippery slope."

Incandati?

Thoughts clicked into place in Gabe's head. He and his friends had been warned, more than once, that their elements would take them over if they let their guard down. He had felt it himself when the voice of the fire had roared and boomed inside his head—he knew how easy it would have been to give in. And if he *had* given in . . .

He thought of the way his mother had seemed on the brink of turning to earth itself.

Is that what we'd become? Incandati?

"Oh, you frown so, Gabe," Thorne said, his green eyes as deep as an abyss. "But is it a frown born of worry or of ignorance? Can it be that no one schooled you on the true risk of your Art? Surely, you know how the elements hunger for power. And if you let them consume you, you'll find their hunger becomes your own. In fact, that hunger is all that you'll have. The Incandati are no more than beasts, left to wander the realms searching for magick. Always hungry, never full.

"Your concern for your mother is most justified." Thorne spoke to Aria over his shoulder as he turned toward Jackson. "But do be a dear and stay with us until you can play your part, though, won't you?" Thorne held out his hand. Jackson readily gave him Kaz's backpack.

Gabe stopped breathing.

Thorne reached into the backpack and pulled out the Mirror Book. "The Mirror Book," Thorne breathed. "Speaking of playing one's part. After the Emerald Tablet's destruction, I knew I would require this for the work ahead." Before Gabe could turn away, Thorne looked straight into his eyes. "Thank you for bringing it to me. You were only ever jumping through the hoops I so meticulously laid for you, but you have my gratitude nonetheless. I think it's important to be gracious when circumstances allow. Manners are essential no matter the dimension, don't you think—grandson?" Thorne smiled his horrible, shifting smile.

Gabe had seen eyes like Thorne's before. He didn't want to admit it . . . *hated* to admit it . . . but every time he looked in the mirror, he saw eyes exactly that shape, exactly that color green. If Gabe had doubted in the past that Thorne was his many-times-removed great-grandfather, that doubt now withered and died.

"And I'm afraid I have need of you yet. When I use this to kill the Crimson Serpent"—Thorne waved the Book in front of him—"you and your mother and your friend Mr. Hernandez will all serve to channel and focus its energies." He clapped Gabe on the shoulder. "I would call it sad that none of you will survive the process, but it's not sad, is it? It is simply the way things must be. Indeed, the way things were always going to be."

From somewhere behind Gabe, Jackson grumbled, "It might have been helpful to know that their deaths were part of the plan."

Thorne grinned at Jackson over Gabe's shoulder, showing his swirling pit of fangs. "Do not fret, young Master Wright! Leave the details to me. But know that the more elementalists I have, the more *power* I command, the better this will go for all of us." He put his face almost nose to nose with Gabe's. "So. To that end. Where might I find Kazuo Smith and Lily Hernandez?"

Gabe kept his eyes on Aria, still collapsed in agony on the ground, at war with her element. Trying so hard to stay alive. To stay human. "They're somewhere you can't get to them, you freaking *monster*."

Thorne straightened up, towering over Gabe. "Ah, well. No matter, really. The power I command now is more than enough to complete the ritual, and at its conclusion, the Crimson Serpent will crumble to dust—and so, unfortunately, will the Mirror Book itself."

Gabe felt as if he'd been punched in the stomach. It was all he could do to keep his face still. He'd seen a huge ritual destroy the Emerald Tablet. He believed the Mirror Book wouldn't survive whatever Thorne had planned.

But what'll happen to Kaz and Lily if they're still in there when the Book bites it?

17

Kaz stared at the figure that had appeared behind him. Every word he'd ever learned vanished from his mind, so that when he opened his mouth to try to speak, there was nothing there.

"That's not like you, Kaz," the figure standing across from him said, in a voice so deep it barely registered as human speech. "You babble. Constantly. Like a brook. Cat got your tongue?"

Kaz shivered, and between one confused blink of his eyes and the next, the mirrored hallway had vanished. All of a sudden, he stood in a vast cavern surrounded by stalagmites and stalactites. The figure with him grinned with a smile Kaz knew well, because it was his own. The boy he faced was himself.

Except it wasn't really him. The creature looked like Kaz, but it was a Kaz made of stone. His feet melded smoothly into the rocky floor of the cavern, and his skin looked like—Kaz squinted—looked like *marble*, gray shot through with quartz maybe. . . .

His eyes were just as Kaz's friends described his own when caught in the full grip of the earth. Slate gray, shimmering with green power.

He *knew* who this other Kaz was, or rather, *what* he was. Gabe's description of fighting the fire elemental in the Arcadian library still hung fresh in Kaz's mind. He was looking at an elemental of earth.

The fire elemental wanted to burn Gabe up. What does this one want to do to me?

The elemental's grin widened, revealing even, translucent crystal teeth. "I want you to be true to yourself, Kazuo Smith." It raised one hand, and an aura of green energy sprang into being around it. "True to your master. The earth."

The ground rumbled beneath Kaz's feet, and as he yelped and threw himself to the side, a massive spike of stone erupted from it. Kaz landed hard on his elbow, hissing with pain, but felt an identical rumble and narrowly avoided another needle-sharp spike by rolling away. Across the cavern, the elemental called out, "Don't resist, Kaz. Let the earth claim you. Let it take your blood and your flesh and meld it with the stone."

Kaz scrambled to his feet. There was no point in running

because there was nowhere to go. To survive this, he had to fight. Cracking the mirror that had separated him from Lily had given him more confidence in his bond with earth. He reached for his element again, and that connection came rushing back into his body with a physical impact. The pulse of the earth beneath him reached up through his feet, through his bones, to his heart and his brain. The ground rumbled beneath him once more. But Kaz snarled and thrust his hands downward, and as the next great stone spike burst out of the cavern floor, Kaz willed it to stop.

No. He willed it to *disintegrate*.

Bits of gravel and pebbles scattered across the floor as the spike burst into harmless pieces.

"Very good, Kaz," the elemental said, and started walking toward him. No, "walking" wasn't right. The creature's feet lifted off the rocky surface, but columns of stone kept it connected to the earth as it moved, anchored to its soles. "Embrace what you are. Embrace the earth. Become *one* with the earth." The elemental raised both of its hands, and stones the size of bowling balls rose up off the floor of the cavern. It pointed at Kaz with both hands, and the stones shot toward him like a barrage of cannon fire.

"Nice try," Kaz gritted out, and a wall of rock sprang up before him. The wall cracked and buckled with the impact of the elemental's projectiles, and as it fell, Kaz's eyes flared brilliant green. Every shattered particle of the wall rocketed toward the elemental, twice as fast as the stones it had thrown at Kaz.

The elemental laughed and raised one hand in a lazy defensive gesture, and the shrapnel parted around it, crashing harmlessly against the far wall of the cavern. "You still do not understand," the elemental said, drawing closer. "There is no need to fight. The earth wants you. It cannot be snuffed out like fire or evaporated like water or dissipated like air. The earth is steady. The earth is strong. The earth is forever."

Faster than Kaz could react, the floor around him cracked and rose and slammed together, pinning him in a vise-tight grip. And as Kaz's ribs threatened to break and all the air whooshed out of his lungs, the stone confining him shifted and melded and became a *giant stone hand*. The hand gripped him tight, squeezing, ever squeezing.

Kaz could only take shallow breaths. He felt his eyes flicker back to dark brown as the elemental finally reached him. The massive rock hand held Kaz six feet off the cavern floor, but the stone columns beneath the elemental's own feet raised the creature to his eye level.

The elemental's eyes stayed gray, glimmering with green power, but it seemed to try to soften its expression. "All this fighting . . . what does it accomplish? It is not who you are, Kaz. It is not *what* you are. You are no warrior. You, Kaz, are a *worrier*."

Kaz's feet had gone numb.

"All the fighting you and your friends have had to do, that's never been what you wanted. You want peace. Serenity. Calm. That's what the earth wants, too!"

The numbness began to spread. Slowly, but steadily.

When it reached his knees, Kaz realized—

No no no please please no.

—his body was turning to stone.

"Think of the mountains, Kaz. Vast. Solid. Immobile. *Unmovable.* The bones of the earth itself. They never have to worry. What occupies the mind of a mountain? Nothing. No pain. No sadness. No danger. The mountains simply *are.*"

As the transmutation crept up into Kaz's stomach, he knew the elemental told the truth. Mountains *never* had to worry. About anything. About other worlds, or magick doomsday cults, or cities full of monsters and hungry buildings.

Kaz's heart became solid rock.

I never realized . . . never realized how much of a burden it is for the heart to beat. Ceaselessly, endlessly, for an entire lifetime. No rest. No time to relax. Just effort, effort, always effort.

Kaz's arms hardened and crystallized, and the numbing stone rose higher and higher, up through his neck, into his face. The more he turned to stone, the calmer Kaz felt.

I could become a mountain. All the worries in my life . . . gone. All the pain, gone. Gone!

"Yes, you see it now. You see the truth. The truth of the earth. No more heartache. No more anxiety. Just peace.

"You'll never miss anything or anyone again, Kaz."

Never miss anyone.

. . . Miss anyone? Miss . . . who?

Kira. June. Carlie.

Dad.

Mom.

Never . . . never see them again?

Gabe? Lily and Brett?

The elemental leaned close, quartz teeth on full display. "You will leave them all behind, Kaz. Just as the earth intended."

Leave my family? My friends?

The floor of the cavern trembled. The motion knocked the elemental off balance, and it wavered on its stone columns, glancing down. "What . . . what is happening?"

When the elemental looked back up, Kaz saw its face bathed in green light. Light from Kaz's own searing eyes. He tore his hand free of the earth's grip and closed a fist around the elemental's throat. The giant stone fist that held him cracked and soon fragmented to pieces in a series of thunder-loud fractures. Then it fell away, leaving Kaz standing atop a stone column of his own. He felt the blood course through his veins, as hot as lava. Felt the ferocious beating of his heart. It wasn't made of stone anymore.

My heart will never be made of stone!

"N-no!" the elemental choked. "No! Kaz! You want peace! The peace of a mountain!"

Kaz yanked the elemental closer, and his own voice rolled

through the cavern, as if summoned up from the planet's very core. "Mountains crumble. Mountains break. And when the earth so desires . . ."

The temperature in the cavern soared. Harsh red light blasted up through cracks in the floor. The elemental clawed at Kaz's hand, at his wrist, but it might as well have been clawing at solid granite.

". . . mountains *shatter*."

The cavern floor erupted with a towering pillar of deep-red magma. The elemental shrieked as it melted away within the vertical blast, and the molten rock slammed into the cavern's ceiling, roaring with a sound like every volcano since the planet began. The roof of the cavern split in half, revealing nothing but empty blackness beyond it. The elemental was gone.

Kaz pulled his hand out of the magma where it had held the creature. It glowed cherry-red but didn't hurt. He wiggled his fingers. The broken bone in his hand had healed.

"*Nobody* tells me I can't see my family again."

The towering jet of magma slowed, wavered, and collapsed, splashing everywhere, so that for a moment Kaz stood on a small, rocky island in the middle of a pool of molten lava. But only for a moment. Because as he looked around, he saw a window a few yards away.

Kaz willed the stone island on which he stood to move closer to the window. It did, and he rode it as it parted the hellish lava around it. As he drew near, he realized the "window" was the same size and shape as the two-way mirror through which he'd seen Lily and her phantom brothers board the sailboat—and when he drew nearer still, he saw that it *was* that invisible barrier. No cavern existed on the far side of it. He looked instead out onto the choppy bay waters, where the air elemental was still attacking the boat and the Hernandez siblings.

Kaz gritted his teeth. "Enough playing around." His fist, still red-hot from the magma, felt as if it was made of diamond. Kaz struck the barrier and shattered it with one blow.

Instantly the cavern disappeared. Kaz still stood on the tiny stone island, but now the bay surrounded him, and the air elemental pummeled the sailboat not twenty yards away. Fierce winds blew in every direction.

"Lily!" Kaz screamed, and hoped his voice wouldn't get lost in the wind. He willed the island to move again, and it pushed slowly through the water, a single stone finger extended up from the bay floor.

The scene on the boat looked hopeless. Brett and Charlie both clung to the mast, their heads down. Only Lily had stayed on her feet, but though her eyes flared silver-white, the malevolent cloud above her attacked relentlessly. Every time she raised her hands to defend herself, the sailboat lurched and spun underneath her, and higher and higher waves crashed over the sides.

"Kaz!" Silver-white eyes locked onto slate gray. *"I could really use a hand here!"*

He paused. *She wants a hand? I can do that.*

He concentrated, and raised one hand above his head.

A massive stone pillar broke through the waters of the bay directly below the sailboat, sprouted five rocky outcroppings, and became a huge stone hand. The boat came to rest in the palm, and the fingers curled around it, anchoring it in place.

The silvery, fog-like mass above the boat seemed to recoil.

On the deck, Lily planted both feet, and bolts of silver lightning whipped and cracked out of her eyes. Cyclones whirled into existence around her hands, and when she spoke, it wasn't so much *words* that came out as it was the freight train roar of a full-fledged tornado. "Leave . . . me . . . *alone!*"

Lily thrust her hands up, and the twin cyclones struck the air elemental like a pair of cobras. The fog-like mass ripped into wispy, silvery shards and vanished.

The cyclones dissipated. Lily bent over, panting, her hands on her knees, and looked at Kaz. "Holy *crap* am I glad to see you. I—"

She blinked.

So did Kaz.

The bay was gone.

Lily and Kaz both stood in the same mirror-fragment-studded cave where they'd landed when they first entered the Mirror Book. Lily stepped closer to him, her huge brown eyes flitting all around, and whispered, "What just happened?"

Kaz groaned. "I think . . . I think that entire labyrinth was an illusion. We never actually left this chamber. The whole thing was a trick. A test."

"A test?" Lily asked. "Then did we pass?"

"Good question," Kaz said.

"Good question indeed," Charlie's voice said from behind them. They both spun to face him.

Lily said, "Charlie . . . ?"

But Kaz put a hand on her forearm. "No. No, that's not your brother. Look at his eyes."

Charlie's eyes glowed luminous, and blue, and reptilian. Kaz recognized them in an instant. *That's not Charlie. That's not anything like Charlie.*

"Hello, Kaz. Hello, Lily. It'ssss nice to finally meet you," said the Crimson Serpent. "I've been waiting for you for a very long time."

18

Gabe stood on a tiny golden platform of magickal energy, just big enough for his feet, hovering six inches off the cracked pavement. He was bound from his shoulders to his shins in broad, heavy chains that glowed with noxious green glyphs. Every time he even thought about connecting with fire, the glyphs flared, and needle-like pain speared into his flesh.

He turned his head. Off to his left, Brett and Aria stood on identical platforms. Brett had been given the same kinds of bonds that Gabe had, but their captors had gone the extra mile for Aria; shackles like the ones she'd chosen to wear at the Presidio clamped her ankles together and her wrists behind her back, and on top of that, twice as many chains wound around her body as around Gabe's and Brett's.

Still she struggled.

Gabe winced as he watched his mother's skin fluctuate between pale and slate gray. Cracks still opened along her arms and up the sides of her face. They didn't break along her skin as deeply as they had, but it was still agony to watch. Aria kept her eyes squeezed shut, grinding her teeth.

You've got to resist, Mom. You can't let the earth take you over! Not if it makes you into an Incandati!

Gabe shifted his attention to Brett, who had finally regained consciousness after that—*Ugh*—that worm bath. He hadn't said anything, though. He just glared the most hateful kind of daggers at Jackson.

All three of them floated on their little platforms behind Jonathan Thorne, his four hench-monsters, and Jackson Wright. Jackson controlled the golden platforms, with thin strands of magick leading from each one to his left hand. They had been traveling for at least twenty minutes. Between the pain of the glyph chains, worry for Aria, and the catastrophic state of the city, Gabe had lost all sense of direction and hadn't the faintest clue where in San Arcadia they were.

A hiss off to his right made him jerk his head around. One of the giant spiders was crouched in the shadow of a collapsed wall. But as their bizarre parade passed by, the creature flinched, turned tail, and ran.

I guess that's the one silver lining here. None of the Arcadian creatures want to mess with Thorne.

Gabe cautiously cleared his throat and when the shackles didn't sting him, called out, "Where are we going, anyway?"

"Turn here," Thorne said to no one in particular, and in the next moment Gabe had his question answered for him. The group made their way around the ruins of a supermarket, and there before them lay a length of the immense body of the Crimson Serpent. This was the first time Gabe had seen the creature up close.

That's . . . Wow. It's huge! How does Kaz think he's going to talk *to this thing?*

Gabe squinted into the air beyond the massive snake and saw a cascade of leaves blowing in the wind.

Except they weren't blowing. They were frozen there, or all but frozen. The Crimson Serpent still represented the border between the normal, safe, noninsane, nonhomicidal world and the screaming madness of San Arcadia.

A buzzing filled Gabe's ears. Just as in the Mirror Cave, after a few heartbeats words emerged from it: "With-five-elements-for-one-act-across-all-worlds." The words repeated. "With-five-elements-for-one-act-across-all-worlds." *They're a loop. I guess that's appropriate.*

Gabe caught Jackson looking at him. Not scowling, or sneering, just sort of . . . *examining.* The way you'd look at a house of cards to make sure it wasn't about to collapse. Before he could even think about stopping himself, Gabe spat out, "It turns out I was right about you the whole time, wasn't I? First chance you get, you stab us in the back. "

Jackson opened his mouth as if to say something but closed it, and turned his head away.

"What, you got nothing? No insults? No hateful comebacks?"

"We trusted you," Brett said. He seemed too disgusted to say anything else.

"That was our mistake, Brett," Gabe said. "Ghost Boy's been looking out for himself from the beginning. Who cares who gets sacrificed. Who cares what city gets destroyed, just as long as lying Ghost Boy gets what he wants."

Jackson looked Gabe in the eye. "You need to be quiet."

"*Quiet?* You want me to cooperate? Is that it? Just go along with you and your freak-of-nature boss while you screw over the whole world? Well, you can forget it, you pasty, skinny, pitiful little *creep!*"

The golden platforms dropped to the ground with a thud, and while Gabe tried not to fall over, Jackson smacked him across the face. Gabe's eyes flared red-orange, but immediately the glyph chains activated, and he screamed. His body felt as if it were being used as a pincushion. He let the fire ebb away again, and the agony from the chains receded along with it.

"Tell you what, Gabriel," Jackson said, his own eyes twin masses of roiling golden power. "Why don't you just *bite me.*"

Magick shimmered and glared around Gabe's head so

brightly he flinched away, and before he realized what was happening, he felt something tighten around his head and—to his horror and disgust—force its way into his mouth. "There, that should do the trick."

Jackson took a step backward and, to Gabe's astonishment and fury, *winked* at him.

Nearby, a single unbroken window still remained in the frame of a house, and Gabe caught his reflection in it. He literally was muzzled. Jackson had fastened a magick gag around his head, and part of it had jammed its way past his teeth, an oblong shape that mashed his tongue against the floor of his mouth and kept him from saying a word.

That little jerk. He'll get what's coming to him. I'll make sure of it.

Jackson relevitated the golden platforms and pulled Gabe, Brett, and Aria over to a clear, circular area about the size of a tennis court, right next to the Serpent. While Thorne stood nearby, his arms folded, watching with eagle eyes, Madam Kureshi and the three pale men scurried about the area. It didn't take Gabe long to realize they were prepping it for an Arcadian magick ritual. One of these had sent him to Arcadia, and the Dawn had used another to sacrifice Uncle Steve in that old theater. Nothing good ever came of rituals like this.

Mr. Humboldt inscribed a circle in the bare earth, the far side of which came within just a few feet of the Crimson Serpent's body. Mr. Grillion and Mr. Kretschmar followed after him, planting odd-colored crystals at what seemed to be care-fully determined points along the perimeter. Madam Kureshi glided out to the center of the circle. From inside her robe, a thick, purple tentacle had emerged, and in that tentacle she clutched the Mirror Book. Kureshi placed it atop a small cairn of stones and glided back out of the circle.

Gabe wished there were some way he could kick himself, hard and repeatedly. *We brought that stupid book right to him!*

If Thorne went through with destroying the Mirror Book, Kaz and Lily would be trapped, maybe forever. He and Brett and his mom would almost certainly be killed. And if Thorne actually did destroy the Serpent . . . well, that was it for Earth, wasn't it? San Arcadia would spill past the Serpent's boundary and take over the whole planet.

This is it. This is the end.

"Now," Thorne said, and waved one hand languidly. "The final piece." From within the wreckage of the closest house, shadowy tendrils slid out and wrapped around an ornate wrought iron chair. The tendrils slithered across the ground, holding the chair up above them, and as Thorne's eyes blazed green, they set the chair in place at the edge of the circle. Thorne turned those green furnaces on Jackson. "I trust you shall find the seat to your liking, Master Wright."

Jackson didn't say anything. He just stood there, golden eyes flicking back and forth between Thorne and the chair.

The ground trembled. Tiny clouds of dust kicked up around

the Serpent, and Gabe realized it was *moving* along its perfectly circular barrier. *Sliding*. Gabe sucked in a quick breath through his nose, filled with awe at the gargantuan muscles that rippled and pushed, rippled and pushed, as the titanic snake's body began to narrow.

That's its tail! But that means . . .

In the next breath, the Crimson Serpent's monumental head heaved into view, its jaws clamped around its tail. A perfect ouroboros. The head had to be at least sixty feet long, and the one eye they could see, blue and glowing and the size of an SUV, shifted in its socket to stare at them all.

Gabe felt like the tiniest, most insignificant of gnats in comparison to this vast, ancient creature.

Brett whispered, "What're we gonna do?"

Because of Jackson's muzzle, Gabe couldn't have answered if he'd wanted to, but it didn't matter. He had absolutely no idea.

19

L ily moved closer to Kaz until their shoulders touched. His ears still rang from the magma explosion in the cavern, so he could barely hear her when she whispered, "You see him, right? You see my brother? My *dead* brother?"

Kaz didn't take his eyes off the glowing-blue-eyed figure. "That's not your brother, Lily. That's . . . I'm not sure how. Or why. But that's definitely the Crimson Serpent."

Charlie—the Serpent—grinned at them. Unlike Jonathan Thorne or any of his spider-eggs-in-your-hair-crazy henchmen, when the Serpent smiled, it just looked like Charlie, smiling. Kaz thought about perhaps starting to relax a little, but the Serpent put a stop to that by running a long, forked tongue out of its mouth. The tongue flicked at the air for just a second, less than a second maybe, before it disappeared again. The Serpent *hissed*, and put a hand over its mouth.

"I am *sssso* sorry about that. I'm not quite used to this human body."

"Why are you bothering with a human body, anyway?" Kaz asked.

Lily put her hands on her hips, her jaw set hard. "Yeah. And while we're at it, why does it have to look like my brother?"

The Serpent strode toward them. It didn't seem threatening. Kaz nonetheless reached out to the earth again, prepared to defend himself and Lily if the Serpent tried anything.

"Well." The glowing blue eyes blinked. "It's kind of like they say in your science fiction movies? 'I chose a form that I thought you could relate to?' Something like that?"

"Is that why you sound like him, too?" Kaz asked.

"You want me to try something else? You want more Obi-Wan Kenobi? Oh, or how about Gandalf? 'You shall not pass!'" the Serpent intoned with a dramatic frown that soon broke into a grin. "*Love* that guy!"

"I don't care what you sound like, but I don't like that you look like Charlie." Lily's eyes wavered between dark brown and silver-white. "I don't appreciate it. And I think you should stop it. Right now."

The Serpent held up his hands. "I swear to you, Lily, I won't take this shape for much longer. I simply needed something that would fit in this cavern."

Kaz frowned. "But . . . wait. Isn't this cavern an illusion? Hasn't *everything* we've been through since we jumped into the Mirror Book been an illusion?"

The Serpent dramatically put one hand over his heart. "Kazuo Smith, you wound me! Am I not real? If you cut me, do I not bleed?"

Lily said, "No . . . Kaz, this mirror business is at least partly real. That dead spike seal was real. And I bet if we'd failed those *tests* he put us through, *we'd* be really, really dead, too. All right, Mr. Serpent. What do you want with us?"

The Serpent's radiant blue eyes sparkled. "First off, I want to tell you exactly what is going on around you. None of this will matter if you don't understand the circumstances."

Kaz said, "Jeez! Finally!"

The Serpent laced his fingers together and cracked his knuckles. The action set muscles in motion in his arms, starting at the backs of his hands and rippling all the way up to the shoulders. Even more than the glowing blue eyes, the gesture reinforced to Kaz how *not* human this thing really was.

"All right, here's the thing: I'm a Guardian Spirit. My life, my whole existence, is dedicated to protecting the balance between the elements."

Kaz and Lily traded glances. Kaz was glad to see Lily's expression mirror his. *Okay, and . . . ?*

"But, you see, Guardian Spirits such as yours truly transect many dimensions. Many worlds. It's a big job, but it's also usually a pretty easy one. Reality chugs along. Not much for us to do. *But . . .* every once in a while there is a colossal, enormous *mess* that threatens to screw up just about the entire multiverse."

"So, wait," Kaz interrupted. "Are there a lot more dimensions than just ours and Arcadia, and, I guess, this place?"

The Serpent laughed. It sounded just like Charlie's laugh, except that it ended with a drawn-out *hiss*. "Oh, Kaz. The things I and some of my brethren have seen? You don't have a *clue*. Good grief, the stories I could tell you!"

Kaz almost had to lean against Lily to keep his knees from buckling.

Brethren? There are more of these things? And then another thought came. *What if Thorne and Arcadia are just the tip of the iceberg? Magick, Arcadia, the Umbra—this might only be a taste of what's out there!*

"Anyway," the Serpent continued, "when Thorne and his followers pulled their shenanigans back in 1906 and ended up creating an entire new realm? That was bad. *So* bad. There aren't even words to describe how bad that was. Imagine a clock with a hundred billion gears and every one of them in the place it has to be, doing exactly what it's supposed to do. And then imagine something that doesn't belong in there suddenly appearing and jamming up the works. First one cog stops spinning and then another thing burns itself out trying to make up for that first thing failing and then—"

"The clock slows?"

"The clock *stops*," the Serpent said. "Bad news all around. And it fell right on my plate to have to try to fix it."

"But how?" Lily seemed to have gotten over her irritation and now sounded just as transfixed by the Serpent's words as Kaz was. "How do you fix something like that?"

The Serpent sighed. "It takes a while. There are rules I've got to follow. I'm a Guardian Spirit, not, like, a god, you know? So, I had to play what you might call a 'long game.' You remember the signet ring with Jackson's family crest on it, yes?" They both nodded. "When I found out what Thorne was planning to do, I decided to inhabit that ring. That way, I was sure I'd be in that room—that place you four called the Friendship Chamber?—when Jackson was sacrificed by Thorne in the ceremony that created Arcadia. And, bonus, since Jackson had been wearing that ring for a while, it helped me forge a direct connection with him. As you know, we need a full circle of five elementalists to do all the really fun stuff. So, long story slightly less long, when Thorne sacrificed Jackson, instead of the poor kid getting killed or booted into Arcadia, I was able to redirect him into the Umbra."

Now the edge crept back into Lily's voice. "*Why?* Why would you do that? Why would you trap him there and torture him like that? Do you have any clue what you put him through?"

"I know in exact detail what I put him through. But I had

to do it. Jackson is the key to destroying Arcadia. Jackson, and this." The Serpent didn't move, but a picture-perfect representation of the Wright family ring materialized in the air in front of them. It looked the same as always, the crest a wagon wheel with five spokes.

The Serpent gave the tiniest gesture with his chin, and the image of the ring doubled in size, and again, and again, growing as big as a beach ball. "Take a closer look. "There. You see? It's hard to spot at the original scale."

Lily gasped. Kaz felt his eyebrows trying to climb right up off his forehead.

The symbol on the ring wasn't a wagon wheel at all. The ring had gone through so much wear and tear that some of the detail had worn away, but up close there was no doubt about it. The ring displayed a serpent, eating its own tail, and the five spokes within it. . . .

Lily stole Kaz's thought. "The spokes represent the five elements!"

"Ten points to Gryffindor!" the Serpent said. "Anyway, Jackson had to stay there in the Umbra for such a long time because, the longer he stayed, the more magick he absorbed, and the more valuable he became. And then, when the time was right, I arranged for him to escape."

Kaz put his hands on the sides of his head. It felt as if his brain were going to come shooting out of his ears, *splortch*, like streams of saltwater taffy. "Are you telling me that the reason

Jackson tried to escape the Umbra—the reason he was able to reach out to Brett, and get us to do the friendship ritual, and go to Alcatraz to find him—all that was because of *you*?"

The Serpent grinned.

Lily picked up where Kaz had left off. "But that means the four of us—Kaz and Gabe and my brother and me—we got dragged into this, bound to the elements, all of it, that was all you, too! You needed five elementalists!"

The Serpent grinned even more widely. Kaz groaned, and Lily stomped a furious foot into the ground.

"This is all your fault," Lily said. Her voice was trembling with anger. "San Francisco is in ruins. Gabe's uncle is probably dead. My brother was possessed by Thorne!"

"No." The Serpent shook his head. "This is Thorne's fault. He made the mess. I just adjusted circumstances so I can clean it up. Actually—" The Serpent reconsidered his words. "So *we* can clean it up."

"But, but," Kaz sputtered. "We could have been left out of it! And . . . and . . ." He tried to imagine what his life would be like if Brett hadn't talked them into doing that first binding ceremony in the Friendship Chamber the night this whole nightmare started. "I mean, yeah, Arcadia would still have been around, but it never would have merged with San Francisco if we hadn't been bound to the elements and done that ritual by accident."

"Arcadia was an abomination, Kaz. It was never supposed

to exist, and it has to be destroyed no matter the cost. Its *wrong-ness* affects more than just this reality. You want an apology from me?" the Serpent went on. "Well, I'm sorry, okay? I wish none of this had happened to you. You're good kids—tough and loyal and brave—and I don't want to see you hurt. But all the good things about you? Those are the reasons I chose you in the first place. And as sorry as I am, I'd do it all again."

"Hmph." Kaz wanted to look and sound indignant, but he couldn't figure out what to do with his hands and finally shoved them into his pockets.

"Brett survived Arcadia and the guilt that weighed him down," the Serpent continued. "Gabe survived the fire inside him. They're ready to play their parts in what is going to happen next. But perhaps you two have the most difficult roles of all to play. That's why I had to test you here in the labyrinth. Not to prove to *me* that you're courageous and smart enough to do what has to be done—I've known that all along—but to show *you* what you're capable of. Now my long game is almost over. Now it's time to destroy Jonathan Thorne and Arcadia's influence for good. Then the balance can be restored.'"

"Yeah, so, about all that destruction or whatever," Kaz said. "Do you have, like, a plan? 'Cause a plan would be *really* nice."

The Serpent's face practically split in half with his biggest grin yet, his forked tongue flicking the air.

20

Gabe's hands and feet had gone mostly numb from the chains cutting off his circulation, and his jaw ached thanks to Jackson's disgusting, glowing, golden gag jammed in his mouth, but he couldn't stop staring at the magickal spectacle shifting and pulsing in front of him.

He and Brett and Aria had been bundled together on one side of Thorne's ritual circle, shackled head to toe in the glyph chains, staring across at the wrought iron chair. Thorne himself stood in the center of the circle, chanting softly over the Mirror Book, which he had picked up from the little cairn Madam Kureshi had built. But it wasn't Thorne who had Gabe transfixed.

Like a twisted version of the defensive dome surrounding Fort Scott, the ritual circle had generated its own magickal energy field, a sliding, shifting, poisonous, purple-black sphere that surrounded them all. Glyphs like none Gabe had ever seen before rotated around them, warping and twitching. He got queasy if he stared at any one glyph for too long, as if the symbols themselves were toxic.

Jackson, Madam Kureshi, and the three pale men stood in a half circle behind Thorne. Gabe guessed they were awaiting instructions. Thorne's hench-monsters turned to watch as Jackson broke away and walked over to stand in front of Brett.

"You are helping no one by keeping Lily's and Kazuo's whereabouts to yourself." Jackson peered up into Brett's eyes. "Tell me where they are."

Brett opened his mouth, then paused and snapped his teeth together. He glanced over at Gabe. "They're . . ."

Brett, what're you doing?

"They're in the Mirror Cave. In the Book."

Jackson's eyebrows shot up. *"Are* they now? Well." He turned on his heel and marched away.

Though bound and gagged, Gabe made a face at Brett like, *What'd you do that for?* Brett winced and tried to shrug. "I heard them setting up the ritual, man. The Book's gonna turn to dust. That might mean Lily and Kaz will, too. They . . . I don't know. They might have a chance out here, at least. With us."

Gabe tried to say something but couldn't. *Not with this stupid gag in my mouth.* He tried to work his tongue over to one side—and felt something weird. There was . . . what was that? Some kind of raised shape on the oblong part mashing his tongue down. Some sort of . . . symbol?

Jackson walked up to Jonathan Thorne and held out his hand. "May I please have a look at that, Lord Thorne?"

Thorne turned and narrowed his eyes at Jackson. He towered over the boy by at least two feet. "I am preparing for the ritual, Master Wright. I do not wish to be bothered."

Jackson put every bit of his trademark smug condescension into his words. "And I do not wish to be a part of a ceremony I do not fully understand."

What is he doing? Why doesn't he just tell Thorne they're in the Book and get it over with?

"Yours is not the place to understand such things, boy. Now step away from me. I must concentrate."

"Do I not deserve the chance to get a look at such a legendary artifact? I only want a few moments to examine it. I am an important part of this ritual, am I not?"

That's Ghost Boy for you. Could he get any more obnoxious?

Thorne's lips slowly peeled away from his nightmare teeth in a snarl that set every one of Gabe's hairs on end.

Madam Kureshi didn't move from where she stood, but the hem of her robes whipped and fluttered as two long, purple tentacles shot out from underneath them, each of them gripping a set of glyph-inscribed shackles. Jackson had no time even to cry out before the tentacles slammed his wrists together behind his back. The shackles snapped closed around them, then around his ankles, and Thorne bent at the waist to glare into Jackson's wide, pale eyes. "Oh, you are important, Master Wright. More so than you know." Mr. Grillion appeared at Jackson's side in a yellowish haze, and as Thorne straightened up and turned away, Grillion blew a noxious cloud into Jackson's face. Jackson coughed violently, gagged, and went limp. Grillion dragged him over to the wrought iron chair and, using more glyph chains, bound him into it.

Wait! What's happening?

"What're you . . ." Gabe could barely hear Jackson's slurred words. "What're you . . . doing?"

Thorne didn't bother facing Jackson as he answered. "I did not lie when I said you and the Serpent were connected through the same magick. And you are indeed a weapon I can utilize to kill the Serpent. Unfortunately for you, my young friend, the exact kind of weapon will be . . . a bomb."

Thorne's using Ghost Boy just like he's using the rest of us!

Thorne set the Mirror Book back down on the cairn and nodded to his hench-monsters. Mr. Humboldt, Mr. Kretschmar, and Madam Kureshi approached Gabe, Brett, and Aria. Gabe's stomach sank as they neared him. But he was surprised when Thorne's followers' attention settled on the chains that bound them. Madam Kureshi said a few words in the horrible, distorted, brain-itching language Gabe had heard members of the Eternal Dawn chant, and plucked at a link of the chain directly over his heart.

At first Gabe wasn't even sure what he was seeing. A strand of metal *peeled away* from the chain, and as Madam Kureshi pulled on it, the chain began to unravel as if she had tugged on a single thread from a knit scarf. She backed away, still holding the metal strand, and even though the chains wrapped around him didn't seem to get any weaker, the strand kept going. Humboldt and Kretschmar joined her, and Gabe realized they had both done the same thing, one unraveling a thread of metal from Aria's chains, the other from Brett's.

Humboldt and Kretschmar handed their strands to Madam Kureshi, and multiple tentacles from beneath her robes joined her human hands in weaving the three metallic strands together. Kureshi glided backward as she worked, heading for the center of the circle. When she reached the Mirror Book, a tentacle plucked it from the cairn, wrapped a loop of the newly formed metal twine around it, and set it back in place.

Madam Kureshi chanted under her breath, still weaving strands together, still moving backward, until she reached Jonathan Thorne, who stood beside Jackson. She handed the end of the silvery twine to Thorne. He favored her with one of his ghastly, mutant-fang-filled grins. And Gabe found it within himself, on top of the fear and anger, to be repulsed when Kureshi blushed and ducked her head like a schoolgirl.

She backed away, and Thorne turned his focus to Jackson.

"You see this conduit, Master Wright?"

Jackson lifted his head, barely opening his eyes.

Thorne went on. "All the power of your elementalist friends shall flow through this . . . from them into the Mirror Book . . . and from the Mirror Book into you. But, you see, the Book will amplify their energies to such a degree that you shall be quite overwhelmed. So much so that you will *explode*, and in so doing obliterate the Serpent and the accursed boundary it has confined us within."

Jackson's eyes opened farther. He struggled against the shackles, but only weakly. To his surprise, Gabe realized he felt bad for the traitorous little twerp.

Thorne pulled something out of his coat that glinted in what remained of the amber San Arcadia sunlight. It took Gabe a second, squinting, to realize what it was, but Jackson seemed to recognize it immediately, and his struggles intensified. Gabe's stomach tightened.

Thorne held the long, slim, silver dagger that the first Primus had used to sacrifice Uncle Steve. "The ritual only needs one last component to be activated, Master Wright."

Thorne began wrapping the end of the braided metal "conduit" around the dagger's handle.

No. No! Gabe tried to move, tried to whip back and forth, anything to give him some room within the glyph chains.

Thorne appeared to be taking a special delight in Jackson's

terror-frozen face. "Yes, you recognize this, do you not? I plunged it into your heart more than a century ago."

Nightmares played out before Gabe's eyes. He knew he was about to die. He, his mother, all his friends, his entire planet, about to be crushed and swept away.

After everything we've been through, this is how we go out?

No. NO.

I can't let this happen! I can't, I CAN'T!

Gabe ground his teeth, the gag pressing painfully into his mouth, the rough patch threatening to rub his tongue raw, and—

Gabe stopped. Sudden realization felt as if it had set his brain ablaze.

That's a circle etched onto the gag. And inside it . . . are they lines? Like the symbol on Jackson's family ring, but why would he—

Then he remembered. "Bite me," Jackson had said when he gagged him.

Jackson never uses modern slang . . . so what if that's not what he meant?

Jonathan Thorne finished wrapping the metal strand around the dagger. He planted his feet and raised the dagger high above his head.

What if it was meant as an instruction?

Gabe bit down on the gag. His eyes flared white-hot as the surface of the mass inside his mouth cracked open and the most intense, purest jolt of Jackson's magick he'd ever felt shot through him as if he'd been struck by lightning.

Even while being charged up with power, Gabe felt a wave of relief. *Jackson meant for this to happen! He's been on our side the whole time!*

Gabe remembered the first time Jackson had ever boosted his fire ability by infusing him with his own magick. How long ago was that? Days? Weeks? It felt like years, but the sensation remained fresh. This was so much more powerful than that. *So much more!* Along with the surge of power, Gabe felt his connection to fire envelop his body, his mind, his *soul*. He'd never felt so attuned to his element before. He didn't just control fire. He *was* fire!

The chains wrapped around Gabe's body flared red, then white, then disintegrated, falling to the barest traces of black dust. Two churning, impenetrable spheres of fire blazed into existence. One around Jackson, then a larger one around Gabe and Brett and Aria. He heard Thorne and the three pale men and Madam Kureshi screaming, and knew they must have been trying to reach him. But he couldn't see them through the flames. With a touch, Gabe destroyed Brett's chains as well as the chains and shackles binding his mother.

"Ah, that feels good!" Brett said, running his hands over his wrists. Aria gave him the biggest smile he'd ever seen on her face. They both followed him as, still shielded within the fire sphere, they crossed the ritual circle—melting the braided magick conduit as they went—and merged with the sphere protecting Jackson so that they all stood within a single, incandescent protective shield.

Gabe had heard an expression before—"drinking from a fire hose"—but he'd never given it much thought. Now, with the fire's energy surging through him, he thought he knew *exactly* what it meant. His body and mind had become conductors for more power than he'd ever felt before. Exhilaration fought with sheer terror in every atom of his being.

"How long can you keep this up?" Brett shouted at Gabe's side, raising his voice to be heard over the roaring of the flames.

"Long enough, I hope," Gabe bellowed back, and at his touch, Jackson's shackles hissed and melted and fell away.

Jackson stood and shouted, "That took you *forever*!" but any trace of smugness vanished completely when he grinned at Gabe.

Gabe would have answered, but he felt the fire sphere beginning to fail. He knew all five of the Arcadian monstrosities outside it must be trying to break through with every bit of energy they had, and that he could sustain the barrier for only a few more seconds.

He turned on his heel, snatched up the Mirror Book, and threw it open.

21

Kaz took Lily's hand as the window appeared on the mirrored cavern wall. His slate gray eyes glimmered with green fire. "Ready?"

Lily's eyes flashed silver-white. Her hand tightened on his. "We got this."

A gust of wind beneath their feet lifted them and propelled them forward, and they stepped out of the cavern into what looked like the middle of a firestorm. Gabe stood right in front of them, red-orange flames licking all around his body, and beyond him Kaz saw Brett and Jackson and Gabe's mom, Aria. Aria didn't look so good. She was down on her knees, and it felt like a punch to the gut when Kaz saw her skin wavering from normal to rocklike and back.

I know what that feels like.

Flames surrounded them, and Gabe snarled and gritted his teeth with effort. "Glad you're back," he ground out. "Better get your game faces on."

Lily tried to get closer to him, but the flames burned too hot. She said, "What's going on?"

Gabe let out an exhausted breath, his shoulders slumped, and the huge sphere of fire that had surrounded them crackled and vanished. For a second, Kaz wanted to jump back into the Mirror Book.

They were in a circular clear spot in the middle of a bunch of San Arcadia rubble. In front of them, the Crimson Serpent's glowing blue eye glared at them, and Jonathan Thorne stood not twenty feet away, his whole head split in one of his monster-show grins, shadows slithering and streaming around him.

Flanking Thorne were three people Kaz had never seen before, and one he'd hoped never to see again: three pale men in old-fashioned clothes, and Madam Kureshi.

He almost flinched away when Lily whispered at his side, "Remember what the Serpent said. Remember what we have to do."

"I know, I know!" Kaz stepped in front of Jackson and Aria, as Jackson helped her move away from Thorne and his minions. She seemed barely able to stand. "I'm just afraid *doing* is gonna be a lot harder than *saying*!"

Jonathan Thorne's words exploded through the rubble around them. "Mr. Smith! Miss Hernandez! How fortuitous that you could join us here!"

A battle line formed. Kaz and Lily, Gabe and Brett, Jackson and Aria on one side, staring across a small stone cairn at Thorne and his four lieutenants. Jackson stepped between Kaz and Lily and, in a fast, terse whisper, told them who Humboldt, Grillion, and Kretschmar were and what they could do.

Thorne lazily cracked his knuckles. One at a time. It sounded as if bones broke with each pop. "You think you have caused me trouble, Gabriel Conway? This is a mere inconvenience. You have done us all a favor, in fact, by summoning the other two elementalists. Re-creating the ritual circle will require but a few moments of my time, and with their added power, the Crimson Serpent shall surely die a most satisfying death."

Off to one side, Aria gritted her teeth, clearly struggling. Her skin cracked and changed in time with her pulse, and it broke Kaz's heart to see Gabe's mother in a kind of pain he knew so well himself. Softly, to no one in particular, Kaz said, "We can't let Thorne do this. We can't let him hurt the Serpent."

Humboldt's awful, faceted eyes glimmered. A clicking, chattering growl emanated from somewhere inside his body, and it somehow made Kaz think of the Serpent's last words to Lily and him, after it had finished explaining the plan: "With five elements for one—act across all worlds." Kaz lifted his gaze to the Serpent's one visible eye, enormous and radiant blue like the world's largest sapphire. The eye narrowed at him.

It's waiting. Waiting for the price to be paid. The buzzing, whirring song of the Serpent reached his ears, the occasional recognizable word emerging from inside it.

"I am not unreasonable." Thorne's voice carried as if spoken through a bullhorn. It cut through the Serpent's song. "Simply surrender yourselves and allow us to get on with the proceedings, and I promise none of you will suffer unduly. I will give you a moment to consider your tragically limited options."

Gabe seemed to have regained his composure. "Did you talk to the Serpent?" he asked.

Did we ever. Kaz nodded, took in the scene, and listened to the Serpent's song.

"Not yet" was the message the song whispered to his heart. *"Not yet."*

"So what do we do?" Brett asked? "What's the plan?"

"Protect the Serpent, protect one another, and stall for time," Kaz said.

"Stall for time?" Gabe asked. "That's *it*? Are you *serious*?"

"Yeah, he's serious," Lily said. "Leave the plan to us. In the meantime, I don't think stalling is going to be all that easy."

"But—"

"Trust us, Gabe," Kaz said. "There's a plan. One that's been in place for way longer than any of us has been alive.

Except for maybe Jackson here." Kaz patted the smaller boy on his shoulder.

"Okay." Gabe sighed. "We stall. We stay alive. That's a goal, I guess. And like Lil says, even that won't be easy. We can't afford to lose control of our elements. And jeez, whatever you do, don't accidentally combine them. But if there's ever gonna be a time to push our limits, this is it."

Brett and Lily nodded. Kaz gulped and said, "Right."

Gabe faced Jackson. "Look after my mom, okay?"

Jackson started to reply, but Aria stood and cut Jackson off in midword. "No one needs to look after me, son." Her body shuddered, and her skin turned gray and stony and . . . stayed that way. The ground trembled as cracks appeared in her arms and neck and face. "We have some cockroaches to squash."

Aria's eyes flared like green supernovas, and massive stone spikes erupted from the ground beneath Thorne and his underlings, and everything dissolved into total chaos.

The air went hazy and yellow as Grillion dispersed, but Lily summoned gusts of wind that swept his poisonous spores away from everyone's faces. Humboldt smashed through one stone spike, then another, but had to veer to one side as Gabe hurled a series of fireballs straight at his head. Madam Kureshi sank into mire as Kaz turned the ground beneath her to quicksand-like soup.

How do you like me now!?

Energy splashed everywhere, green and gold and oily black,

and bursts of fire boomed out like cannon shots, and Kaz realized there was no way he could keep track of everything.

Thorne, towering over everyone on a pillar of shadow.

Gabe, his eyes white-hot, gouts of fire blasting from his hands.

Lily, hovering ten feet off the ground in the middle of a cyclone, bolts of lightning cracking all around her.

Then Humboldt let loose another clacking, chittering growl and charged straight for him. Kaz lifted a hand, and a wall of rock eight feet tall and three feet thick erupted from the ground in front of him, directly in Humboldt's path.

Humboldt smashed through it as if it had been made of Popsicle sticks.

Kaz dived out of the way as the hulking man barreled past him.

Nearby, Brett and Gabe stood back to back, one projecting hooked spears of ice, the other firing off a barrage of flaming projectiles faster than a machine gun. Kaz heard a loud, horrible sucking sound and had just identified it as something pulling itself free of dense, wet mud when a thick, sucker-covered appendage snaked around Brett's body too fast for him to react. With a shout, Brett disappeared.

Above them, Lily screamed her brother's name, and a blue-white glare of lightning left Kaz seeing spots—before Lily crashed to the ground, enveloped in a cocoon of writhing, oily shadow.

"Get away from them!" Kaz recognized Aria's voice. It rose to a shriek. *"Get away from those children!"* A wave of power blasted the shadows away from Lily, but she only rolled over, unconscious. Aria stepped over Lily, and Kaz sucked in a breath at how beautiful and *awful* Aria looked. Green light flared from every crack in her stone-like skin, and her voice echoed and rumbled like the roar of an avalanche. "I won't let you hurt them, you monster! I—"

But a wave of foul yellow dust rose around her. Aria gagged, choked. Fell to one knee. Two seconds later she collapsed.

"Not yet," he heard somewhere within the Serpent's song. *"Not yet."*

Well, it better be soon, *because I don't know how long we can keep this up!*

With Gabe and Jackson, he scrambled behind a pile of half-burned wooden rubble and willed the ground to rise, providing shelter underneath a rocky overhang.

From somewhere on the other side of the overhang, Thorne's voice rang out. "Where are the other three? *Find them!*"

"How much longer are we going to have to stall?" Gabe asked. "Because—"

Jackson's scream cut him off. The pale boy whipped about, flailing, clawing at his own skin. Kaz realized that Jackson's body was covered with small, white worms at the same moment he felt them on his own skin. Gabe screamed, too, and the worms rose up all around them. The ground *became* worms, and Kretschmar's disembodied voice called out, "Over here, Lord Thorne. These three were trying to hide."

The worms were *everywhere*. Kaz couldn't pull them off fast enough, and they wriggled higher, higher. They rode his hands to his face. They pulled at his lips and slithered into his nose and wriggled inside his ears—

—and Kaz called on the earth at the same time he saw Gabe's eyes ignite, and he realized what was about to happen; but it was too late to stop it—

—and the *ground exploded* as their elements combined.

The fiery impact from directly beneath them lifted all three boys in the air, destroyed the overhang they'd been hiding under, stripped every last worm from their skin, and pelted them with what felt like hundreds of pounds of burning-hot sand.

Kretschmar's disembodied voice screamed as tens of thousands of scorched, stinking worms rained down amid the rubble. Kaz, Gabe, and Jackson hit the ground in a jumbled heap, and Kaz's forehead fetched up directly against the small stone cairn he'd seen earlier.

We're back in the circle.

He struggled to sit up and made it, partially.

Gabe and Jackson lay nearby. Kaz grunted—he couldn't tell how many burns covered his skin from the sand, but it felt as if every inch of his body had been cooked—and turned his head to see Brett and Lily and Aria huddled on the other side of the cairn. Aria seemed to have shut down completely. She hugged her knees to her chest, her face hidden, and rocked silently back and forth.

Kaz was about to try to get to his feet again when smoky tendrils of ink-black shadow rose from the ground all around them. "No, no," Thorne said. The tips of the shadow-tendrils narrowed. Hardened. Became jet-black blades that hovered less than an inch from everyone's throats. "You shall all remain exactly where you are. Until I command you to move."

Madam Kureshi glided over to Thorne's right to join Humboldt, and Grillion, and finally Kretschmar—charred and smoking, but very much alive—all standing, glaring, triumphant.

For a moment no one spoke, and the only noise Kaz heard was the buzzing, ever-present sound of the Serpent.

And the words whispered within it.

"With five elements for one act across all worlds."

Kaz dug his fingers into the ground and pitched his voice low enough so that none of Thorne's monsters could hear him. *I hope.* "Guys. We still need to buy time, but I think I know what the Serpent's words mean."

Thorne turned to Madam Kureshi. "We need more of the glyph chains." Kureshi nodded. Her robes writhed and undulated, and she began pulling loops of the chain out of the shadows the robes concealed.

Kaz whispered, "Five elements! One act! We have to cut

loose with all our powers at the same time!"

"The Serpent didn't tell us that part, though, Kaz," Lily said.

"The Serpent didn't tell us a lot of things! Some of them we have to figure out on our own. But everything it does, it does for a reason, and those words we keep hearing have to mean something!"

Jackson winced as he moved. "Kazuo, that is insanity! Every time our powers have combined, it has resulted in disaster! Combining your elements at once and amplifying them with my magick would be—"

Gabe groaned. "We've gotta do *something*. If we let them get us in chains again, we're done."

Kaz looked around. One by one, all five of them nodded.

Kaz heard Lily say, "*¿Listo, hermano?*"

"*Sí.*"

Kaz felt his eyes turn slate gray, and welcomed it. "Straight up, everybody. Right into the clouds."

Gabe said, "Now!" and all five of them unleashed their power into the churning, amber sky overhead.

22

Flames engulfed Gabe's body as a column of fire as thick as a tree trunk blasted up from his hand. It didn't hurt. It only felt warm. Inviting. Like a crackling fireplace in the dead of winter. He heard the fire's voice whispering in the back of his mind—*"Burn . . . burn . . . burn. . . ."* Gabe snapped the voice off with terse internal words of his own.

Quiet. I'm concentrating.

The column widened, widened, spread down from his hand, until it surrounded him completely, rendering the world around him in shades of red and yellow and orange. He heard screaming, felt the ground shake with running footsteps, but glances to his right and left showed him similar pillars of force beaming up from Kaz and Brett and Lily, along with Thorne's tendril-blades recoiling as if they'd been stung. He couldn't even see Jackson. The Ghost Boy's tower of golden magick roiled and shimmered and hid him completely.

It finally occurred to Gabe that the screams and running footfalls belonged to Thorne's minions.

He raised his head. Twenty or thirty feet above them, the five beams of elemental power combined into one and rocketed into the clouds, and the amber-gold sky of San Arcadia burst into eye-searing, dazzling incandescence. Gabe stared. He couldn't stop. *The whole sky . . . it's burning!*

He'd never seen a color like this before.

He didn't think anyone had.

Gabe knew he hadn't moved, that the ground hadn't shifted. But he felt suddenly raised up, thrust far into the air, because the sky above San Arcadia *became a sun.* All of it, horizon to horizon, burning as bright and hot as a star, in that color-not-a-color that threatened to engulf Gabe's mind, his entire world.

Tears leaked from his eyes.

It's beautiful.

Then the ground did buck and tremble beneath him as a massive shock wave blasted out from the five of them. With a lurch in his stomach, Gabe watched channels of elemental power flowing away from him and his friends to combine at their center. He realized that the shape was a familiar one.

"It's like the symbol on Jackson's family ring!" he shouted

to the others. "The wagon wheel!"

"It wasn't a wagon wheel," Lily shouted back, her eyes dazzling like stars. "The circle is the Serpent. And, Gabe, the lines, they're—"

"They're us!" Kaz finished. "From the beginning, it's always been us!"

Gabe's mind spun and hitched. Everything had been leading to this. Everything, for centuries.

The shock wave faded, as did the channels of elemental magick, and Gabe knew he and his fellow elementalists had accomplished what they'd set out to do. *What the Serpent wanted us to do.* The fire flickered and died from around him. And one by one, Kaz, Lily, Brett, and Jackson let their own power dim. . . .

But above them, the combined pillar of force remained, pulsing, the same color as the sky, like a scar in the fabric of the world. Nearby, breathless, Lily said, "Is it—is that like the thing on Alcatraz? The rift between here and Arcadia?"

Kaz gaped at it. "Yeah, except a thousand times bigger."

Gabe got to his feet. He knew he should be looking around for Thorne and his hench-monsters, but as he gazed at the great streak in the sky, something deep within him saw it for what it was. He swallowed hard, and his fists clenched. "It's a door."

From behind him, Aria said, "Oh no . . ."

"Mom?"

She was still there, on the ground, and seemed to be unhurt. Gabe helped her stand. He barely recognized her anymore. Her skin had taken on a gravel-like texture, and her voice grated out like the grinding of a huge millstone. Aria tilted her head back, stony eyes fixed on the phenomenon hanging in the sky. "They're coming. . . . I can feel them getting closer. . . ."

Jackson, Brett, and Lily stumbled over. Jackson said, "Feel *what*, exactly?"

"What have you done?"

Jonathan Thorne's voice smashed and scraped over them. Lily and Jackson covered their ears, and Gabe winced as his eardrums came close to rupturing. Thorne slammed down in their midst, his shifting-horror mouth wide in a snarl, oily black shadow-tendrils writhing around him. "To me! Everyone!" Out of the corner of his eye, Gabe saw Madam Kureshi and Mr. Humboldt emerge from behind a broken wall. As they headed for Thorne, a yellowish mist coalesced and became Mr. Grillion, who fell into step beside Humboldt. The three of them stopped a few yards away. The ground around them wriggled, squirmed, and rose up into a disgusting column that became Mr. Kretschmar.

Thorne rounded on Gabe, and everyone flinched again as Thorne screamed, *"What chaos have you brought upon us?"*

Only Aria seemed unaffected by his sonic onslaught. She summoned a weak smile and pointed upward with one finger. "See for yourself."

Thorne looked up.

Gabe had never imagined he'd see fear on the cult founder's face.

With a clap of thunder that should have split the sky in half, *something* came through the doorway into San Arcadia. At first Gabe thought the portal had opened onto a mountain range and sent an entire mountainside sliding through into this dimension.

Then he realized what he was seeing was a *leg*.

The immense slab of stone cast a shadow over Thorne's minions. And while Madam Kureshi, Mr. Humboldt, and Mr. Kretschmar screamed and scattered, Mr. Grillion seemed to be frozen in place and only stared up in horror as the four-hundred-ton foot came down on top of him. A cloud of yellow puffed out from either side of the monstrous appendage.

Gabe struggled to understand what he was witnessing. It wasn't like the grotesque Arcadian prison guards he had encountered in Alcatraz Citadel, where their bodies made no sense and caused his brain literal pain to try to comprehend them. This was a matter of *scale*. The stone giant had to be eighty feet tall, maybe a hundred, and for several long seconds Gabe's mind simply refused to accept that such a thing could be possible. The creature's earthen body creaked and rumbled as it moved, and its massive, barely humanoid head opened a mouth like a cavern and . . .

It *spoke*.

Gabe knew they were words. He had no hope of understanding them, no way even to identify the language, but their general meaning made itself crystal clear within seconds as the colossus turned and—Gabe felt his blood freeze—*beckoned* to the doorway.

"Destroy the giant!" Jonathan Thorne screeched. "Destroy it and close that accursed portal!"

Thorne, Humboldt, Kureshi, and Kretschmar threw themselves at the giant, attacking with every shred of power at their disposal.

Gabe hissed, "Guys! Mom! We need to get out of here!"

Lily looked from Aria to Gabe and back. "What is that thing? *What is that thing?*"

Aria whispered, "Incandati," and Gabe understood with a wrenching thump in his chest.

"What's an Incandati?" Brett grabbed Gabe's shoulder. "You know what it means! I can tell from the look on your face!"

The giant roared, a sound like a thousand earthquakes, and Gabe led his friends and his mother around to the far side of a ruined store a hundred yards away. "An Incandati is what an elementalist turns into if they let their element take them over."

Kaz's face turned pale. "Like . . . like when the earth tried to get me to transform into stone? I—" He broke off, eyes wide, as he stared at Aria's rough, gray, rocklike skin. Aria turned her back on the group, her head bowed.

Brett gestured at the incomprehensibly huge stone giant. "So that's an Earth Incandati? Why'd the Serpent want us to bring that here? What's the point?"

Kaz rubbed the back of his neck. "It, uh . . . it said it wants to restore balance to the elements. And get rid of Thorne's influence. I didn't know this was how it meant to do it."

Lily groaned, and everyone turned to watch as the Earth Incandati fell to one knee. Thorne's shadow-tendrils had burrowed deep inside it, and the cracks in its stony skin began to widen. The giant roared again.

The doorway in the air thundered and split open twice as wide. Gabe pulled everyone down behind a charred wall, and they watched through a broken window as a silver-gray mist shot through the portal and slammed Thorne away from the earth giant. The mist rushed through, faster and faster, growing more and more solid, until it solidified into the figure of a woman. Easily as tall as the Earth Incandati, the air giantess had long, snow-white hair, skin the color of storm clouds, and electric-blue eyes from which bolts of lightning cascaded in a never-ending barrage. She raised her arms, and though Thorne and Madam Kureshi gripped bits of rubble and held on, the sudden ripping, shredding wind picked up Mr. Humboldt and sent him skittering down a side street like a stone skipping across the surface of a pond.

The Water Incandati flowed out right behind the air giantess. Less like a human form and more like a living wave, the water giant flowed into and through the Air Incandati, her lightning traveling through it so that it flared blue-white. A separate wave split apart from the greater mass, became something like an immense, liquid fist, and slammed down directly on Jonathan Thorne. When the water flowed away, Thorne was nowhere in sight.

"Thank God these guys are on our side," Brett whispered.

Gabe might have said something, but the Magick Incandati arrived, and he had to remember how to make his lungs work.

The Magick Incandati looked the way Gabe had always imagined an ancient Greek god would look. Definitely male, and even more beautiful than the air giantess, his body seemed to be composed of shifting, interlocking, golden polygons— planes of energy that came together to form a seamless surface, only to split apart seconds later, rearrange themselves, and form the same shape again. The magick giant fixed his great, shimmering golden eyes on Madam Kureshi, extended one hand, and a sixty-foot-long, needle-sharp lance of pure energy pierced the woman just below the collarbone. The lance punched through her body and buried itself in the ground behind her. She collapsed on it.

That's the last of Thorne and his hench-monsters! Holy crap— have we won?

As if in answer to his question, the earth giant rumbled to his feet, turned to the ruins where Gabe and his friends were hiding, and brought both fists down on them with catastrophic force. The impact sent everyone tumbling, and they had no time to regroup, because the air giantess sent a hurricane-force wind battering down on them at the same time that both the Water and Magic Incandati unleashed waves of destructive power, flattening building after building around them.

"I thought they were on our side!" Brett screamed, hanging on for dear life to a bit of foundation. The wind had blown them into a demolished dry cleaning store.

Gabe could barely breathe. He felt as if the air giantess were sucking all the oxygen out of the atmosphere, and as the Water Incandati rose up to tower over them, he wondered if breathing would matter much longer.

But the water giant faltered. The living wave undulated, turned back on itself—and went from the blue-gray of the ocean to a foul, poisonous green. Gabe spotted Mr. Grillion, reconstituted, standing on a half-collapsed balcony nearby, grunting as he forced a stream of noxious particles into the Water Incandati.

The Magick Incandati crashed to the ground beyond the water giant, clawing at its eyes. Gabe stared in horror as tendril after oily, black tendril wrapped itself around the golden giant's head, Jonathan Thorne's awful laughter echoing through the ruins.

"What do we do?" Lily grabbed Gabe's elbow. "The giants and Thorne's hench-monsters are going to destroy the whole city at this rate! Do we run away? *How?*"

Brett came up behind Gabe and Lily, and when he spoke, his voice sounded strange. "Whatever we do . . . guys . . . we better do it fast." Gabe saw something odd reflected in Brett's dark eyes where he stared off over Gabe's shoulder. Something red-orange and flickering. Gabe felt the rush of heat before he even turned around.

The Fire Incandati had arrived.

The other elemental giants shied away from him, the air giantess in particular, as one of her limbs hissed and evaporated with his passing, only to re-form seconds later. The earth giant hissed in pain and stumbled and fell, part of his face glowing red-hot.

Gabe stared.

The Fire Incandati looked like an erupting volcano made human. Not as amorphous as the water giant, but not as clearly defined as the colossus made of magick. Sheets of dancing, destroying flame draped the Incandati's limbs and hid its face. Great gouts of plasma roared from its hands and took the shapes of medieval maces. And with a scream like the heart of a raging wildfire, the giant smashed its blazing maces down, each blow incinerating the remains of an entire ruined building.

It was coming straight for Gabe. And his friends. And his mother.

And it was coming *fast*.

"Gabe, we've got to move," Aria said. She tugged on his arm. "We can't face that! Let's go!"

But two things had settled into Gabe's mind with unwavering certainty. The first was that there was no way to outrun this creature.

The second was that he had to stop it.

"You are fire," Gabe gritted out. "You are the element to which I am bound."

The fire giant raised one crushing, charring, devastating mace and swung it directly at Gabe—and, his eyes ablaze and his heart pounding hard enough to burst, Gabe reached up, reached out, took hold of the mace, and shunted it aside. The massive weapon smashed into the ground ten feet to Gabe's left, and when the giant pulled it back up, the earth beneath the impact had fused into glass.

"You are fire!" Gabe shouted. "You do not control me! *I* control *you!*"

The other mace flashed down after the first one, and though it pushed him back so hard his feet dug paths in the dirt, Gabe shoved it aside as well, so that it slammed down ten feet to his right.

The fire giant yanked the weapon back, roaring.

"You are fire!" Gabe screamed. *"And so am I!"*

The Fire Incandati raised both maces at once—and before it could begin its last downward blow, Gabe sent a blast of white-hot power as intense as the heart of a star straight into its chest.

The fire giant faltered. Stumbled backward. Dropped to its

knees, its head hanging down, chin on its chest . . .

And the Fire Incandati raised its head. The obscuring sheet of flame flickered and died away, revealing its face.

Gabe gasped. The fire dimmed and died in Gabe's eyes, leaving them normal and human and green.

The Incandati had the face of Gabe's father.

Oh my God. Oh my God. It can't be. It can't be!

If the rest of the conflict still raged on, if Jonathan Thorne still attacked the golden magick giant, if Humboldt had come back to rip and tear at the earth, Gabe didn't know.

". . . Dad?"

The Fire Incandati snarled—and paused. His brow furrowed. Enormous eyes filled with the blaze of a hundred infernos narrowed at Gabe. He snarled again.

From over Gabe's shoulder, he heard his mother's voice. "Sam? Is that you?"

Aria stepped up beside Gabe. Shoulder to shoulder. She extended a hand, and Gabe marveled that her skin had returned to normal. Once again, his mother had long black hair, perfect blue eyes, and fine, smooth skin. Emotions chased one another across her face. The Incandati's focus shifted to Aria. Gabe held his breath . . . and choked back a sob as the fire giant's features creased with an infinite, soul-crushing sadness.

"Mom . . ." Gabe struggled for words. "Mom, how . . . ?"

Aria didn't look at Gabe as she spoke. "Ten years ago. The ritual, when I was lost to Arcadia. Your father fought so hard to save me . . . gave everything he had. Oh, Gabe." Her fingers found Gabe's and entwined through them. "He fought so hard to save me, the fire overtook him, Gabe . . . this is your father."

She stepped forward. Slowly extended a hand upward. Toward the fire giant's face.

The white-hot mace in the giant's right hand flickered and vanished. He moved as if to touch her . . .

. . . and jerked his hand away. The obscuring flames roared over his face again, and he lurched to his feet, the mace blazing into existence once more. He turned, the mace crackling in a deadly arc, and slammed the weapon straight into Madam Kureshi, who was still alive and had been bearing down on Gabe and Aria without them noticing.

The Fire Incandati rose to his full height, squared his shoulders, and *roared*.

Gabe felt sure he had just gone deaf, that the impossible volume of the creature's bellow had destroyed his hearing, but then realized he could still hear just fine. The fire giant's roar was . . . something not of Earth. Something human ears were not equipped to perceive.

But the effect it had on the other four Incandati was nothing short of profound.

The earth giant, the movement of its body like a living rockslide, reached down to the shadow-wrapped Magick Incandati, dug its fingers into the bands of greasy shadow wrapped around its head, and tore them free. Jonathan Thorne's laughter turned to screams as the earth giant shook the soot-black scraps loose from its rocky fingers.

The air giantess turned to the Water Incandati, whose body quivered and convulsed as waves of yellow spores writhed and swirled inside it, and with a snarl brought her hands together. A thunderclap washed over the scene, and forks of lightning speared the water giant's liquid body. The spores inside blackened and fell, lifeless, out of the Water Incandati, piling on the ground around its base like ash.

"Gabe," Kaz said, coming up to him. "What did you *do*? Why aren't the giants attacking us anymore?"

Gabe shot a glance at Aria, but her head was bowed again. As he watched, the gray crept back into her flesh. He shook his head. He couldn't answer.

Thorne's voice boomed and echoed across the rubble: "To me, my lieutenants! These lumbering beasts shall not dissuade us!" The combat moved off to where Gabe couldn't follow the action.

Gabe turned to Lily. "We need to get to higher ground. We have to see what's going on."

Lily turned in place, scanning the city around them, and pointed to a snapped-in-half steeple of a church a block away. "Would that work?"

Gabe nodded. Lily's eyes shimmered silver-white, and she beckoned everyone to come in close. "It'll probably help to hold hands," she said, and wind rose under their feet, buoying them up off the ground. She guided them to the steeple and set them down as gently as if they'd just stepped off an escalator.

Gabe started to say "You're getting *really* good at that," but Brett tapped him on the shoulder and pointed, and the words died in Gabe's throat.

The battleground spread out below them, a four-block-wide circle of carnage with the Crimson Serpent at one edge.

The five Incandati smashed and roared and burned and flooded as they fought, but Thorne and his minions seemed to have gotten a second wind. Thorne flitted through the ruined city like a living shade, too fast for Gabe to track, and his shadow-tendrils shot out from every angle. The Incandati screamed, and more than one faltered.

That left openings for Madam Kureshi and Mr. Humboldt to launch themselves at their opponents. Despite the impaling and the fiery blunt force from the fire giant, Kureshi still seemed to be fine. Her suckered tentacles seemed to have grown saw-toothed edges, and along with Humboldt's brute strength, the two of them tore huge chunks out of the Incandati. The earth giant, finally overwhelmed, bellowed and crumbled to the ground, split in half and pulsing with greasy, black tendrils.

The Magick Incandati slammed a fist down directly on Mr. Grillion, but the same thing happened as before: a vile yellow cloud puffed out from the point of impact. Then the air giantess clenched one immense fist, creating a narrow cyclone spinning faster than any tornado Gabe had ever seen. The shrieking vortex sucked every bit of Grillion's mold and spores inside of it—and the cyclone lit with a blinding blue-white glare, utterly incinerating anything that might have been inside it.

The cyclone dissipated.

No trace of Grillion remained.

"Enough!"

Thorne's voice rolled across the battlefield. Gabe spotted him, not far from the Crimson Serpent, standing atop a mostly intact print shop, Madam Kureshi and Mr. Humboldt beside him. Thorne held up the Mirror Book. "You want to see power?" Even at this distance, Gabe saw the abominable green glare of Thorne's eyes. "Then it is power you shall have!"

Thorne channeled his shadow-tendrils *through* the Mirror Book—and it was like a ray of sun focused through a magnifying glass. What had been powerful now became devastating. A bolt of shadowy destruction leaped out from Thorne and speared the Magick Incandati through the head, punching in one temple and out through the other. The magick giant moaned as it fell, dying.

It sounds like whale song.

"We've got to get down there," Gabe said. "We can't let the Incandati just die!"

"Gabe, no!" Lily turned him to face her. "You see the kind of damage *both* sides are doing! We'd get flattened in a heartbeat!"

Thorne's words reached them, their malice amplified by the

Mirror Book's power. "Die, you beast! *Die!*" The black energy flashed out again, and when it struck the water giant, it splintered like light passing through a prism. Within seconds, the Water Incandati had turned as black as ink, and with another whale song–like cry, it collapsed and died. Hundreds of thousands of gallons of water blasted out in apocalyptic waves, scraping clean the city blocks around it.

Gabe's knuckles turned white as he gripped the edge of the ruined steeple. "This is *our* fight. Not theirs. We can't let them all get killed! We can't let D—"

His voice broke off.

Kaz spoke up. "Gabe, did you fry your own brain? Thorne's hench-monsters are just way too powerful. They're killing the Incandati! *We'd* be toast!" He shrugged helplessly. "We're way outnumbered."

Behind them, Brett said, "Oh . . . my . . . *God*," and a rasping cry sounded out over their heads.

Jackson grinned, wide and a little sharklike. "What were you saying about being outnumbered, Kazuo?"

At least three dozen null draaks swept down out of the sky from the direction of the Presidio and rocketed past the steeple, spraying volley after volley of corrosive acid all over Thorne, Humboldt, and Madam Kureshi.

The battle wasn't lost. Not by a long shot.

23

Each null draak sported a robed Eternal Dawn rider, and when one wheeled back and approached the steeple, Eva waved to them from her saddle. She might have said something, but the whipping winds carried her words away.

The acid attack had sent Madam Kureshi on the run, and now she dashed and skittered through the waterlogged ruins of the city, propelled by half a dozen long, muscular purple tentacles. The air giantess chased after her, bolt upon searing, blinding bolt of lightning crashing down around her. Kureshi screamed as she ran.

Mr. Humboldt, too, had left the side of his lord and master. Displaying strength that Gabe figured *had* to be magickally boosted—no physical body could be this strong—Humboldt ripped up great sections of pavement and hurled them at the fire giant. At first the Fire Incandati smashed the chunks of asphalt aside with his blazing maces, but Humboldt was so strong, and threw the impossibly huge projectiles so fast, that soon more than one made contact, smashing into the giant's torso. It staggered backward, bellowing in pain.

Jackson came to Gabe's side. "Did the null draaks take out Thorne, at least?"

Gabe squinted. When he finally did make out Thorne, he wished he'd been looking somewhere else. Thorne still stood, and he was covered by—Gabe fought back the urge to vomit— a thick layer of small white worms. *Kretschmar*. When one of the null draaks swooped in and unleashed a spray of acid, the worms *absorbed* it . . . and a long, needlelike spike of shadow lashed out, stabbing the null draak straight through its body. The beast and rider both crashed to the ground below.

"That's it." Gabe turned to face his friends and his mother. "We can't just sit by anymore. Or I can't, anyway. You're right. Thorne's a monster, he's way more powerful than we thought, and now that he's got the Mirror Book, he's not gonna stop until the Serpent's dead and the world is freaking screwed." He turned to Kaz. "Do you feel like telling us any more about this plan the Serpent has?"

Kaz and Lily glanced at each other. Kaz said, "For now, we just have to—"

"Oh my God, please don't say 'stall,'" Brett muttered.

"—stall," Kaz finished. "And trust that the Serpent's right."

"Well, if we're gonna make a difference here, we've got to do it now," Gabe said. "Right now, while the riders have them distracted. Jackson? Lily? Can one of you get me down there? Maybe I can burn those worms off him. Let the null draaks do their thing."

Jackson and Lily, both nodding, tried to talk over each other. Gabe couldn't make out what either one of them said, until Jackson rolled his eyes and gave an exaggerated bow. "Please, after you, madam."

Lily scowled at Jackson, but to Gabe she said, "I'll get you down there, but I'm also going with you."

Brett and Kaz nodded, too.

Kaz said, "Earth makes the best shields. Don't want to go into a fight without earth."

"Magick has some potent defensive measures as well, if it's not too boastful of me to say so," Jackson said.

"You? *Boastful?*" Brett said. "*Never!*" This got a smile from everyone, even the smaller boy. "And no way are you going down there without me, buddy." Brett's eyes flickered blue-green. "Who else is gonna whip up a wicked hailstorm or some icicle blades when you really need them?"

"Thanks, dude," Gabe said. This felt right, the five of them. Together. He wished he had more time to enjoy it.

"Sounds like the full roster," Lily said.

Gabe's eyes caught fire. "Then let's do it. Mom, you stay here, okay? . . . Mom?"

Aria had crouched next to a low wall and didn't look at him. "Yes, yes. I'll stay here." Gabe could barely make out what she said. Pain wrinkled his face. *I don't want to leave you! I don't want to lose you!* There was so much to say, and no time at all to say it. He gestured to Lily.

Five elementalists rose on a column of air and descended into chaos.

Gabe grew disoriented as soon as his feet touched the ground. The Water Incandati had flooded the battleground when it died, and the debris piled everywhere made the ruined city look even more damaged than it had before. Not only that, but he'd also lost sight of the Fire Incandati—*my dad!*—and the air giantess had chased Madam Kureshi several blocks away. He still heard the cracks of thunder.

"Come on," Gabe said quietly. "Thorne is this way. I'm pretty sure."

The brilliant sky overhead had begun to darken, and the scar-like doorway had disappeared altogether, so that Lily's silver-white eyes left luminous trails in the dimming air as she walked. "What're we going to do when we reach him? I mean, what exactly? Do we have a plan?"

An explosive impact right behind them sent all five of them stumbling forward. Gabe's knees ground into sharp gravel, but he spun around to see Humboldt, his Victorian-era clothes torn and singed, stalking toward them. "Won't be a plan," Humboldt said in his clicking-ticking voice. "You'll all be dead. No plans when you're dead!" The hulking man ripped a huge rock out of the ground and threw it. It seemed to take him no effort at all.

Lily screamed, and a massive burst of air made the rock veer off course, but not by enough. Its edge clipped her head right at the hairline, and she left droplets of blood in the air as she fell.

"No! *Lily!*" Gabe screamed, and his eyes blazed so hot he felt his eyebrows singe off, and he turned the scream into a gout of flame that washed over Humboldt, covering every square inch of his body. Humboldt ignored it. He kept walking forward as if the fire had been nothing more than a cool summer breeze, and when Jackson sent a razor-edged golden disk hurtling at his head, Humboldt batted the disk aside.

"I think you'll find . . ." Humboldt paused, his words clotting with a frenzy of clicks. "The elements have little effect on me. I have what you might call . . ." He whipped more rocks. One caught Brett in the pit of his stomach, sending him to the ground in a painful heap, and though Kaz managed to turn another stone away, he wasn't fast enough. ". . . rather thick skin." A pointed rock sliced into Kaz's shoulder. He went to his knees, hissing in pain, one hand clapped to his wound as blood seeped through his fingers.

Humboldt looked Gabe up and down as he got closer and closer. "You'll make . . ." *Click click click click.* "You'll make a great plaything, won't you?" Humboldt reached out his great, block-like hands—

—and Gabe heard a sound like a cat bringing up a hair ball, right before a fist-size greenish glob splatted squarely against the side of Humboldt's face, making him falter. A giant Arcadian spider crashed into Humboldt and sent him tumbling sideways into a pile of soggy, charred wood scraps. The spider stopped and wheeled, and Gabe's jaw flopped open when he saw who was *riding* it.

"Uncle Steve . . . ? *Uncle Steve!*"

"Gabe!" Uncle Steve leaped off the creature and grabbed Gabe up in a bear hug. "You're alive! Thank God! *Thank God!*" He set Gabe down, and though Gabe had about a million questions to ask, the only sounds he could make were a near-hysterical combination of sobbing and laughter. Finally Gabe sniffled and wiped his face on his sleeve and said, "I thought you were *dead*!" He took a step back from his uncle and saw the giant spider regarding him calmly. "Uh . . . Uncle Steve, you're *friends* with the *spiders*?"

Steve and the giant spider traded a casual glance. Steve said, "Eh. We've come to an arrangement. This is their queen. Her name's Jasmine." The spider raised her front right limb and bumped fists with Uncle Steve. "They're not actually spiders. Some of them used to be people. Eternal Dawn members."

Nearby, flat on his back, Kaz wobbled a weak hand in the air and said, "I knew it! Square-cube law!"

The enormous spider fixed all eight eyes on Gabe. *"Apologies about the bite,"* she said.

"Fools!" Humboldt came slamming and crashing out of the pile of rubble. "I'll tear you apart! All of you, limb from limb! I'll—"

He broke off in midword and had just enough time to look truly, profoundly surprised before a mass of several hundred slightly smaller spiders rushed past Gabe and Uncle Steve and swarmed all over Humboldt, hiding him from sight completely. Gabe stared. Humboldt never made another sound. Not voluntarily, anyway. Gabe didn't think the ripping and tearing and sort of wet *squelching* sounds that came from beneath the writhing pile counted.

Kaz, Lily, Brett, and Jackson warily approached Uncle Steve and Jasmine. Lily kept one hand on her head, and wobbled a little, but seemed more or less all right. Kaz's eyes shifted from dark brown to gray and back as he packed a line of mud into the cut on his shoulder. Brett rubbed his midsection gingerly.

Uncle Steve focused on Gabe. "What's the situation? Tell me everything. And tell me fast."

Gabe took a deep breath. "The Crimson Serpent told us to combine our powers, and it opened a doorway and five Incandati came through, but Thorne and his people have killed three of them, maybe more, and Thorne and Kretschmar and Madam Kureshi are still here and they want to wire us all together and use Jackson as a bomb to kill the Serpent and the null draak acid isn't doing anything to Thorne because Kretschmar keeps turning into worms and absorbing it." He paused, panting.

A long black tongue emerged from Jasmine the Spider Queen's mouth and ran over her mandibles. Gabe couldn't tell if she was smiling or not, but a kind of twinkle appeared in all eight of her eyes. *"Worms, you say?"* She raised her head, and the swarm of spiders immediately abandoned Humboldt and rushed over to her. Gabe saw what was left of Humboldt out of the corner of his eye, and decided that was as much as he wanted to see. Jasmine said, *"Let us take a look at these . . . worms."*

Thunder boomed overhead. As the spider swarm swept away toward Thorne's position, Gabe looked up and saw Madam Kureshi locked in combat with the air giantess and the Fire Incandati at the same time. Kureshi's tentacular body had grown huge, the "human" part just a minor feature of it; she looked like a woman in robes riding atop a gigantic, violet monstrosity that reminded Gabe of the leviathan that had destroyed Argent Court.

Kureshi had grabbed up half a dozen long, steel I-beams, and every time the air giantess launched a bolt of lightning, Kureshi somehow used the beams to turn it back against her. The giantess weakened visibly with each impact, but when the fire giant moved in to try to strike Kureshi with a white-hot mace, Thorne's shadow-tendrils lanced out, stinging him, piercing his molten skin.

Kaz and Lily faced Gabe. Kaz said, "Come on! If the spiders

can get Kretschmar's worms off of Thorne, we might be able to move him!"

Lily said, "Right! He needs to be over by the Serpent's head!"

Gabe frowned. "What? Why?"

Lily took off running. "Just come on!" The rest of the group had no choice but to follow her.

Uncle Steve fell in beside Gabe. "Where's your mother?"

Gabe gestured over his shoulder. "We left her back there—in a safe place. As safe as we could find, anyway."

With another heartbreaking, whale-song cry, the air giantess folded and died, and Gabe barely kept his feet as a gale-force wind exploded from where her body had stood seconds before. *That just leaves Dad. Can he take on Kureshi?*

That turned out not to matter. Madam Kureshi clung to the top of a badly damaged, ten-story office building; and as she turned to face the Fire Incandati, brandishing her I-beams much the way he wielded his plasma maces, six null draaks landed on her back, dug their claws into her knotty purple skin, clamped their jaws around the base of her robes, and *tore off the human section of her body.*

The huge tentacular form shuddered. All the I-beams fell from her grasp. Effectively headless, Madam Kureshi slithered down the side of the building and crashed to the ground with a sound like a vast, wet sponge being slapped against a hard surface.

Thorne's scream at his favorite lieutenant's death sent a piercing pain through Gabe's head. He touched his ears and couldn't believe they weren't bleeding.

Thorne hadn't moved from his spot on the low roof, less than half a block from the Crimson Serpent. The null draaks had peeled off. Thorne devoted all his fury to the fire giant now, stabbing and stinging, over and over, with needle-sharp, oily, black tendrils. Thorne himself still wore the thick coating of worms, courtesy of Mr. Kretschmar. Gabe thought Thorne looked as if he'd been turned inside out.

Uncle Steve said, "Wow. That is really disgusting."

The swarm of spiders had reached the base of Thorne's building. *"Guys!"* Gabe hissed. "Thorne will tear those spiders apart. We've got to get his attention!"

Lily said, "Okay, but *how*?"

Gabe shook his head. "We don't have time for a plan. Just hit him! Hit him with everything you've got, but take turns— let's not accidentally combine powers and blow ourselves up!"

Gabe attacked first, sending a stream of fire straight into Thorne's midsection. The worms burned away from the point of impact but immediately covered it over again, and Thorne didn't seem to care about the heat at all. But then Kaz shattered the concrete wall of the building where Thorne stood, and he tumbled down to street level, where Lily's whirlwind, combined with Uncle Steve's, swept him up and slammed him into the pavement, once, twice, three times. Before Thorne could even raise his head, a gigantic golden cylinder appeared above him and rammed him into the ground so hard it cratered the earth. Water seeped up through the cracked pavement. With a hiss of effort, Brett raised both his hands, his fingers like up-curled claws, and spears of ice erupted from the ground and impaled Thorne's body, pinioning him like a bug on an entomologist's specimen board.

Thorne raised his head and fixed his blazing green eyes on Gabe and the rest of the group as Kretschmar's worms began eating away at the ice spears. The ever-shifting, ravenous display inside Thorne's mouth flashed as he spoke. "You cannot kill me, you worthless little *pigs*. This is nothing more than an inconvenience. A *distraction*."

Gabe shrugged. "You said it yourself."

The spiders swarmed over Thorne's body. Instead of the ripping and tearing Gabe had heard when they'd attacked Humboldt, now a truly hideous *slurping* sound rolled across the battlefield, followed by Mr. Kretschmar's voice. Kretschmar said no words.

He only screamed as the spiders ate him.

Worm by worm.

As soon as the last of Kretschmar's screams died away, a dome-like explosion of black energy flung the swarm off Thorne. The giant pseudo-arachnids scurried into the shadows and disappeared. Thorne stood there, chest heaving, inhuman teeth grinding, ripples and waves of oily, black power undulating all around him. He raised a finger, pointed straight at Gabe, opened his mouth—

And the Fire Incandati brought both of his maces straight down onto Thorne, smashing him flat.

Gabe gasped.

A single black ribbon of energy lashed out from the center of the plasma inferno and punched through the Incandati's chest. The fire giant recoiled, staggered backward, and fell out of sight behind a ruined house. Flames rushed out from the building, but Gabe heard no whale song.

In the tiniest of voices, he said, "Dad . . . ?"

Please be okay, Dad! Please!

He had no more time to think about the giant with his father's face, though, because once again, Jonathan Thorne climbed deliberately, confidently, to his feet.

"The longer you defy me, the longer I shall take to *eat* you," Thorne growled, and might have said more, but Eva's null draak swooped down from the sunset sky and *bathed* him in acid.

The ground beneath them vibrated. The buzzing, thrumming, static-filled song of the Serpent filled Gabe's head. And for the first time, it changed. Instead of the looping, cryptic message, the Serpent's voice bellowed a single word: *"NOW."*

"It's time!" Kaz shouted.

"Finally!" Brett said.

"We can't wait for Thorne to recover again!" Kaz said. "Lily, get him into position!"

As Lily summoned another whirlwind, Gabe grabbed Kaz's arm. "What position? What're you two talking about?"

Kaz didn't answer. He seemed to have all his attention focused on Lily. "Now! Do it now!"

Thorne's soot-black clothing hung in tatters around his body, and streams of putrid-smelling smoke rose from his flesh as the null draak acid corroded it. Before he could raise his head again, Lily's cyclone jerked him up off the ground and then hurled him back down. Thorne looked like a rag doll, his ruined clothes and long, gaunt limbs flailing as he spun, and Gabe was sure he heard the snap of bones breaking as Lily drove Thorne into the ground.

As Gabe and Kaz and Lily reached the site of impact, with Jackson, Brett, and Uncle Steve close behind them, low, rasping laughter filled the air. Thorne's body had made another crater in the earth, and the first thing to come out of it was his hand, still clutching the Mirror Book. Thorne's flesh had melted away from his bones, but as Gabe watched, the tissue knit back together. Thorne dug his fingers into the dirt as he pulled himself out of the crater, and the tiny rocks that had embedded themselves in him fell at his feet one by one, pushed out as his corpse-like body repaired itself.

"Enough talking." Thorne's eyes seemed to burn green tunnels through the air. "There is nothing left now but . . . action. . . ."

Gabe saw Thorne pause as everyone else gazed past him, at the Serpent. Gabe didn't know what to say. Didn't know what to do. He knew his slack-jawed stare left him open to whatever attack Thorne wanted to launch, but . . . it didn't seem to matter anymore.

Thorne turned his head.

The Crimson Serpent had let go of its tail. Its head had risen high in the air, both of its enormous, radiant blue eyes fixed squarely on Jonathan Thorne.

Thorne trembled. He said, "I just—"

The Serpent struck. Its massive jaws closed around Thorne, and its vastly powerful, muscular neck shook the man's body like a terrier shaking a lizard. Thorne's screams shattered glass and concrete in every direction, but cut off abruptly when the Serpent threw its head back and swallowed Thorne whole.

Something fluttered out of the sky and fell to Earth in front of them. Gabe recognized it as the Mirror Book, rattled loose from Thorne's grasp, just as Kaz scooped it up.

Lily screamed, "Kaz! *No!*"

Ripples of power undulated along the Crimson Serpent's length, and the barrier between San Arcadia and the rest of the earth shimmered and vanished, reappeared, vanished, and reappeared again.

Kaz ran to stand right beside the Serpent's heaving body, the Mirror Book clutched to his chest, and turned flickering, slate gray eyes on Lily. "I'm doing this, Lily. Don't try to stop me."

Lily's whole body shook with a sob, and Gabe grabbed her shoulders. "Lily! What's Kaz doing? *What's going on?*"

She scrubbed at her eyes. "We didn't—didn't tell you guys everything. From when we were in the Mirror Cave. The Serpent . . ."

"What? The Serpent *what*?"

"The Serpent said, once it takes all of Thorne's power, absorbs it all, it'll be able to pull all the magick back with it, into the Mirror Book. But . . . Gabe, somebody's got to hold the Book open for it to work. And whoever does that—it'll consume them. The Serpent called it 'the final sacrifice.' He said Arcadia was born in blood. And it has to be sealed with blood."

As far as Gabe was concerned, the rest of the world disappeared. The whole of the human race was just him, Lily, and Kaz. "Why—Lily, why didn't you *tell* us any of this?"

She sobbed again. "Because I didn't want anybody doing anything stupid! Gabe, *I* was going to do it! *I* was going to hold the Book open! And if I'd said anything, Brett would've tried to stop me!"

Gabe shouted, "*I* would've tried to stop you!" He turned to Kaz, who still stood in the same place, fifty feet away, the Book held in both arms.

No. NO. None of my friends are going to die!

Gabe muttered, "Sorry, Kaz," and as he sprinted toward his friend, his eyes caught fire.

24

The world wavered and warped around Gabe as he ran. The Crimson Serpent's building-size body twitched, its muscles clenching beneath its scaled, red skin as ring after ring of power ran from its snout down its length.

Kaz saw Gabe coming and put out one hand. "Gabe, don't! Don't try to stop me! This has to be done!"

Glad he took one hand off the Mirror Book. Gabe's blazing eyes narrowed, and the cover of the Book flared red. Kaz yelped and dropped it, clutching his burned hand, and Gabe grabbed it before it even hit the ground.

Another pulsing, wavering shimmer distorted the air around him, and Gabe looked up to see the magick of San

Arcadia pushing beyond the border the Crimson Serpent had maintained. From somewhere, he heard Uncle Steve's voice— "Gabe, no! Don't do it! *Don't do it!*"—but Kaz had been right about one thing.

"It has to be done."

Gabe opened the Mirror Book.

The Crimson Serpent's chanting, humming song sounded out again, this time with no words. Just pure, unstoppable, triumphant force. The mighty, blue-eyed head swung around, the immense red body reared off the ground like a cobra set to strike, and the Serpent dived into the Book.

A spike of pain rammed through Gabe's mind. It was as if the pages of the Mirror Book had become a black hole. The Serpent's head, easily the size of a building, narrowed to a point no more than a foot wide and disappeared into the Book, its body following after. Faster. Faster and faster. The miles-long beast vanished into the pages with such speed and force that Gabe could barely stand, the wind blowing his hair back and forcing him to shut his eyes. It was like holding a hurricane in his hands.

And it only got worse.

Once the tip of the Serpent's tail had vanished, it left a *pit* in the Mirror Book. A pit into which—Gabe understood what was happening on a deep, primal, molecular level—every bit of magick in San Arcadia was being pulled. It wasn't like one of Lily's whirlwinds, sucking everything into it with brute force. It was more like . . .

Like explosive decompression.

Gabe had seen enough science fiction movies to know what happened when a spaceship had a hole blown in its hull. All the pressurized oxygen inside rushed to get outside, out into space. That was how this felt. As if all the world's magick had been pent up, pressurized, and now, given the chance to escape, rushed into and *through* the Mirror Book with devastating force.

Through the Mirror Book . . .

. . . and through Gabe as well.

He knew, the same way he knew that all the magick was being torn out of the world, that he wouldn't survive this process. A hole like this had to be plugged.

Gabe gritted his teeth and held the Book open.

None of my friends are going to die!

The violent, bomb-blast force of magick's exodus became visible in the sky first. The amber air, the bloodred streaks, all of it ramped down out of the clouds and funneled into the Book. Gabe gasped at the beautiful blue this revealed. Bit by bit, the golden hue of magick tore free of buildings, of pools of water, of the ground itself, blasting through the Book's pages and away from Earth.

He felt the fire leave him. The energy peeled away from his body, from his soul, and suddenly Gabe was *freezing*. The heat he hadn't realized he'd grown accustomed to had vanished, and he shivered, his teeth chattering.

Gabe knew his body was about to come apart. He could feel it. Soon this explosive vortex would disappear, and the Mirror Book would fall to the ground, alone. As if Gabe had never been there.

He closed his eyes.

None. Of my friends. Are going to die!

And then . . .

. . . then Aria's hand touched Gabe's shoulder, and time seemed to stand still.

"Let go, honey."

Gabe gasped at Aria's appearance. Her rocklike skin had turned smooth, and though deep cracks still ran through it, warm green light shone out from each one. Her long black hair had been replaced by a cascading shower of sand. Her deep-blue eyes had turned green, and Gabe knew that it was the green of the earth. The green of life itself.

She's beautiful. She's . . . she's like a goddess.

Aria's mouth didn't move as she spoke. Her words came from everywhere. From the earth, from the air. From inside her, and from inside Gabe as well. "Let go. It's time now. I must leave you, Gabe. But always remember. Remember we'll always be a family."

A wave of gentle warmth and a comforting orange glow came from behind Aria, and Gabe blinked back tears as his father—still molten, still a being of fire itself, but now the size of a man—stepped up beside her. Beside his wife. Sam didn't speak, but he reached out to touch Gabe's face. Flames caressed Gabe's cheek, his chin, but they didn't burn. Instead they made him feel safe.

Around them, the world slowly churned as reality itself trembled. But in this moment Gabe had never felt more safe and loved.

"Do we have to say good-bye? Do you . . . do you have to go?"

Aria gave him the saddest smile he had ever seen. Gently, she took the Mirror Book from Gabe's hands, and the passage of time returned to normal.

Gabe stumbled backward and raised one hand to shield his eyes against the punishing winds rushing past him and into the Book's pages. He could still see his mother and father, and expected them to get pulled into the Book along with everything else . . . but instead they began to *grow*. His father became, once again, the towering fire giant—and Aria grew along with him.

She's becoming an Incandati.

The last thing Gabe saw was an image etched into his mind, deeply and permanently: his mother and father, earth and fire, embracing each other. Together again. Whole again.

Then a blast of light and power struck him and he saw only darkness.

The warmth of the sun on his face woke Gabe. He lay on his back and, near as he could tell from a quick wiggle of fingers and toes, still had all his parts in working order. He opened one eye and then the other, and the thick white clouds scudding across the deep-blue sky above were the most gorgeous things he had ever seen.

He lurched up to one elbow. A patch of grass nearby was *so green*—he hadn't realized how much the magick-infused San Arcadian energy had changed the colors of everyday objects. The dirt had turned brown again. A wrecked cab nearby was yellow.

Gabe sat up. He could tell he was in the same place where the explosion had happened, but . . . the Crimson Serpent was gone. So were the Incandati. So was the Mirror Book.

So were his mom and dad.

A bird landed nearby, dug into the dirt with its beak, and pulled up a fat red earthworm. A chill bay breeze ruffled Gabe's hair, and he stood and raised his arms, turning slowly as he drank in the sensation.

San Arcadia had disappeared. San Francisco was back.

"Gabe?"

He spun around to see Lily wobbling toward him. "Lily!" He ran to her and wrapped her up in his arms, laughing with delight. "Are you okay? Where's everybody else? Where's my uncle?"

"Over here," Uncle Steve called. Gabe spotted him sitting

on an overturned slab of concrete, wrapping some cloth around the end of a thick piece of wood. Steve stood, with the aid of the improvised crutch, and Gabe saw that his magickally restored leg had once again disappeared, leaving only the long-healed stump.

Gabe ran to his uncle. "Uh . . . wow. I'm, uh . . . sorry about your leg."

As Brett, Jackson, and Kaz all freed themselves from piles of nearby rubble, Steve pulled Gabe into a one-armed hug. "Don't be." He squeezed Gabe tighter. "I've got everything I need."

25

Gabe straightened up from the ankle-deep mass of debris in what used to be his living room and put his hands on his hips. "I swear, I've gone through half this stuff, and it doesn't look like I've even made a dent."

Uncle Steve thumped over to him, moving carefully on his crutch. They'd just received their insurance check the day before, and his uncle had a chunk of it earmarked for a new, more advanced prosthesis; but for now he still had, as he put it, "a leg and a half."

At least he got a real crutch.

Sure would be easier helping him out if Mom were still here—
Gabe grimaced, breaking off the thought.

Quit it. Quit it. You got to meet her. You got to spend time with her. That's more than you had before. More than a lot of kids ever have.

He tried not to dwell on how much he missed her. His dad, too. Gabe had only spent a couple moments with him. In that time, he never even uttered a word, yet Gabe was sure that his dad had saved all their lives.

Brett, Lily, and Kaz helped pick through the mess in the dining room. There wasn't much of a second floor left now. The whole house was more like a huge pile of junk and soggy, charred wood in between bare brick walls. Gabe glanced around. "Hey, where's Jackson?"

"Right behind you."

Gabe turned and saw the Ghost Boy coming through the front door, or what had been the front door. Now it was just an empty doorframe. Jackson held a king-size bag of Snickers bars, and grinned as he popped one into his mouth. He held out the bag and, around a huge mouthful of gooey candy, said, "Want one?" It turned out Jackson had an endless appetite for sweets. Lily and Brett's grandmother had sent over a loaf of freshly baked banana bread, and he'd already devoured most of that.

Gabe took a bar. Uncle Steve took one as well and said, "Where did you get these?"

Jackson hooked a thumb in a vaguely northern direction. "The residents of San Francisco seem in a frenzy to rebuild. Only a month since the crisis, and one of your convenience stores has reopened on the next corner." He swallowed his mouthful of candy and pulled his smartphone out of his pocket. "I shall text you some pics!"

Gabe let one corner of his mouth twitch upward at Jackson's pride in the phone. He knew Jackson prized it, since it symbolized his first step toward being a real *kid* in modern society, and had been made possible by the new identity Uncle Steve had cooked up for him. Gabe wasn't sure how his uncle had pulled that off, and was even less sure how well Jackson would fit in. The boy was crashing with Kaz for now, but they had all decided he'd come to live with the Conways once Uncle Steve bought a new house—a situation Gabe had promised himself he'd try to make work. He'd never had a brother before. It would be a new kind of adventure.

Since a large section of his front wall was no longer there, Gabe could look straight out through the ruined foyer onto the San Francisco landscape. He knew that the official story, the story the rest of the world had been told, was that the city had suffered another catastrophic earthquake, just like the one in 1906.

Not that anyone who lived through it bought that.

He'd been amazed at how many people *had* lived through it. Eva Terrington had found herself helping to coordinate relief efforts for the survivors. Gabe and Uncle Steve had located her a few days after the crisis ended and shared a pleasant meal with her, if you could call eating turkey sandwiches on top of a huge pile of rubble pleasant.

"So what are people saying?" Gabe had asked her.

Eva had wiped a trace of mayonnaise off her mouth with a napkin. "Oh my God. I can't believe how much I missed mayonnaise. This is just the *best*. Um. Yeah, so, there's some wacky stuff out there. People are trying to tell reporters that it was, like, aliens, or dinosaurs, and I heard one guy saying it was alien dinosaurs. But there's no evidence. All the technology quit working inside the barrier, and the rest of the world didn't even know anything had gone wrong thanks to the time distortion. The media's running with 'hallucinations caused by gas leaks.'"

Uncle Steve had snorted with, Gabe thought, equal parts amusement and disgust. "The brain comes up with reasonable explanations for things it can't explain. Compared to leviathans and sawjaws and Jonathan Thorne, I guess dinosaurs don't seem too implausible."

Around another bite of sandwich, Eva had said, "That's the thing, though—I bet, in about a week, we're the only ones who are gonna remember *any* of this."

Now, standing in his living room, Gabe stared out at the once-again-normal-if-somewhat-battered Golden Gate Bridge. *Magick is gone, our powers are gone . . . but I got to spend time with Mom and meet Dad.* He promised himself he'd never forget any of it.

"Are you going to buy another row house, Dr. Conway?" Jackson asked. "Or one detached from other domiciles?"

Gabe said, "Domiciles?" and Jackson blushed. They'd

been discussing ways for Jackson to sound less like a hundred-and-eleven-year-old English professor and more like an eleven-year-old kid. It was slow going.

"That depends," Uncle Steve said. "Having a large portion of the city destroyed is doing odd things to the housing market. We'll see."

Gabe didn't care what kind of house they got. Row house, detached, whatever. He couldn't wait because he knew, Uncle Steve had *promised* him, that the new house would be permanent. No more running. They were setting down roots.

"Hey!" Lily called out. "I found something!"

Gabe, Jackson, and Uncle Steve went through into the dining room, where Lily held a framed photo. The glass had long since disappeared, but the photo itself was only a little wrinkled. Gabe peered at it.

"Look how young I am," Uncle Steve said with a sigh. Gabe and Brett and Lily and Kaz had seen the photo in Uncle Steve's office . . . *ages* ago. Uncle Steve posed in it, smiling, along with Gabe's mother and father, and Greta Jaeger. It stung Gabe to see Greta, who'd been so kind to them all, and his parents again, knowing he'd never get to be with them, but . . .

"We did it, didn't we?" Gabe gently took the photo out of Lily's hands and looked at his uncle. "What you guys set out to do. Destroy Arcadia. We did it."

A crack sounded out. Dust rained down as the mortar around a wedge of loose masonry in the living-room wall gave way. Uncle Steve shouted, "Kaz! Look out!" as the mass broke free and fell straight at Kaz's head. Kaz yelped and threw his hands up—

—and the wedge of stone and concrete crashed to the floor, two feet to his left.

No one moved. *Everyone* stared. The rest of the group gaped at Kaz, while Kaz's eyes bugged out at his own hands. "How'd I do that?" He looked around. "Guys? Did I move that stone? *How'd I do that?*" His words sped up. "Magick is gone, right? I mean, without Arcadia, none of us have powers anymore, right? I mean, I felt the whole earth thing get pulled right out of me when the Serpent left. *Guys, I'm seriously freaking out here!*"

"N-no need, Kaz," Uncle Steve said, though Gabe thought he sounded sort of uncertain. "I'm sure that was just an optical illusion. The rubble only *looked* like it was going to hit you."

Kaz exhaled. "Yeah. It must have been. I guess."

A faint memory bobbed up to the surface of Gabe's mind. An explanation he'd heard, he couldn't place where, about why Arcadia was formed in the first place. Jonathan Thorne and the Eternal Dawn had wanted to increase the amount of magick in the world, but they botched it.

Before that, the world had always had a little magick. . . .

Gabe turned away from the group and held up a palm.

Nothing happened.

Gabe stared at the bare skin in the center of his hand, concentrating as hard as he could. *Come on. Come on.* He visualized a ball of fire. Nothing fancy, nothing huge, just *something*.

Still, nothing happened.

Behind him, someone might have said his name, but he wasn't sure. Gabe closed his eyes and thought of Aria. His mother. *Mom*. He remembered how she'd saved him. He thought of Greta, so scary at first but ultimately just filled with kindness. She had taught him so much.

Thought after thought flashed across his mind—everything that mattered to him. Everything truly important. San Francisco, this big, crazy, beautiful, impossible city. Uncle Steve, and Kaz and Brett and Jackson. Lily. The worlds they had crossed together to save their home . . . to save the whole planet.

To save one another.

Gabe opened his eyes and saw a tiny sphere of pure, red-orange fire blossom in his palm. Weak, no bigger or stronger than a candle flame, but as warm as the sunrise.

The spark of a smile lit up his face.